MW01633073

Moonlighting in Vermont

by

Kate George

Mainly Murder Press, LLC
PO Box 290586
Wethersfield, CT 06109-0586
www.mainlymurderpress.com

Mainly Murder Press

Senior Editor: Judith K. Ivie
Copy Editor: Judith K. Ivie
Cover Designer: Patricia L.Foltz

All rights reserved

Names, characters and incidents depicted in this book are products of the author's imagination or are used fictitiously. Any resemblance to actual events, organizations, or persons, living or dead, is entirely coincidental and beyond the intent of the author or the publisher.

No part of this book may be reproduced or transmitted in any form or by any means, electronic or mechanical, including photocopying, recording, or by any information storage and retrieval system, without permission in writing from the publisher.

Mainly Murder Press
www.mainlymurderpress.com

Copyright © 2009 by Kate George
ISBN 978-0-615-29202-1

Published in the United States of America

2009

Mainly Murder Press
PO Box 290586
Wethersfield, CT 06109-0586

Dedication

For G and the four junior members
of the madhouse crew.
I love you more than I can say.

~

To my friends and beta readers -
couldn't do it without you.
Special thanks to Sara, Buffy, Danny and Beaux -
for inspiration in one form or another.

One

"Why. Won't. You. Open!" With every word I pushed my shoulder into the door. I gave the wood a two-handed shove, but all that got me was stinging palms. "I just love being a housekeeper," I muttered, put my back to the panel, bent my knees, and drove my weight backward. The door gave a little, and I rammed it again. The gap widened, and I turned to put my eye to the crack between the door and the jamb.

"Oh, my God." I sank to my knees. The thing blocking the door was my boss. My dead boss, if the amount of blood on the floor was any indication. Crap! I knelt down and squeezed my arm through the space to see if I could feel a pulse, but she was cold. Dead cold. I sat down on the porch floor, put my head between my legs, and willed myself not to throw up.

Not throwing up is something I'm definitely not good at. A life skill I haven't developed. My name is Bella Bree MacGowan. Bella is Italian; Bree—well technically, Brie, but my mom couldn't spell—is French, and MacGowan is Scottish. Basically, my name means good cheese. Or maybe, beautiful cheese. Either way, it's cheese, and what kind of life skills can you expect a cheese to develop? Luckily, I'm okay in the looks department, or I'd totally be screwed. Five-foot-six, not too wide in the hips. Straight, medium brown hair and medium brown eyes. I look kind of like Rachael Ray without the benefit of a hair and makeup stylist. I smile a lot, and that seems to help.

It wasn't helping me now. I sat gulping air and trying to focus on not shaking, but I wasn't having much luck. I was telling myself to breathe when the two-way radio on my belt went off.

"Bree! What's taking you so long?" The hotel manager's voice came through. "I need you back here."

I fumbled for my radio. "Brian, you need to get out here." I still had my head between my knees.

"Bree, you know I can't come out there right now. What's going on?" I heard the aggravation in his voice.

"You're going to have to come out here, Brian. I think Vera's dead."

The radio was silent. I pictured Brian trying to wrap his head around that last statement. Like a lot of people in South Royalton, we'd known each other since childhood. We'd grown up on the same hill, a couple of farms apart. My parents lived in town, but I spent as much time as I could on my grandparents' place. Brian and I were friends from way back.

The radio squawked again. "Bree, did you say Vera is dead?"

"Yes." I could understand how he felt. It didn't seem like it could be true, if it wasn't for the all-too-real body.

"I'm on my way."

I scooted to the edge of the porch and sat in the sun waiting for Brian to get there. The evening light was dappled with the color of the autumn leaves. I was thankful for the cool air and tried not to think about Vera ten feet away from me in the housekeeping closet. All that blood. I had my head back between my knees and my eyes closed when Brian showed up.

Brian dressed like the manager of a five-star hotel, which is good, because he is one. He wore Armani pants and jacket and a crisp, button-down shirt. His chestnut hair was immaculate, his face smooth shaven. But to me he'd always be the neighbor kid who knew how to talk his way out of hard work. He hadn't grown any taller than me and was a shade on the chunky side. And he'd never gotten over his love of a good practical joke. I had a feeling he was counting on news of Vera's death being just that. Good luck.

The cottages at Whispering Birches have secret rooms inside them. They're referred to as housekeeping closets, even though they're big enough to hold a king-sized bed. These storerooms have two doors. One opens from the outside porch of the cottage, and the other is a hidden entry into the guest quarters. With the outside door to the closet blocked, Brian let himself in through the cottage entrance and then used his key to turn the hidden latch that opened the inner door.

He came out a few minutes later, white faced and thin lipped, and sat down next to me on the porch.

"You gonna be all right?"

"She's dead isn't she?" I couldn't stop the tears from running down my face.

"Yeah. I called the cops." He glanced my way. "We're going to have to move Ericson to another cottage. Don't think we'd better do that before the cops come, though."

"Ericson's still at dinner in the main house?"

Brian nodded

"He likes to drink. You could probably keep him up there for most of the evening. Break the news about having to move him when the other guests have gone back to their rooms. We can have his stuff moved to another cottage before dinner's over." I was glad to have a problem to distract me.

"As long as the cops will let us move his stuff," Brian said gloomily. "Ericson will pitch a fit if he has to be separated from his clothes. He's such a fashionista."

We sat together on the porch, waiting. The sun glinted through the windows of another cottage on the hill above us. I wondered how the other housekeepers were doing. The team was down by two now, Vera and me. We had a full complement of guests, and the housekeepers had only a couple of hours to freshen up and turn down all the rooms. It had to get done without anyone being seen or heard while the guests were at dinner.

Whispering Birches, the secluded resort that locals call simply The Inn, consists of the main house, the pond house, and ten individual cottages. The main house is a renovated 1800s farmhouse that holds the lounge, dining rooms and four guest rooms. The pond house overlooks a small lake and holds six guest rooms. The cottages are scattered through what used to be cow pastures and woods, each containing a luxurious suite. There are stands of trees, hills or valleys between each cottage for privacy. The whole place is a gated, exclusive five-star hotel that guarantees the rich and famous freedom from the paparazzi—for a price. The least expensive room goes for a grand a night.

It was past sundown when the state troopers came down the narrow dirt road that led to Coydog Cottage. The housekeepers' two-way radio told me that turndown was well under control. The girls were tearing around like crazy, and there'd be plenty of bitching later, but the work would get done on time.

While Brian let the officers into the cottage, I sat in the cool evening getting goose pimples from the breeze and trying not to think. A tall, sandy blond trooper named Steve Leftsky squatted on the porch beside me. Steve wasn't a handsome guy. His face was pockmarked from teenage acne, but he was kind, and he had the sort of eyes that wrinkled at the edges when he smiled. We had known each other since high school. He occasionally stopped me for speeding, but he almost never gave me a ticket.

"Trying to get my attention, Bree?" He smiled at me. "You know if you want to see me, all you have to do is call."

"Very funny. I'm not likely to be going through withdrawals from the state police. You pull me over just about every other day." I glanced back at the cottage. "How'd she die?"

"Won't know anything officially until the medical examiner sees the body. How'd you get to be the lucky one who found her?"

"We store the extra carafes out here. Dotty broke one and asked me to grab another one for her. I couldn't figure out why the door wouldn't open."

"Did you touch anything, move anything around?" Steve took his notebook and pencil out of his shirt pocket.

"I must have moved her when I shoved the door open. And I reached in and touched her wrist to see if she was alive." A shiver ran through me.

"Was she warm?" I shook my head. He lowered his voice. "Know anybody who didn't like her?"

"Are you kidding? Everybody around here hates her. Even her sister Dolly won't speak to her half the time." I took a couple of breaths. "Can I go soon? I'd really like to get out of here."

"Yeah, I think it would be a good idea for you to leave before the meat wagon gets here." He glanced at me appraisingly. "Are you going home from here? It might be better if you're not alone."

"I have to feed my animals. But I think I'll go to Jim's house after that."

"Jim? You're still seeing James Fisk? God, I thought that would be over by now. He's got a stick up his... uh." He looked around to see one of the other officers watching him. "You're too laid back for him." Steve smiled and dropped a hand on my shoulder to steady himself as he stood.

"You got somebody else in mind?" I raised an eyebrow at him. "I know you're not thinking of going out on Shirl. She'd kill you before she let any one else have you."

"Not me." He scowled. "But I've got a couple of buddies in the unit that might be interested."

"Oh, and you think a state trooper is going to be laid back? I don't think so. I start dating a trooper, and I'll have every cop in the place keeping an eye on me. I do way too many stupid things to date a cop." I could imagine being stopped for every illegal U-turn I ever made. "Shouldn't you be investigating the scene or something instead of trying to find me a date?"

"I'm interrogating a witness." Steve winked at me. "You'll need to make a statement down at the barracks tomorrow. I'm thinking the V.B.I is going to want to investigate this and they'll want to talk to you."

"V.B.I?"

"Vermont Bureau of Investigation. They'll be involved. At least until murder can be ruled out."

* * * * *

Halfway home, I started to shake. The memory of the blood pooling on the floor around Vera flooded my brain, and I had to pull over. I gulped air and willed the shaking to stop. When that didn't work I tried clearing my mind, but I wasn't any good at meditation at the best of times. My breathing was ragged, and tears were welling in my eyes, so I decided drastic measures were in order, and I checked my cell phone for service.

Cell phone service in Vermont is a crapshoot; you never know when you'll have it and when you won't. Besides that, if you have service and move ten feet in any direction, you're likely to loose it. Luckily, I'd stopped in one of the pullouts that had a reputation for good reception.

"Hey, MacGowan, how's it going?" Jim's voice was warm and cheerful on the other end of the line.

"Hey back." I tried to sound cheerful, but my voice shook, and my eyes were starting to tear up again. "You'll never believe this, but I found Vera dead at work today. I was driving home, but now I'm shaking so hard, I can't keep the car on the road."

"Where are you?"

"At the top of the hill, about three miles from my house."

"I'd come get you, but I won't be able to break free from work for a while. Is Meg or Tom around?"

"Dunno." Meg is my best friend and Tom is her husband.

"Why don't you call Meg? She's a lot nearer to you than I am anyway. It'd be a couple of hours before I could get there."

"I'll call Meg."

"That's my girl. Keep your chin up. I'll be over around eleven."

"Can you bring pizza?"

"Barbecue chicken with pineapple?"

"Yeah. Thanks." I wiped my eyes with my sleeve.

He hung up and I didn't call Meg. She had enough on her plate already. She had four kids, and her husband was the captain of the state police barracks. I was a little surprised I hadn't seen him at the Inn with Steve tonight. I rested my forehead on the steering wheel and closed my eyes. Why did Steve ask me if Vera had enemies? She was mean and petty, someone you avoided if you could. No money or property to speak of. Why murder Vera Post?

Thinking about what a pain Vera had been calmed me down. Gradually, the shaking subsided, and my eyes stopped running. I began to think Steve was just yanking my chain. I couldn't think of one good reason to murder Vera. She just didn't have that much of an impact in the world.

Ten minutes later I pulled into my drive, and my dogs mobbed the car. I'd like to think they were welcoming me home, but they were just looking for food. I tossed Lucky, my old pony, some hay. I dug a carrot out of a bin and fed it to him. Then I gave him a rubdown and told him about my day. I fed the horses that my elderly neighbor Max boards on my property, the rabbits, and the barn cat.

I threw pellets to the chickens. They'd stopped laying again. I was feeding twenty-eight chickens and getting three eggs a day in return. My neighbors thought I was nuts, but I couldn't bring myself to eat them. How could I fry up Speckles or Hermione? Meg's kids had named every single one of those chickens. Besides, I didn't know which three were laying. With my luck I'd eat the only three hens that gave me eggs.

After that, I fed my four dogs. I'm a magnet for unwanted animals, so I've recently collected a ten-month old, oversized, male Irish wolfhound who thinks he's a lap dog. That's in addition to a large, two-year-old male yellow Lab who is a total wimp; a two-year-old boxer with a shoe fetish; and a three-year-old female beagle cross who calls the shots. Their names are Ranger, Hank, Diesel and Annie. Top that off with a furball tabby of a housecat named Annabelle.

It was late when I finally walked into my kitchen, and Jim was already there eating pizza out of the box. There was an open bottle of beer and a jar of Parmesan cheese on the table. His legs were stretched out in front of him, long and lean, with his hiking boots propped on the rungs of my kitchen stool. He was dressed in his casual clothes, tan Dockers and an immaculate golf shirt. The hiking boots were his fashion concession for coming to my house. In town, he wore loafers.

Jim's brown hair curled around his ears, too long for a lawyer. He smiled at me when I walked in, and the smile reached the corners of his lash-rimmed, grey-green eyes. It was his eyes that had attracted me in the first place. In the spring I had attended an evening lecture at Vermont Law School, and Jim had introduced the speaker. I almost flattened him in my rush to leave after the mind-numbing presentation, and he asked me out to coffee. I liked that he wasn't put off by the fact that the law lecture had put me to sleep.

Jim reached out as I walked by, pulling me down into his lap. He dropped a kiss on my head. "So, what happened at work today? You were kidding about Vera, right? Did one of those rich snobs ask you to do something perverted?"

"I wasn't kidding about Vera." I reached out, snagged a slice of pizza and stuffed half of it in my mouth. "I found her lying in a pool of blood." I shivered and slid off his lap. I needed a beer.

"You sure she was dead?"

"Yeah, I'm sure." I shuddered with the memory, grabbed a beer from the fridge and popped it open. "I touched her. She was cold."

Jim stood up and slid his arms around me. I rested my head on his chest, and he held me tight against him. I could feel his heartbeat and the warmth of his chest against my face. He smelled good, like sandalwood. He leaned down and kissed my neck.

"Hmmm. You're warm." I tipped my head and kissed him back. His mouth was soft and cool from the beer.

"Bet I know how to make it better." His breath was hot on my ear. I suddenly lost all interest in pizza.

* * * * *

The sun was shining in the window when I woke to Jim's cell phone ringing. He reached across me to grab it off the night table. His hand hit the lamp, and the phone was knocked to the floor.

"Shit!" Jim dove across my body, caught the lamp before it toppled off the table, and slid off me onto the floor in a tangle of sheets. He rolled over, handed me the lamp, and felt around under him for his phone. "What? Yeah." He untangled himself from the sheets and walked into the hall. He closed the door behind him.

Laughing, I put the lamp back on the table and headed for the shower. I needed to be at work early. Housekeeping at Whispering Birches is my second job. By day, I'm a paste-up artist for the *Royalton Star*, the local weekly paper. My best friend, Meg, owns it. Used to be we actually had to paste the ads and articles onto big sheets of grid paper, but these days the work is all done on the computer.

I could hear my cell phone ringing when I walked out of the bathroom. I wrapped my towel tighter around my body and went searching for it. When I got downstairs, Jim was standing in the kitchen holding my phone in his hand. "I'll give you your phone back if you promise to show me what's under the towel."

I rolled my eyes, dropped my towel on the floor, and laughed when his mouth fell open.

"Gimme." I grabbed the phone from him. Jim slid his arms around my waist as I reached down to pick up my towel.

"No way, I'm not done looking yet."

I scowled at him and flicked open my phone. "Hello?" I gasped as Jim ran his fingers up my spine.

"What took you so long to answer? Are you out at the barn?" It was my mother.

"No, Mom, I'm dealing with inside animals at the moment." I shot Jim an elbow in the ribs. "Stop it!" I hissed at him. "Hang on," I said into the phone. Jim was running his hands down my thighs. I batted him away, grabbed my towel, and scooted into the living room. I put the phone back to my ear. "I'm back."

"Is that James Fisk? You should be nicer to him. You'll never get married if you keep bossing your boyfriends around like that."

"I'm not bossing him around, Mom." I tucked the phone between my ear and shoulder and headed for the bedroom.

"Well, it sounded bossy to me." She had her resigned, what-am-I-going-to-do-about-my-daughter voice on. "When are you coming to visit? We haven't seen you since July."

My mom and dad moved to South Carolina a couple of years back. My mom decided she didn't fancy being old in the snow and bought a condo on the beach with the money her mom had left her. My dad followed along. I think he figured South Carolina with mom was better than Vermont without her. He was still suffering from culture shock.

"I'll come down at Thanksgiving. And maybe Christmas if I can get someone to take care of the animals." I rooted around in my closet and shrugged on my robe.

"I guess I'll have to be content with that. I know it's hard for you to get away. But when you have children, I'll expect you to come more often."

Sheesh. I rolled my eyes as I clicked off the call. When I walked back into the kitchen, Jim was on the phone again. He was scowling and scribbling notes ferociously on a scrap of paper. "I told you earlier." He had the phone between his shoulder and ear. "I don't think that's necessary. Besides, it's intrusive. My personal life is not their business at this point." He glanced up at me. "I've got to go. I'll discuss this with you further when I get to the office."

"Trouble?"

"Just the usual." He picked up his coffee cup. "I'm going to take this with me. All hell is breaking loose in Hanover today, and I still have to go home to shower and change." He gave me a quick kiss, took his coffee and left.
I was chewing a piece of toast when the phone rang again. A truck rumbled by on the road as I answered, and the dogs all started barking.

"MacGowan?" It was Officer Steve. "You there?"

"Yeah, wait a sec." I opened the door and let the dogs out.

"Sounds like all hell is breaking loose over there. You need me to come rescue you?"

"Nah. It's just the dogs warning me that a truck is going by. They feel it's their duty to protect me from harmless strangers. I suppose you need me to come down to the barracks?"

"Yeah, first thing."

"Okay. I'll be there, soonish."

"Good. I'd hate to have to come up there and arrest you."

"Very funny. I bet I could get you in trouble for saying stuff like that."

"Yeah. But you won't."

Shit. I was going to be late for work. I headed back upstairs to stand in front of my open closet. What did you wear when you were giving a statement? Would it help if I dressed like a slut? What about a business suit? Should I dress casually and look unconcerned, or should I wear church clothes to make a good impression?

I sat down on my bed without choosing anything from the closet. I felt numb, and my mind refused to focus. *Relax, it doesn't matter what you wear.* "But it does matter. First impressions are the most important. The credibility of my statement could be determined just by how I look. Oh, shit. Now I'm talking to myself."

Finally, I grabbed my usual jeans and tee-shirt. I slid a blazer over my top so I wasn't too casual and pulled on my favorite footwear. Slouchy black cowboy boots that made me feel braver. Just like Calamity Jane. *Calamity Jane? Surely there were some other cowgirls? Cow women? Cattle women? There had to be lots of strong dames in the old West. Running ranches. Holding down the fort.*

What was wrong with me? Thinking about cowgirls instead of getting my butt down to the barracks. I went into the bathroom to brush some color on my face.

* * * * *

The state police are housed in a brand new building on Route 107, right on the line between Royalton and Bethel. I pulled into the parking lot and took a couple of breaths. The barracks intimidated me. I gathered myself together, squared my shoulders, and swung out of the car.

"Hey, MacGowan," Steve called as I walked in. "I saw your car by the side of the road last night." He walked over to me. "Everything all right?"

"Yeah, I'm fine." I grimaced. "Just had a little reaction to finding a dead person."

"Your first time?" He grinned. "Don't worry, it gets easier."

"If it's up to me, that will be the last time. Do you want to take my statement?"

"Not me. Lieutenant Brooks. Like I said yesterday, the V.B.I. pulled this case. I can't really say anything, but I hope you have a good alibi." He laughed. "By the way, the inspection sticker on your car has expired. I didn't want to ticket you, knowing you'd had a bad day and all, but you might want to get that taken care of before someone else does. There are lots of cops around here that would love an excuse to stop you."

"Give me a break. Most these guys are married. I'm too old for the single guys. Nobody around here would take a second look at me."

"Not true. Officer Smith's looking for a companion." Steve laughed. Officer Smith looked to be about a hundred years old. "You're not married to the boss, and that's a plus." Meg's husband was in charge of the barracks. Meg had a way of charming the men with cookies and a sympathetic ear. Mostly, they thought of her as a second mother, but it was rumored that a few of the officers wouldn't mind being in Tom's shoes.

A uniformed officer stepped into view, and Steve motioned to him. "Looks like Lieutenant Brooks is ready for you. See you later. Don't forget to get that car inspected."

I'd never seen Lieutenant Brooks before. It was all I could do to keep my eyeballs in my head. Brooks was dark haired and had clear blue eyes. He had to be over six feet tall and was muscular without being bulky. I guessed him to be in his early thirties. His uniform made him look well put together. It amazed me that women weren't crashing their cars into the barracks every day just to catch a glimpse of him. But if he was with V.B.I., he was probably based out of Montpelier. Maybe they were crashing into things up there. He'd be the cop I'd most want to be arrested by.

"Ms. MacGowan." Lieutenant Brooks offered me his hand. "Miles Brooks. In here, please."

I followed Brooks into a conference room and couldn't help but notice he had a nice backside too. I wrenched my mind back to the matter at hand. He smiled at me as I sat down, and I hoped like hell he couldn't tell what was going on in my head.

I ran Brooks through yesterday's event. I couldn't think of any new details, and frankly, I wanted to forget what I did remember. At the end of our interview Lieutenant Brooks looked me in the eye. "Did you have reason to dislike Vera?"

"Everyone disliked Vera. Even her sister couldn't stand to work the same shift with her."

"Why's that?"

"Because she liked to make trouble. If two girls weren't getting along, she'd team them up just watch the fireworks. She lied and spread rumors. And while everyone else was busting their butts getting rooms done, she'd sit on hers and eat. Besides that, if you got on her bad side, you get assigned all the shit jobs to do." I'd been on the wrong end of that stick a number of times.

"I understand you are employed at the *Royalton Star*. What do you do there?"

"Typesetting and paste-up."

"Do you like that job?"

"Yeah. I get to work with my best friend. What could be better than that?" *Where was he going with this?*

"Why work part time as a housekeeper? It can't pay all that much."

"I have a lot of animals. Feed and vet bills ad up after a while."

"And you're content to remain as a housekeeper? You aren't gunning for a management position? To earn more?"

"The general manager is a friend of mine. He needed a couple of housekeepers he could rely on to show up. I needed the extra cash. Management isn't flexible enough to accommodate my job at the *Star*."

"Do you usually work in teams at the Inn?" He was making notes on his pad now.

"Yes, we do."

"Why's that?"

"To protect the guests from getting their stuff taken and to protect us from being accused of theft."

"But last night you were working alone?"

"We were short staffed, so I offered to work by myself. Brian trusts me."

"It was your idea to go off by yourself?"

"Yeah."

"And why did you go to that particular cottage?"

"I was there because Dotty broke a carafe, and we keep the extras in that closet. I would have eventually been the one to find Vera anyway. That cottage was on my list of rooms to turn down last night."

"Do you turn down that cottage every night?"

"No. I never know what rooms I'll be doing on any given night until assignments are made. Why do you want to know this stuff?"

"Someone suggested you might want Vera's job."

"Lovely." My heart sank into my stomach, and I wondered who would tell him that. And why.

"Thank you for the information, Ms. MacGowan. Please let us know if you intend to leave the area."

I could feel his eyes on my back as I left the room. I wanted to ask Steve what he thought, but he wasn't at his desk or in the break room. I even took a quick look into the briefing room, but he wasn't there either. I changed tactics and tracked down Tom in his office.

Tom was on the phone when I peeked in his door. He motioned me in, and I sat on one of the wooden chairs in front of his desk.

"What's up, Bella? I don't usually see you down here."

"I had to come see Lieutenant Brooks about Vera's death. I'm the one who found her."

"That's right. Steve told me he'd seen you there. I wouldn't worry, Brooks probably just wanted to talk to you in person. That's pretty standard."

"Do you know how Vera died?"

"I can't hand out details about an ongoing case without talking to the O.I.C. first." Tom smiled. "Especially to a newspaper shark like you."

"Yeah, right. What's an O.I.C.?"

"Officer in charge. In this case, Brooks. Not to change the subject, but I haven't seen John lately. Do you know what he's been up to?" John, my older brother, had been friends with Tom since pre-school.

"He's around. I think he's been hanging out with one of his girlfriends a lot lately."

"That man needs to settle down. He's too old to be tomcatting around. Last I talked to him, he had three girls in three different cities."

"He's always been like that. Not settling down kind of runs in the family."

Tom laughed. MacGowans were notorious for not making long-term commitments. The exception was my father, who fell hard for my mom in high school and never looked back. His brothers and sisters had never married. I had plenty of cousins; they just had parents who had never tied the knot.

"I have no doubt that someone will bamboozle you into making a commitment one of these days. In fact, I'd put money on it. I even know who I'd put money on and it ain't James Fisk."

"What do you mean you know who you'd put money on? You have no reason to believe that I won't commit to James Fisk. He's got as good a chance as anyone."

"James is too sedate for you." Tom was enjoying himself a little too much for my comfort. "You need someone with a little spark in them. A touch of the devil. James is a good boy. He's all about upholding the law. I'll bet you fifty bucks that when you get caught, it'll be by a bad boy."

"And you've got someone in mind. Well, that's just dandy. I hope he's not sitting somewhere pining away for me, 'cause he'll be pining a good long time. I may marry Jim Fisk just to spite you, Thomas Maverick."

Tom grinned.

"Got you, didn't I? You jump for the bait every time, Bella. Every single time. Well, not to worry. I've got plenty of time to collect on my bet. Speaking of time, aren't you supposed to be pasting up the paper? I'm not going to be too happy with you if my wife comes home cranky tonight because you couldn't get the paper done before midnight."

"Talk to your Lieutenant Brooks. I would have been at work hours ago if I didn't need to come down here. It took me forty minutes just to figure out what to wear. So if you're going to blame anyone for Meg's cranky mood, blame him."

Two

I zipped down Route 107 to Route 14. I was feeling lucky because I didn't get stuck behind a tractor, and it only took me ten minutes to get into town. South Royalton is a typical New England village with a big green, two gazebos, two war memorials and a cannon, smack in the middle of town. Chelsea Street runs along the north side of the green, hosting a row of brick buildings. Windsor Street borders the east side, with a few shops and houses. Residences and what used to be the South Royalton Inn sit on Park Street, opposite Chelsea. The bank is housed in a converted train station and sits next to the post office, sandwiched between Railroad Street and the train tracks on the west side of the green.

A hair salon, a print and copy shop, a deli, a video store, a grocery, book store, laundry, two restaurants and a pizza place occupy the lower floors of the buildings on Chelsea Street. The upper floors house apartments and various professional offices. The *Royalton Star* has offices over the laundromat.

I parked next to the green across from our office, jogged across the street, and took the stairs two at a time to the second floor. Meg was sitting at my desk, frowning, when I flung open the door to the office. Her curly bangs had fallen over her eyes, and she absentmindedly blew them out of her face. She looked up at me and blinked.

"I don't know how you stare at this computer screen all day. I've only been here a couple of hours, and already my head hurts. Nothing fits right on the page."

"Sorry I'm late." I tossed my blazer over a chair. "I got called into the barracks"

"It's okay, Tom told me." She squinted back up at me. "You should have called me, though. I might have worried. Here, take your desk. You can do your job for a while." She pushed away from my computer. "See what you can do with that mess, will you, or we'll never make it to press tonight."

We went to press every Tuesday night. The paper came out on Wednesday mornings. Every Tuesday, we worked like madwomen to finish the paper, and every Wednesday morning, we slept in. Normally, we'd both be in here early, inhaling coffee and working out the bugs together. My visit to the barracks had messed up our schedule.

I turned to Meg. "This whole Vera thing has me discombobulated. I didn't sleep great last night. I let my mom get the better of me on the phone this morning, and now I've got the impression that Brooks doesn't think Vera's death was an accident."

"What makes you say that?"

"They asked me to notify them before I leave town."

"Are you leaving town?"

"I wasn't planning on it. Lieutenant Brooks just told me to let him know if I was thinking of leaving town. Maybe I should."

"No. You should not leave town. They'll probably have this whole thing straightened out within the week." Meg looked at the ceiling. "Oh, by the way, Tom says your car needs to be inspected. It's four months overdue."

I spent the first couple of hours double-checking ads I'd designed last week. Then I checked to see if anyone had requested specific page placement. I always try to place ads in logical places, the fundraising dinners near the calendar, the employment ads in with the classifieds, and the birthday announcements that read, "Ain't it nifty, look who's fifty" with fifth-grade braces pictures near the local interest articles. Sometimes, someone wants to shake things up and get prime placement for their ad on the third page. I'm fine with that as long as everything fits.

Except for the occasional "Crap!" it was quiet. Our reporters avoid the office on Tuesdays. They know they'll get roped into running errands, bringing coffee and lunch. Locals who might be tempted to drop by other days of the week knew better than to show up on a Tuesday. Meg and I could get pretty testy during paste-up.

At three o'clock, Meg looked up. "I'm going down for a sandwich. Do you want anything?"

"Yeah." I fished around in my wallet for some bills. "And I need caffeine. A soda would be good."

Meg took my money and headed down the stairs. I turned my attention back to the computer screen, but my concentration had been broken. I put my head down on my desk and thought about Vera and why I shouldn't leave town. I had a hard time believing her death could have been murder. Not that half the people in this town wouldn't love to see her brought down a notch. But murder?

Somewhere in the back of my mind, I heard Meg come back in the room, and I jerked my head up off my desk.

"Too late," Meg laughed. "I know you were sleeping. And I know why. You let Jim sleep over last night." She started singing, "He likes you. He wants your babies…"

I threw an eraser at her head and missed. "Give me a break. Where's my soda? We'll never get the paper done if I don't get some caffeine. The *Royalton Star*, the only paper in Vermont that comes out on a different day every week."

Meg scowled at me and set our sandwiches and sodas on my desk. She grabbed her chair and rolled it over. "How far are you from finishing?"

"Hmmm, I'm guessing I'll be zapping it over to the printer around ten tonight. Why?"

"I wanted to talk to you about something. I've got a problem."

"What? Is Jeremy giving you trouble again?" Meg's oldest was fourteen and a great kid, but he had a mind of his own, and puberty wasn't treating him kindly.

"No it's not the kids. It's me. I have a problem. A huge, horrible problem."

"You're not sick are you?" I was puzzled. Meg's life seemed so perfect. "You're not pregnant?"

"No. Tom and I haven't had any time alone together in ages, so I'm not pregnant." Meg looked down, her face flushed. "You know Scott Howe? The guy we hired to build the new barn."

"Uh huh," I nodded. "Hotty Scotty." Scott Howe is Brad Pitt in a tool belt. He's in his early thirties and has a reputation as a good, honest contractor and a nice guy. I'd seen him over at Meg's. He was easy on the eyes and had a quick smile.

"Well." She sighed. "I'm attracted to him."

"Jeez, Meg. Every woman within a fifty-mile radius could say that. You're married, not buried, as Val would say." Val is a good friend of ours. She's a ton of fun to hang out with but has a tendency to get her friends in trouble. She's also a lawyer, so she has the ability to get us back out of trouble, if she has to.

"No, it's more than that. I'm really attracted to him. If he made a pass at me, I'd drag him into my bed kind of attracted. And I can't stay away. Whenever I have three seconds free, I find myself down at the new barn, flirting."

"Does he flirt back?" Bells were going off in my head. If Scott made a pass at Meg, things could get really ugly. Tom wouldn't tolerate another guy hanging around his wife.

"God, I don't know." Meg sounded miserable. "He's always been friendly. And Tom is never around any more. There are so many new hires at the barracks that he has to be there all the time. He works every weekend, and when he does come home, he has a bunch of chores to do. Jeremy does what he can, but he's in high school now and has tons of homework."

"So what are you going to do?"

"I'm thinking of telling Scott that I'm attracted to him. I thought that might cut some of the tension. Maybe he'd be more careful around me. Maybe if he knew, I'd be embarrassed enough to stay away from him."

"On the other hand, if he's not as nice a guy as everyone thinks he is, he could take advantage of the situation and ruin your marriage. Or he might be so uncomfortable that he quits and leaves your barn half built. Tom would want to know why. You still love Tom, don't you? You don't want to leave him?"

"I never even see Tom anymore. I need companionship, I need affection, and I need sex! If I don't get some soon, I'm going to burst. And don't tell me to take care of myself. Doing it alone in the shower is not the same thing!"

"Hey I didn't say anything about a shower." I looked over at her. "So what do you want to do?"

"I don't know. I just get so worn down from all the bickering up at the house. Those kids are at each other all the time. Even with the banging and hammering, the barn seems peaceful and quiet. And Scott is nice to me." Meg eyes started to tear up. "No one is nice to me any more. The kids are horrid, and Tom doesn't notice them or me. He comes home late and exhausted, shovels dinner in his mouth, and disappears into the den. I guess he still loves me, but it's hard to tell for sure. I thought things would be better when he was promoted to captain, but they've gotten worse. No money was better than no Tom."

I made a mental note to corner Tom next time I saw him. Tom Maverick is my older brother's best friend, and we had a long history together. Ignoring Meg was going to stop now. I'd threaten him, beat him, whatever it took.

Meg sniffed and blew her nose on a tissue. "We'd better get back to work." She pushed her chair back over to her desk.

"Listen, if you do decide to have an affair with Scott, I don't want to know about it. This is not a secret I could keep."

"What if I have an affair with someone besides Scott. Can I tell you about that?"

"No! I've known Tom my whole life. I don't think I could keep a secret from him if I tried. He'd get it out of me. You know he would."

"I know." Meg spoke quietly. "I'm not planning an affair. I don't want to ruin what I've got with Tom. But if something happens I promise not to tell you. Shoot, I promise not to tell me. I can't keep secrets from Tom any better than you can."

Meg proofed pages while I worked on getting everything laid out. It was a system we'd been using for a couple of years. After I'd worked on something for a while, I couldn't see typos or missing lines, and Meg had hawk eyes when it came to that stuff. We printed a hard copy and laid it out on a master so Meg would have copy to mark up.

It was nine-forty before I made the last change and transferred an electronic copy to the printer, and we were done for the night. Meg and I tromped down the stairs together and out into the chilly night air. I contemplated heading down to the corner bar for a drink, but I knew Meg wouldn't go with me. It felt kind of pitiful to sit in the bar by myself.

*****

The next morning, I called our local auto shop, Rockin' Rob's Automotive Repair. Rob could fit me in for an inspection if I got there before ten. So I fed my animals, spent a little time grooming my old pony, Lucky, and made myself coffee and an egg sandwich. I ate the sandwich in the car on the way to the auto shop. Eating while driving on the narrow back roads isn't always the best idea, but I got lucky and didn't meet anyone coming the other way.

Rob's shop is always spotless inside. He's the cleanest mechanic I've ever seen. No tools lying around, grease and oil kept to a minimum. Floor always swept up. I've never been in his bathroom, but I'm willing to bet the toilet and sink aren't black with dirt like they are in the male-owned video store down from the paper.

Rob McCullough is tall and solid with short, dark hair, dark brown eyes, long lashes and an engaging smile. He likes to listen to French music while he's working on cars, and he keeps himself as clean as his shop. He's got pictures of his motorcycle hanging in the shop, and if you encourage him, he'll stand around talking about riding across Canada for half the day. When I was younger, I used to have a crush on him. Who am I kidding? I still think he's fabulous, but we've never been more than mechanic and the girl with the Junker. The Junker changes every so often, but I keep my mechanic.

I strolled into the shop, and Rob went out, pulled my car into the bay, and put it up on the lift. He fussed around underneath it for ten or fifteen minutes, then came to join me by his workbench.

"I'm guessing you were hoping to drive out of here today." I nodded, and he shook his head. "You've got a bad ball joint. I can't give you a new sticker until you get it fixed."

"How much is that going to cost me?" I love my old Toyota, but it's starting to fall apart. I'm afraid I'll be driving on the back roads one day, and the thing will just rattle itself to death, leaving a string of car parts in the road behind me.

"I'll call you with an estimate. I'll need to get in touch with the parts shop. I can get you a quote today, but I won't be able to finish the work right away. I could get it back to you the by end of next week."

"Oh, crud. If I don't get the dang thing fixed, I'm going to end up with a ticket. If I do get it fixed, I'm going to have to stop eating for a month." I puffed out some air. "Do you want me to leave it with you?"

I called Jim to see if he could pick me up and take me to the office, but he wasn't answering his cell. So I called Meg. Meg was home with a sick seven-year-old, so she called Tom to see if he could pick me up. Tom sent Steve to come get me.

Rob laughed when he saw the cop car pull in. "Nice taxi you got there. This is going to be good for a few laughs at the bar tonight. I don't know what's going to be better, teasing Steve for picking you up, or teasing you for getting picked up by a cop." He grinned and disappeared back inside his shop.

I slid into the passenger seat of Steve's car. "Thanks for coming to get me. Pretty sad when the state trooper doesn't have anything better to do than give rides to stranded women."

"The only reason you're getting a ride is that the boss thinks he needs to watch over you. Otherwise, you'd be walking like everyone else." He smiled.

"Anything cooking on Vera's death? Lieutenant Brooks asked me not to leave town. That doesn't sound like accidental death to me."

"Not my case," Steve replied, his eyes fixed on the road.

"But you've heard something, haven't you?"

"Not my place to say," Steve looked unhappy. He shot me a look. "I don't want to lose my job, which is what will happen if I tell you anything at this point."

Steve dropped me at my house. I was majorly bummed about my car but I did have a back-up. My dad's old 750 Kawasaki Spectre was stored in my barn. The weather was getting a little chilly for riding, but it was better than puttering around town on a tractor. A tractor could put a real damper on a person's style. I'd discovered this in high school when hunky Bucky Osborn dumped his truck in the river and had been reduced to driving his John Deere into town. His date-ability factor dropped dramatically.

I tromped into my barn and pulled the sheet off the bike. It wasn't too dusty. I'd ridden it during the summer and only put it up for the winter a couple of weeks ago. I got my motorcycle license in my early twenties when my dad bought himself a Honda Goldwing and lent me the Kawasaki. We used to ride together a lot, zipping up Route

100 on warm summer evenings and riding the scenic road up Stowe Mountain.

I checked to see that no essential parts had been chewed by critters and rolled the bike out of the barn. I picked up the gas can and put a couple of gallons in the tank. The engine turned right over, purring like a big cat. I rode it up to the house and went inside to grab my helmet, gloves, and leather jacket. My Dad had drilled the importance of protective gear into me. "I don't ever want to have to watch someone picking gravel out of that pretty face," he'd say to me. I didn't want anyone picking gravel out of my face either.

The phone rang while I was in the house searching for my gloves.

"Hey, Bree, it's Rob. It's four hundred and fifteen dollars to get your car repaired and inspected. And I don't take credit cards, in case you forgot."

"Okay, Rob. Go ahead and fix it. Thanks, I guess." What kind of businessperson doesn't take credit cards? And where was I going to find four hundred big ones by the end of next week? Crap and double crap. I pulled on my gear and mounted the bike. I shot off to work so I could raise the money to fix my car.

* * * * *

I'd been sitting at my desk at the paper for a couple of hours when the phone rang.

"MacGowan." It was Jim on the phone. "I'm downstairs in the diner. How about coming down for a coffee?"

Our local cafe is small. Three booths are crammed against one wall, and four tables crowd the blue and white tile floor. Opposite the booths is a counter normally packed with locals. Most of the time, it's so tight in there you have to reach over someone's head to pay the bill.

I joined Jim in one of the booths against the wall. Jim studied the menu like he'd never seen it before. He could be quiet sometimes but not usually when we were out together. I felt a big, fat ball of unease building in my stomach. There was too much weird stuff going on these days. I touched Jim's hand.

"You're powerful quiet." I used my best Vermont drawl.

He smiled at me. "I like it when you talk like an old Vermonter."

"I am an old Vermonter. My grandparents were born here."

"Yeah, but usually you talk like an educated American, not an old timey Vermonter. I like it."

"I'll keep that in mind, especially as now you've come out of your quiet spell. Is there something going on?"

"Just work stuff. Nothing to worry about. At least I don't think it's anything to worry about. Guess we'll have to wait and see."

"We'll have to wait and see, or you'll have to wait and see?"

"I can't tell you about it, so I guess technically it's I'll have to wait and see."

I stuck my tongue out at Jim. I don't know what it is about his job that drops my maturity level down about five notches. I guess I'm just a Nosey Nora. I don't like being the one that isn't in on the secret. I was worried the secret might be about me.

"I hate that we can't talk about your job. It makes me feel like I don't really know you."

"You know me as well as anybody. You can't ask for more than that."

"Well, yeah, I can ask for more. But that doesn't mean I'll get it, does it?"

Sandy interrupted us with a pot of coffee. I ordered my usual muffin. Jim finally settled on a bagel with cream cheese.

"So," Jim said. "Have you recovered from your little adventure the other day?"

"As long as I don't think about it. It's not an experience I'd like to repeat."

"Not thinking of taking up a life of crime? Or is that a life of crime busting?"

"Neither. I'm not taking up anything that offers up the opportunity for viewing bodies. Or blood."

"Then I guess you're going to have to give up your job at the Inn. Because so far that's the only place you've seen a dead body."

"I wish I could give up that job. In order to do that, I'd have to get rid of most of my animals. I just keep getting more and more. They seem to be collecting me."

"You could just stop bringing them home."

"I can't just leave them in the street. And after I pick them up, they adopt me. I tried to find Ranger a home. But no one else is nutty enough to take on a goofy, giant puppy that thinks he's the size of a Corgi. So he ends up with me. Next thing I know, I'll be overrun with hamsters. Or guinea pigs. Or pot bellied pigs."

"Those, at least, you could eat."

"As if. I can't even eat chickens that aren't laying eggs."

"You have a serious problem. You can't get rid of your animals, you can't eat your animals, and you can't quit working at a dead-end job because of your animals. You'd never make it as a lawyer. There's not an ounce of logic in that brain."

"If I was a lawyer, I wouldn't be lacking in money, which would solve the animal problem. But I'd probably shoot myself in the head out of boredom, which would leave my animals homeless, and then you'd have to take care of them."

"I'd have no problem eating those birds. Every time I had chicken for dinner, I'd think of you and how if you only had fewer animals, you'd still be alive."

"Jeez. You're such a prince." I reached across the table for the sugar and knocked over my cup. The coffee ran across the table toward Jim. I grabbed a handful of napkins and tried to stop the hot liquid from running off the table into his lap. As I reached for a second handful of napkins, my hand hit Jim's coffee cup, sending it flying off the table right into his lap.

"Shit!" Jim jumped out of his seat, a gigantic coffee stain spreading across his lap. "MacGowan, you're a disaster."

The waitress ran over with a damp cloth and made as if to mop Jim's lap. Jim took the rag from her and blotted his pants. I felt horrible about the hot coffee, but there was a bubble of laughter rising in my throat. I forced the urge down again but the effort must have shown on my face.

"What's wrong with you?" Jim asked. "Did you get coffee on you?"

"No." A smile spread across my face despite my efforts to stop it. "I'm fine." A snort of laughter forced its way out of me.

"Are you laughing at me? This isn't exactly funny, you know. My legs are burned. To say nothing of other, more sensitive, parts."

"I know it's not funny." My eyes started to water with the effort. "I'm sorry. I don't know why I'm laughing." Another snort of laughter burst out of me. I got up and ran for the ladies room. I got through the door and leaned against the wall, my shoulders shaking with mirth. I stood laughing for a few minutes before I could pull myself together.

Jim was pulling his overcoat on when I made it back to the table. "You're hilarious. I could hear you laughing from here." He didn't sound happy. "I'm going home to change. Then I have to take this suit to the cleaners and make an afternoon meeting. This has got to be the tenth time you've spilled something on me. Remind me not to ask you for coffee again."

"Last time it was Coke. At least that didn't burn you. And I paid to have your suit cleaned."

Jim rolled his eyes at me. "You're an accident waiting to happen."

"I'm sorry, I'll pay for your suit to be cleaned again. I didn't mean to laugh. I just couldn't help it."

He shook his head at me as he stiff-legged it out the door. I paid the bill and apologized to the waitress for making a mess. Then I made my way out the door. I was going to try and put a dent in the pile of work sitting on my desk.

I tripped on the way up the stairs and hit my knee. "Damn!" I sat on a step and rubbed my stinging knee. Tears welled up in my eyes, and a sob rose in my throat. *Pull yourself together,* I said to myself. *First you're laughing at things that aren't funny and now you're crying over nothing.* But I couldn't stop. I sat there sobbing until tears ran off my chin.

I was afraid that someone might come through the lower door and see me crying, but didn't want to go in the office either. Meg could have dropped in, and she'd want to know what was wrong. I couldn't tell her, because I didn't know myself. I gulped in air and wiped my face on the sleeve of my coat.

I got up and limped up the stairs into the office. It was empty, thank God. I slipped into the bathroom and blew my nose. Then I splashed water on my face and blotted it off with a paper towel. I rummaged around in my purse and pulled out some mascara. I blinked it through my lashes and took a look at myself in the mirror.

I went out and sat down at my desk. I rubbed my knee while my computer came back to life. I'd probably be limping for a couple of days. I shook my head. If I didn't pull myself together they'd be carting me off to the funny farm.

At the end of the workday, I dialed Jim's number and was a little surprised when he actually answered.

"Hey. Just callin' to see how you're doing. Did you recover from having coffee with me?

"The trouble with you, MacGowan, is that you never know when to leave something alone." He disconnected.

I couldn't even pretend to myself that he was kidding.

Three

I shut down the office, pointed the Kawasaki towards the Inn, and headed to my night job. I wasn't really looking forward to going back, but I needed to fix my car before the snow flew, and I couldn't pass up a night's pay. The evening air was cold against my face, and the sharp scent of winter was in the air.

The direct route to Whispering Birches had me riding over five miles of dirt road. I rode slowly and kept my eyes sharp. The last thing I needed was to lose traction and go down in a corner or get taken out by a deer. Or, worse, a moose. A broken leg would put a big crimp in my ability to get around.

I pulled into the employee parking lot, yanked my bike up onto its center stand, and buckled my helmet to the back. I ran my hands through my hair to minimize helmet head and strode down the path to the laundry building. The gravel crunched under my feet as I stepped carefully on the slope. I could feel the stones underfoot threatening to roll and send me falling.

The laundry building was up the hill behind the main house, hidden from view behind a stand of evergreens. It could be seen from the road but not from any of the guest rooms. The windows were cracked open, and bits of conversation floated over the sound of the radio. There was a constant battle between the women who listened to rock and those who listened to country. Country must have won today. I could hear Toby Keith singing.

A covered entryway let us pull our Jeeps right up to the sliding door. In theory, this kept the rain and snow out of the clean sheets and towels. The gravel turned to cement as I stepped under the portico. I brushed past a Jeep parked outside the entrance and pushed the button that opened the door. The warm air rushed out at me. The dryers and the huge roller iron used for ironing linens and bedding kept the building nice and warm--too hot in summer or when we were working hard.

Kim and Hailey were working at two tall tables, folding towels. Vera's sister Dolly, who I assumed was taking over as supervisor, was standing at the iron with Terri. Terri works days in the elementary wing of the school as an aid. Kim and Hailey are high school girls from the next town working nights for a little extra cash.

Kim flipped her blond hair off her face and glared at me. "I didn't think we'd see you in here tonight."

"Why not?" I was puzzled by her hostility. Kim could get in a snit on occasion, but as far as I knew, I hadn't done anything to get on her bad side.

"Everybody knows you hated Vera," Hailey chimed in. "It's indecent for you to be here."

"I found her dead. I didn't kill her." I was angry now. "Every single one of you had a problem with Vera. Kim, you stomped out of here early last Thursday because Vera pissed you off."

"Yeah, but we didn't have the opportunity to kill her." Kim flipped her hair. "We were all working in teams when you found her. None of us could have killed her."

"Wait a minute. I thought her death was an accident."

"The cops have been hanging around asking questions," said Dolly. "Seems like they think it was murder."

"Great. And you've all decided that I did it. Jeez."

I walked into the break room and clocked in. I wasn't exactly surprised that Vera's death wasn't accidental, but it still disturbed me. I couldn't tell if the girls seriously thought I would murder someone. On top of that, niggling around in my head was the thought that I was working where a murderer was lurking.

I had my head in my hands when Dolly walked in. "Those girls are just being nasty. Don't pay any attention to them. It must have been awful finding Vera lying in the blood like that." Dotty patted me on the shoulder. "I need someone to go down to the kitchen and get the treats. I thought you might like to get out of here."

"Yeah. Thanks. You want me to check the office and common rooms while I'm down there?"

"We've already done the office. Go ahead and check the common rooms. Take your time. We've got a while before people start leaving their rooms for dinner."

I grabbed the plastic container we used for carrying turndown treats and walked down the hill. I could have driven, but I wanted to be away as long as possible. The air felt good, and there was the beginning of an awesome sunset over the Green Mountains. I was tempted to sit on the grass and watch the sky change color, but I didn't feel like getting chewed out.

I slipped into the kitchen and hunted down the dessert chef, Amy Kruse. Amy was a petite blond who'd been with the Inn for about six months and was getting rave reviews. The last dessert chef had made things like tiny nuggets of crystallized ginger or mint leaves dipped in chocolate to put beside the beds at night. I don't know what he was thinking. More of those ended up in the trash than in anybody's mouth. Probably why he wasn't working here anymore.

Amy made decadent brownies and cookies, special truffles or chocolate-dipped fruit. She always set aside a few treats for the turndown crew, even though the head chef frowned on staff eating treats. I didn't know what the big deal was. The kitchen and wait staff ate extras and goof-ups all day long. If the presentation wasn't perfect, it couldn't be served to a guest, so an employee ate it. Otherwise, it just went to waste.

Amy had chocolate caramel brownies today. She hadn't finished frosting them, so I helped myself to an unfrosted one and went to tidy up the common rooms. I flew through the double set of swinging doors that separate the kitchen from the dining room, sweeping my eyes around the room for any detail out of place. I was tidying magazines in the tearoom when Gunnar Ericson, the man in whose cabin Vera had died, sauntered in.

Gunnar stars on a daytime soap opera called, "The Unfaithful." I'd guess his age to be thirty-ish, and he's tall, well built, and handsome in a daytime TV kind of way. He's got the classic Matthew McConaughey thing going for him: blue eyes, blond hair, great smile. Women swoon over him wherever he goes. I wondered if he came to Vermont to take a break from all that.

"Excuse me." I started to brush past him to make for the door. Housekeepers were supposed to be invisible. If a guest showed up in a room where I was working, I was supposed to disappear, pronto. Only the wait staff were allowed to talk to guests.

Gunnar slid around me and blocked my exit. "Wait a minute. You've got something on your face." He brushed a brownie crumb off my lip in a gesture that was far too familiar for a complete stranger. He slid his hand under my chin. "You know, it's pretty lonely around here. Why don't you come to my room later and cheer me up?"

I refrained from saying that after work I would be stinky and sweating from busting my fanny all evening.

"I'm sorry. I'm not allowed to socialize with the guests. Company policy. I'd lose my job." I backed away

"I'm sure I could get Brian to bend the rules for me." Gunnar smiled his gazillion watt smile at me. "There is a hot tub in my room. Come share it with me."

"Sorry, I really can't. I have to get back to work." I slid around him and almost ran out the door. I made a beeline for Brian's office. If a guest approached a staff member, we were supposed to let him know right away. That way, if anyone made a stink later, Brian would know the truth about what happened. Or at least his employee's version of the truth.

Brian gave me a guest/staff incident report to fill out. "How are you doing, Bree? Finding Vera was tough."

"I feel kind of weird, but it'll be fine."

He nodded his head. "If you need anything, let me know. Your dad would never forgive me if I let anything bad happen to you." My dad had been Brian's dad's boss, way back when. "Oh, and I noticed your car needs inspecting. Better take care of that."

"It's in the shop now. Sheesh. You'd think no one in this town had anything better to do than to check other people's inspection stickers." I hurried back to the kitchen and picked up our treat box, now filled to the brim. It was dark and chilly now, and I moved quickly up the hill. I was feeling sort of creeped out being back here and having Gunnar hit on me.

I was relieved to step into the light and warmth of the laundry. The crew was all sitting on one of the low sorting tables waiting for rooms to be called out. Normally, we divided into teams of two, but my partner hadn't bothered to come to work, so we split into a group of two and a group of three. Dolly and I took the main buildings, while the others worked on the cottages. I was glad not to be with the younger women and relieved that I wouldn't have to drive by the empty cottage where Vera died.

We spent the evening zipping silently along secret passageways and getting supplies out of hidden cupboards. The whole place was designed to give us as little exposure to the guests as possible. We were the proverbial house elves, traveling through underground corridors and popping unseen into rooms. We'd tidy up, turn down the beds, and leave brownies before disappearing again.

At the end of the evening, we carted trash, wet towels and rumpled sheets back to the laundry and dumped them all on the sorting table. It took us another thirty minutes to sort everything into piles, take out the trash, fill the washers, recycle and clean everything up. It was nine-thirty when I finally clocked out, jumped on my bike, and motored out of there.

I knew that I should go home and feed my animals, but I wanted to check on Meg, so I headed down the hill into Royalton. I live in an old farmhouse up in the hills. Meg and Tom live in an old farmhouse on the edge of town. That means the road they live on is actually paved, and in the winter it gets plowed on a regular basis, unlike my road.

The wind was whipping over the White River and up the flood plain when I got off the Kawasaki. I shivered. There is a reason this part of town is called Windstorm Valley: it blows nonstop three seasons out of the year. I scrunched my shoulders and hurried to the house. I knocked out of courtesy and let myself in.

Meg was at the kitchen table with Jeremy, their heads bent over a book. I pulled out a chair and sat across from them. Meg looked up and smiled at me. "Hey, there."

"Whatcha doin'?" I peered over the table at the textbook.

"French test tomorrow," said Jeremy. "Dad's better at French than Mom, but he's at the barracks again."

"I know just enough to be dangerous," said Meg, "but I think he's got most of this stuff memorized now. It's all weather vocab."

"So, Jeremy," I asked. "How do you say it's colder than a witch's, uh, toe outside?" Meg was giving me the beady eyeball.

"C'est froid et venteux à l'extérieur."

"Sounds good to me. You'll get an A."

"Go on upstairs, now," Meg said to Jeremy. "Bree and I need to talk."

Jeremy raised a hand in farewell and headed out of the room. We listened to him tromp up the stairs, heard his door close and his stereo go on. Sounded like he was listening to Nine Inch Nails.

"So," I said. "Have you heard anymore about Vera's death? The girls at work were telling me that the cops have been hanging around, and the cabin she died in still has crime scene tape all around it."

"Tom's not talking. Not that he would, but it's tougher this time. He's got to be seen as impartial, or they'll move the investigation."

"So it really is murder then. I was hoping this was all going to go away." I put my head in my hands. "The girls at work think it was me."

"That's just sour grapes. They're just jealous 'cause you're friends with Brian. You know that."

I opened my mouth to answer, but the door swung open, and Tom banged in with three of Meg's dogs surging around his feet. He pushed the door closed, avoided tripping over the dogs, and planted a kiss on the top of Meg's head.

"Hey, Babe, Bella," he said. "How's everything here? The kids doing okay?"

"Jeremy could have used your help with French tonight," Meg replied. "But I think he'll do well on his test tomorrow. I'd better go up and tell him it's lights out. I'll be back in a minute." Meg wasn't fooling me. I knew she still sang a goodnight song to each of her kids. The fact that Jeremy stayed up later than she did half the time didn't stop her.

I waited until she was out of earshot and turned to Tom. "You are on my list, mister." I pointed my finger at his chest. "You keep neglecting my best friend, and I'm going to kick your butt."

"Jeez, Bella," Tom rubbed his hand across his head. "I've got a lot going on down at the barracks right now. Meg knows that. She understands."

"What Meg understands is that you haven't taken her out in months. And when was the last time you two hit the hay together? The woman needs some attention, Tom. There are plenty of guys around here that would be happy to fill in the gaps you're leaving. All they're waiting for is half a hint that she's unhappy, and they'll be following her around like these guys." I tilted my head toward the dogs and jabbed him in the solar plexus with my finger.

"Shit, Bella. I know she needs attention, but she seems to be making out all right. I thought I could concentrate on the job for a while. Get things up at the barracks under control."

"That place has always been a madhouse. It's going to take more than a few months to make it anything else. It's not worth losing your marriage over." I poked him again.

He grunted and pushed my finger away. "I didn't even consider that was a possibility."

"Take her out to dinner. Better still, go somewhere tonight. Drag Meg down to Crossroads, dance, get drunk, then bring her home and take advantage of her. That's what I'd do if I were a guy."

"What about the kids? Can't leave them here alone. Gemma might wake up. And I doubt the animals have been fed."

"I'll stay with the kids. And I can feed your animals while you and Meg are getting changed. You won't get this offer every day, so you'd better get moving."

"What about *your* animals? Have they been fed yet?"

"No, but my neighbor Max owes me a favor. I'll call and ask if him to throw them some food. It's no problem."

"Thanks, Bella. I'll go ask Meg if she wants to go."

"You'll go *tell* Meg that you're going." I grabbed my coat and headed to the barn. I knew the barn routine by heart. I'd fed their animals when each of the kids was born, when Meg and Tom were on their honeymoon, and any number of other times. I checked to see that the cows had round bales and water. I threw the horses good hay and grained them. I stopped and scratched Meg's old Morgan, Falstaff, behind the ears.

I latched the door to the chicken house to keep out foxes and weasels and started down to the duck pond at the bottom of the hill. I was about halfway down when I stepped on a slick patch of earth, and my feet slid out from under me. I landed on my butt in the mud. A few choice words escaped me, and I heard laughter from behind me.

Rob, my mechanic, was standing on the road above the barn looking down at me. "Nice language," he called down.

"What are you doing here? I've never seen you lurking around here at night."

"Farmer Ron's cows got loose. I was helping him herd them home."

"Why don't you come down here and help me? We'll see what kind language comes out of you."

"No, thanks. I know what kind of language would come out of me. I always swear in French."

"So you're going to walk away and leave me sitting here in the mud?"

"Yep. But I'll make for it up by taking you to coffee tomorrow. I'll pick you up at the paper around ten-thirty." He sauntered off down the road.

"Bastard," I muttered under my breath, not really meaning it. I knew he was too smart to try and extract me from the mud. He was probably on his way to meet his girlfriend in town. I got up, slopped down the hill, and fed the ducks. I stepped in a puddle at the edge of the pond and made my way back up to the house, squelching with every step.

I went through the back door and into the mudroom. "Hey, guys," I called out. "I've got a small mud problem." I bent down and undid the buckles on my boots. I slid them off and put them by the door.

Tom looked in at me and laughed. "What happened to you? "We don't even have ice out there yet."

"Ran into a little trouble with that muddy spot on the hill. I'm going to have to take these jeans off, or you're going to have mud all over your house."

Tom disappeared into the laundry room and came back with a pair of clean sweats. "Here, you can wear these. I don't think you'd fit in Meg's jeans. You're about a foot taller than she is."

"And just about as big around as you are. Nice of you not to say so. Now you guys get out of here before you turn into pumpkins."

Meg came into the kitchen and gaped at me standing in the mudroom. "Oh my God, Bree, I'm so sorry. Tom should have warned you about the hill. He slipped on it yesterday. Came in head-to-toe in mud. There's a spring running at the top of the hill, and it's turned the path into a mire."

"I'm all right. Rob McCullough was walking on the road and saw me fall, so my pride is hurting, but other than that, it's just a little wet dirt. Now get on out of here before I change my mind and take my muddy self home."

Meg and Tom left for the bar arm in arm, and I was feeling pretty smug. I was thinking that this might be the end of Meg's attraction to Scott Howe when Tom stomped back in the door.

"Bella, before I forget, I've got some bad news. Vera's death wasn't caused by a fall. It's being handled as a murder. Unfortunately, you're on the suspect list. I wanted you to hear it from me before word got around."

"Great. Not only do I have to deal with the trauma of finding a corpse, but now I'm accused of murder too. I've had better weeks."

"Not accused, just a suspect. You'd be on the list even if you hadn't found her body, because you worked with her." Tom sighed. "But it definitely puts you in the spotlight. For what it's worth, I don't think anyone really thinks it was you. At least, no one that actually knows you."

Meaning I was number one suspect in Lieutenant Brooks' eyes. Great.

"Get out of here. Meg's waiting for you. I promise not to kill anybody while you're out."

Tom grinned at me and headed back out the door. I stripped off my mud-covered jeans, pulled on Tom's sweats, and slumped in a kitchen chair. *Crap*, I thought, *crap, crap, crap.* I would have yelled, if the kids weren't supposed to be sleeping.

I dug my phone out of my jacket pocket and flipped it open. Jim picked up his phone on the third ring.

"I'm having a very weird week. Got a minute to talk?"

"Not really. I'm right in the middle of something. I'll call you tomorrow." And he rang off.

I stared at my phone. It was ten-thirty at night. What could he be in the middle of now? Something didn't feel right to me, but I shook it off. Everything seemed bizarre at the moment.

*****

I was sitting in front of the TV when Meg and Tom walked in. It was one-thirty in the morning, not too bad considering they hadn't left home until after ten. Meg was laughing and hanging onto Tom.

"Had a few too many." Tom grinned at me. "I think I might get lucky tonight."

"You'd better believe it, Big Boy." Meg giggled. "You are mine tonight." She stood on her toes to whisper in his ear.

Tom blushed bright red. "Easy girl, Bella's still here."

"She couldn't hear me." Meg giggled. "Anyway, Bree's a grown-up. She knows the birds from the bees by now."

"Yeah but she may not know about what you just suggested."

I stood up. "I'm outta here before I get roped into something we will all regret later."

"Chicken." Meg laughed.

"Yeah, I'm Chicken Little. See you tomorrow Meg. Later, Tom."

I grabbed my jacket and muddy jeans and headed for the door.

"Hey, Bella," Tom called after me. "Thanks for the advice." He grinned at me. "Hanging out at the barracks is definitely overrated."

* * * * *

Next morning, I dragged myself out to the barn early and gave my animals some overdue attention. It was drizzling steadily, turning everything to mud and muck. The chickens liked it. They were spreading their wings and preening, taking a rain bath. One of the roosters was splashing around in a puddle trying to make the ladies look at him. I swear those hens were rolling their eyes.

On the way back to the house from the barn, I slid in the mud and went down on my knees in some horse manure. "Crap."

"Yeah, literally," said a voice from the road. Rob was sitting in his Toyota 4x grinning at me. I hadn't heard him drive up. I struggled to my feet.

"What? Are you stalking me? I don't really need an audience for every stupid thing I do, you know. If I did, I'd date a cop." I trudged toward the road, flicking mud off my hands.

"You date a lawyer, isn't that the same thing?"

"No. Anyway, you can only be dating if you actually talk to someone, which I haven't for at least, uh," I thought a moment, "since yesterday. I guess I can't really complain."

"He's probably just working on a case. You know how those lawyer guys are. Serious about their work." He leaned out the window to rub Ranger's head. "Anyway, I just dropped by to see if you wanted a ride into work. It's kind of wet for the bike today."

"Yeah, I could go for that. Just give me ten minutes to get ready." I looked down at myself. "Make that twenty minutes." I headed for the house.

Rob parked his truck and followed me into the kitchen. I stood just inside the door for a minute, undecided. I didn't want to track mud and manure through my house, but I wasn't comfortable getting undressed in front of Rob. My loathing for cleaning overcame my embarrassment.

"Turn around for a minute. I don't want to track mud all over the house, so I'm going to take my clothes off here."

"That's fine. Go ahead and do what you need to do."

"Be nice," I gave him what my mom would call the beady eyeball. "Turn around and look out the window, or I'll tell your girlfriend on you."

"Spoilsport." But he turned and looked out the window.

I shucked my boots and peeled off my wet, stinky clothes. I left them in a pile near the laundry room door and took off across the kitchen in my bra and panties. A wolf whistle stopped me. I looked over my shoulder to see Rob watching me leave the room.

"Nice undies."

"You cheated. Better watch your back, McCullough. When you least expect it, I'm going to take you down."

"Can't wait." He winked at me.

I sighed and took myself upstairs to get cleaned up. I intended to take a quick shower, but washing off the animal smell and mud took a while. I had to shampoo twice and then figured I might as well shave while I conditioned my hair. My conscience started to bother me, and I wondered if Rob had a customer waiting for him. I gave my hair a quick rub with the towel and combed it out. I pulled on a pair of jeans and a tee shirt and shoved my feet into a pair of dry hiking boots. My motorcycle boots from last night were still soggy.

Rob was sitting on my couch when I came down the stairs into the main room. He was wearing jeans and a long-sleeve undershirt with a flannel open over the top. Hank had his head in Rob's lap with his eyes closed. Rob was stroking his ears, and I swear you could almost hear that dog purr. Rob smiled at me.

"Mud all gone?"

"Yeah, mud, horse shit and whatever else I picked up out at the barn. Sorry it took me so long. Shall we?" I tilted my head toward the door.

"I don't know. Hank here seems to think it's my job to scratch his ears."

"Hank is a big baby. He may not like it, but he's going outside with the rest of the dogs."

I shooed the dogs out the door and we headed for Rob's truck. It was a twelve-minute drive to town from my place when the roads were dry, and I wasn't stuck behind a tractor. With Rob driving, it took us fifteen minutes in the mud. I'm pretty sure he was a dirt track driver in another life. He turned to me as we pulled up in front of the launderette.

"I'll pick you up at ten-thirty for coffee. Are you working at the 'dairy' tonight?"

"No, it's an off night for me. Not too many guests this week."

"Good. I'll come after work and give you a ride home, too. What time do you think you'll be done here?"

"Six-ish, I think. But I'm flexible, if that doesn't work for you."

"No, six is good. See you later. Don't forget coffee."

I jumped out of the truck, and he drove off. *Nice guy,* I thought, *too bad he's seeing Lisa Clarkson. Wait a minute, I'm seeing someone too. So cool it. Rob is a friend. A friend.* I finished talking myself out of a relationship with Rob and headed toward the lower door to the office. Before I could push the door open, my feet veered off course and took me to the coffee shop. I wanted a muffin.

I stood at the counter trying to catch Sandy's eye. I heard laughter from a table behind me and took a look around. Lucy Howe, one of our reporters, who also happens to be my archenemy, was sitting at a table with a group of women. Several of them had been looking my way but swung their heads away as I turned toward them. Lucy made a comment under her breath, and they laughed again.

I thought about going over to find out what the big joke was, but Sandy came up the counter, and I figured if I didn't order now, I'd never get my breakfast.

"What's with them?" I jerked my head toward the twittering women.

"Lucy Howe has been holding court all morning. She shuts up when I come around, but she's finding something highly amusing."

"Why do I feel as if this has something to do with me?"

"Well, it could just be paranoia. Then again, it might be the way they all look at you when they're laughing. Don't know. Coffee and a muffin?"

Four

I took my coffee and muffin upstairs to the office. Meg hadn't arrived yet, no surprise. She was probably sleeping off a night of drunken debauchery. I powered up my computer and downloaded my email. Most of our articles came from the reporters electronically. Some of the local interest stuff about the ladies club and school lunches got called in, but luckily for me, most everything else came to me already typed.

I was hard at work putting together the calendar of events when Meg finally waltzed in. She had a smug smile on her face and a swing in her walk. Good stuff.

"Everything hunky dory at home again?"

"Things are good." Meg smiled. "Tom said he'd make sure that we get more time together, no kids, at least once a week. More if he can manage it. So things are good."

"I'm glad. Problem solved, then?"

"Well, not exactly," Meg grimaced and looked down at the rug. "Yesterday, I told Scott I was attracted to him."

My eyebrows just about shot off the top of my head. "You didn't! God, Meg, what got into you? What did he say?"

"He said he was attracted, too, but thought I was just flirting for a little fun. He was embarrassed. He doesn't want to cause a rift in my marriage, and he had to think about what to do."

"What to do about what?"

"I think what to do about getting the barn finished." Meg sighed. "Man I really blew it. If Scott tells Tom he isn't going to finish the barn, Tom is going to want to know why. He'll make him talk. He's good at that. Guilty guys always confess to Tom. That's one of the reasons he's such a good cop. They take one look at his face and spill the beans."

"Well, maybe if you tell Scott you'll stay away from the barn, he'll feel like he can finish it. Why, why, why?" I hit my head with the base of my hand. "This is the kind of dumb stuff I do. This isn't you."

"I got flustered. I was wound up, and I didn't really want anything to happen. Well, I guess part of me wanted something to happen, or I wouldn't have kept hanging around. I just blurted it out."

"I think you should lay low for a while. Come to work more. Stay away from the barn. Spend time with Tom and the kids. Maybe it will all blow over."

"God, I hope so. Man, I'm so stupid sometimes."

We went to work on the paper, and silence fell over the office. It was a quiet day, no phones ringing, no reporters hanging over our shoulders. The time passed quickly, and before I knew it, Rob was standing next to me holding my jacket.

"Time to go, Cinderbella. I owe you coffee."

Meg raised her eyebrows at me as I waved goodbye. Let her wonder, I thought, and grinned. I knew I'd get a grilling when I got back to the office.

"What are you grinning about," Rob asked me. "I know you're not that happy to be going to coffee with me."

"Sorry. Just a thing between Meg and me."

"You going to tell me about this thing?"

"Uh, no. I don't think I could without sounding like a complete idiot. Besides, it's good for a girl to be mysterious sometimes."

Rob's rolled his eyes at me, but he didn't say anything. We got into his truck and motored over to The Sugar House on Route 14. The place was packed, as usual, but the hostess was a good friend, and she slid us into a little table for two.

I ordered coffee and a muffin. Rob ordered hot tea. The rain was pounding on the windows, and leaves were blowing and sticking to the glass. I was silently thankful that I wasn't riding the bike today.

"So when do I get my car back? I'm going to miss it, if this keeps up." I pointed my chin at the window.

"I'm waiting on parts. I'll get it to you as soon as I can." He paused for a minute, considering me. "Don't take offense, but are you going to able to eat if you pay me next week? I'd hate to see you starving."

"Don't have much choice, do I? I'll just buy groceries with my credit card. Not my favorite, but better than trying to ride the bike in the snow. Anyway, it's a fair trade. I'm paying your bill with cash."

"The reason I'm asking is that I'm pretty flush right now. Lots of inspections and tire swaps. Fast money stuff. I'd be fine with it if you needed to pay installments. Only don't tell anybody I do that. I only offer payments to people I trust to pay. And folks who really need the favor."

"So which am I? Someone you trust or one that needs the favor? Wait. Don't answer that. I don't want to know. Anyway, I'm fine. My grandparents left me the house, so I don't have payments. I don't make a whole lot of money, but as long as I don't have vet bills, I don't need a whole lot of money."

"Keep it in mind if anything changes."

We sat with our hands wrapped around our mugs and talked motorcycles. Rob's face lit right up when he talked about bikes. He laughed when he told me how he rode through a puddle that just keep getting deeper and deeper until his engine died and he tipped over and landed in a foot and a half of water. The guys riding with him laughed so hard they cried, but then they had to wade into the water to help him pick up his motorcycle, and they all ended up soaked.

I told him about the time I rode into a grass meadow to check out a camping spot. I stopped on a hill and leaned the bike downhill instead of uphill and couldn't hold the weight of the bike. Fell right over and slid down the hill. The guys with me were laughing so hard that it took them twenty minutes to get my bike back up on two wheels.

Rob laughed. "Got to appreciate a woman who can laugh at herself."

I smiled at him. "Back at you." He really was a nice guy. *Whoa,* I said to myself. *He's seeing someone, and so are you.* I shook my head to clear my thoughts.

"What was that?"

"Oh, uh, nothing. Just a mental head slap. I probably should get back to work."

Rob paid the bill, and I left a couple of dollars on the table as a tip. I'd waitressed for a while in college, so now I tended to over-tip. It's hard work, and waitresses get paid next to nothing.

Rob and I walked out, pulling on our jackets. A state cruiser sat in the dirt lot in front of the Sugar House, and a trooper got out of the car and walked toward me. I veered off course to meet him.

"Bella Bree MacGowan?" I didn't know his name, but I'd seen him before, and it was apparent he knew who I was.

"That's me." I had known this was coming since Tom had talked to me the night before. "Do you need me to come down to the barracks?"

The trooper looked a little surprised. "Yes, and I need to drive you there myself."

"Actually, I don't have a car here, so it works out fine for me. Can someone drive me back to work when you guys are done with me?"

"I'll come get you if you're stuck," Rob broke in. "Just call."

"You can sit in the front. Maverick says you're not armed or dangerous." He opened the passenger side door. I pulled my cell phone out of my purse. "I need to make a quick call to work. Is that okay?"

I called Meg and told her I didn't know when I'd be back to the office and slid into the front seat of the cop car. I waved to Rob who was standing there with his arms folded, looking murderous. I rolled down the window.

"Go back to the shop," I called out to him. "I'll be fine. I'll make one of the guys take me back to work." But he stood watching as the car rolled me away.

I was back in the same interview room as before. I'd been sitting by myself for at least thirty minutes, and I wondered if someone was watching me through the two-way glass. At least, I assumed the mirrored wall hid a viewing room. It would if this was TV.

I supposed I should be more nervous. I knew I was a suspect in murder case, but I couldn't take it too seriously. I couldn't see myself as a potential murderer. You couldn't pull a murder out of thin air. There had to be motive, evidence.

Lieutenant Brooks finally entered the room after I'd been sitting for about an hour. He grabbed the chair across from me and sat down. He was quiet for a moment doing the cop routine, staring at me from under lowered eyebrows, the tips of his fingers pressed together.

"The word around here is that you didn't kill Vera. But if you ask me, anyone can commit murder, given the right circumstances."

The door opened, and a female trooper entered the room and stood with her back to the closed door. She shot Brooks an angry glance, and I figured he wasn't supposed to start without her. But she didn't say anything, and her face betrayed only that one quick emotion. *Cop face, gotta love it.* I wondered if they gave classes in shutting facial expressions down.

Lieutenant Brooks had his baby blues fixed on me. Actually, they were brilliant blues with beautiful dark lashes. *Good lord, what is wrong with me? I'm attracted to just about every guy I meet.* I did a mental headshake and tried to concentrate.

"So. Why don't you tell me again how you found Vera's body?"

I went through the story again, shuddering at the memory of Vera's cold arm. When I finished Brooks was considering me again. He had his hands folded into a steeple and the tips of his fingers against his lips. I wondered if he knew how sexy that was. He had a great mouth. Jeez, I needed to get a life. All a guy needed was a good pair of lips, and I lost my head. I must have low blood sugar or something.

"You must know that your coworkers think you are the only person who had the opportunity to kill Vera. You were the only one working alone that night. Didn't you, in fact, insist on being the one to work alone?" All of a sudden, Brooks wasn't so attractive. Funny how that worked.

"I offered to work alone. I grew up with the general manager, and he trusts me not to do anything stupid."

He just looked at me.

"Do my coworkers know when she was killed? Because when I found Vera, she was stone cold. She could have been killed long before I found her. Anybody could have killed her." I had a thought. "You must know when she was killed by now. When did she die?"

"I'm not at liberty to release that information at this time. But I don't believe you have an alibi for the time in question."

"I don't get the opportunity to say for myself if I have an alibi or not?"

"You haven't been charged with a crime, so I don't think it's necessary."

Boy, this guy was starting to piss me off. "So it's necessary to keep me at the barracks half the afternoon, when I should be working. It's necessary to tell me that the people I work with think I'm suspected of murder, necessary to make me relive that awful evening, but not necessary to tell me when the crime I'm supposed to have committed took place." *Nice. Very nice.*

I stood up. "If you are waiting for me to confess, it's not going to happen. I didn't kill Vera. I had no reason to kill Vera. And unless you have cause to hold me longer, I'd like to go home now."

Brooks let me go. I left the room a little forcefully and heard my mother's voice in my head telling me not to slam doors. Steve was waiting for me. I figured he'd watched the whole thing behind the mirrored wall and knew when I'd be done.

"How you doing? You were stuck in that room for a long time."

"Pissed off, is how I am. I've got things to do, and he's wasting my time. Is he even looking for the person who really killed Vera? I bet he's already nailed it on me, and he's figuring I'll crack if he holds me long enough. I bet you anything he doesn't have any evidence at all. I found her, Steve, I didn't kill her."

"Don't sweat the small stuff, Bree. Nobody who really knows you thinks you killed her." Maybe Brooks doesn't really think you killed her either. Maybe he has the hots for you and wanted an excuse to spend a couple of hours in your company."

"Oh, shut up!" I gave him an open-fisted shot to the shoulder. "God, you are so one-track-minded."

"Minded? What's minded? Is that a real word?" He was laughing at me now.

"You know what I mean. Can you find someone to take me home? I need some time before I go back to work."

Steve took me home. We pulled into the dooryard where the dogs were, and they barked and raised their hackles at the car. I pasted a smile on my face and thanked Steve. The dogs swarmed me and I bent to rub Annie's brown velvet ears before dragging up the steps and letting myself into the house.

The house calmed me. I moved through the kitchen and dining area, inhaling the quiet. I'd inherited a little money with the farm when my grandmother died. Most of it, I'd used fixing up the old house and putting in modern windows. Sunshine fills the rooms, making them glow. I love the windows, especially during the winter, when every shaft of sunlight is like a gift. I made my way up the stairs to my bedroom.

I'd stripped the room of everything except my bed, a dresser and my grandma's old rocking chair. It was full of space and light with a little blue in the quilt and rug. A room you'd expect to see in a beach house with a view of the ocean. My view was of the pastures and the pond.

When my grandmother had lived in this house, the windows all had heavy, insulating drapes covering them. I'd pulled them all down, declining to put up any curtains at all, except in this room, where I'd hung lacy white sheers that fluttered when the windows were open. My favorite room in my favorite house.

I slid off my shoes and pulled down the quilt. I hoisted myself onto the mattress and sunk into the bedding. Then I grabbed the covers and pulled them up over my head. This was a place I could find peace.

The dogs were barking to come in, but I ignored them. I lay under the covers for a while, willing myself to go to sleep, but my stomach was growling and my mind wouldn't slow down. Fragments of my conversation with Lieutenant Brooks were popping into my head, making me crazy. My stomach felt full of rocks, and there was a miniature jackhammer drilling into my skull above my left eye. Finally, I threw the covers off in a fury and stomped downstairs for something to eat.

I cast around my kitchen for something suitable and snagged a cup of chocolate pudding out of the fridge. I ate it standing at the window, but I wasn't seeing anything. My mind was focused on the events of the last few days. I grabbed another pudding out of the fridge and started on that one too. About halfway through, I started to feel sick and threw it away. Time to go back to work.

I pulled on my rain gear, an old yellow slicker with matching pants. Then I stomped outside and dragged the bike out of the barn. Riding the bike in the mud wiped my mind of the events of the day. I was concentrating on finding the firmest ground and not letting the bike slide out from under me around corners. I made myself relax when I got to the pavement, rolling my shoulders and releasing my breath.

Meg wasn't at the office when I got there. I powered up my computer and rifled through the ads to be set, looking for something easy. I pulled a couple out of the pile and tried to concentrate on them, but what I really wanted to do was talk to Meg. I called the house and got Jeremy on the phone. Yeah, his mom was around the house someplace.

I locked up the office and headed over to Meg's and Tom's. I let myself into the house. Louise was sitting in the kitchen with papers spread across the table. She had a pencil in her mouth and a scowl on her face.

"Homework? Need help with anything?"

Louise pulled the pencil from her mouth. "Nah. I just have to do a science project for Mr. Morse. I'm making a poster that shows the life cycle of this plant, and I'm trying to work out how I want to lay it out."

I looked over her shoulder. She had drawn up several diagrams on letter-sized paper. These were strewn over the table. Even if she had needed help, I doubt she would have asked me for it. This was out of my league.

"Are these going on poster board or something?"

"Uh huh. I've got a big piece of cardboard in my room. I'm going to cover it with butcher paper and glue the parts of my presentation on it."

"Sounds good. Have you seen your mom around anywhere?"

"I think Mom was going down to the barn for a while. You might find her there."

I retreated out the door and made my way down the slippery hill to the new barn. I gave myself a mental high five when I arrived without landing in the mud. I stepped into the doorway and waited for my eyes to get used to the dim light. Meg was leaning against a stall door watching Scott sanding the bottom of the support beam. She said something I couldn't hear, and he looked up and smiled at Meg.

They didn't notice me. Meg said something else, and Scott laughed. She reached down and touched his shoulder. They laughed together some more. Scott didn't seem the least bit uncomfortable with Meg. And Meg wasn't acting like she had any qualms about being there.

"Hey," I called. "What's up?"

They both jumped, and Meg scooted away from Scott. I didn't know what to think. I certainly didn't want to be thinking the thoughts that were currently running through my head.

"Hey, Bree. Are they any closer to finding who killed that woman at Whispering Birches?" Scott asked.

"I don't think so. But the cops don't really tell me anything."

"Too bad. It would be interesting to be in on the investigation."

"It might be interesting, if I wasn't a suspect. But as it is, I'm not finding it amusing."

"Point taken."

"Meg." I turned my attention to her. "I need to talk to you about something. I was looking for you up at the house." That, at least, was the truth.

"Oh." Meg frowned "I took a break from the office. I just came down here to give Scott a message for Tom. We can go back up to the house now if you like. See you later, Scott."

Meg and I walked out of the barn together. I was telling myself to mind my own business, but I couldn't do it. "What the hell do you think you're doing down here with Scott?" My voice came out two octaves higher and much louder than I intended.

"I was just telling Scott about a saddle rack Tom wants Scott to add to the tack room. He saw a new design up at Stillson's Barn."

"Well it sure didn't look like you were discussing saddle racks. I thought the point of telling him you like him was to be too embarrassed to go down to the barn." I sounded like a bitch, and I knew it. But, jeez, what did Meg think she was up to?

Meg stomped up the hill toward the house. I tried to catch up with her, but my boots had smooth soles, and trying not to slip in the mud was slowing me down. Meg was part mountain goat, and she had her lugged hiking boots on. She motored on up the hill. About halfway to the house Meg stopped and whirled around.

"I want to know what you think you're doing here?" There was an undertone of anger in her voice.

"I called your house looking for you." I stopped walking and felt the mud sucking my feet down the hill. "Jeremy told me you were somewhere around the house, so I came over to talk to you about what happened at the barracks today. Apparently, your little fling with Scott is way more important than that." I took a few steps to keep from slipping any further backwards. I cast around for a solid place to stand, but Meg seemed to have staked out the only firm spot on the hill.

"I have the right to hang out in my barn with whoever I choose to, Bella MacGowan," Meg shouted in my face, "whether it's Scott Howe or anyone else. You have no right to come here and accuse me of God knows what. Get right off my property right now!"

Tom chose that moment to walk out onto the back porch. "What are you two shouting about?"

Meg jumped and spun around. I jerked back when she jumped, startled by the movement. I slid backward again for about a second, and then my feet slipped out from underneath me, and I was face down in the mud. Again. I pushed myself up out of the muck and onto my knees. Tom started down the porch stairs, but I waved him away. No point in both of us rolling around in the mud.

Meg was looking down at me with her mouth open. I had a momentary impulse to pull her down in the mud with me. I let it pass and gingerly got to my feet. Meg had snapped her jaw closed but the corners of her mouth were twitching, and her shoulders started to shake. I took a step up the hill toward my bike, but my foot slipped again, and I went down on my knees.

A snort of laughter escaped Meg. Then another. Pretty soon, she was laughing so hard that tears were running down her face. I could hear Tom telling Meg to stop, but it was too late. I grabbed her pant leg and yanked. She went down hard, landing on her butt in the mud.

Meg looked at me with disbelief. Then she reached out and knocked my shoulder, knocking me off balance and sending me backward to the ground. I could hear Tom yelling now, but the words were lost in the roaring in my ears. I struggled to sit up. Meg was laughing again. I picked up a handful of mud and smeared it over the front of her blouse. She gasped and launched herself at me.

We were rolling over and over in the mud. Meg shoved a handful of wet muck down my shirt, and I smooshed mud down her collar. She tried to get on top and straddle me, but I swiped some slop up off the ground, and it splattered in her face. I rolled her off me while she was trying to wipe her eyes with the inside of her jacket. Apparently, it wasn't really clean, because it wasn't doing any good. Finally, she swore and pulled the jacket off. She turned it inside out and wiped her face with the inside of her sleeve.

"Damn!" Meg started to launch herself at me again, but Tom grabbed her and hauled her away from me. I saw my chance to get in one last shot, but before I could move, I was grabbed from behind. Scott grasped me around the waist and hauled me backward away from Tom and Meg.

"That's enough of that." Scott was trying to sound stern, but I could tell he was trying not to laugh. He had his arms locked around my waist.

"What's so funny?"

"I haven't seen a fight like that since I was in college. We used to watch mud wrestling at the local pub on Wednesday nights. Even in bathing suits, those girls couldn't beat you two for entertainment value." He was laughing hard now.

"Sorry to be a killjoy, but I'm going home now." I twisted out of his arms and stomped back up the hill, stumbling and sliding as I went. I made the top of the hill and turned to see Tom dragging Meg up the steps to the house. She grinned over at me.

"See you tomorrow at the paper?" she called.

"Yeah, I'll be there." I dragged my muddy butt across to the bike. It was beyond me how Meg and I could have a knock-down, drag-out fight and come away feeling better. I did feel better, though, and I could tell Meg did, too. She'd looked positively delighted as Tom dragged her into the house.

I shivered; it was too cool for my clothes to dry. I wiped my boots in the grass, but the rest of me was a lost cause. I swung my mud-plastered leg over the seat of the bike. I'd be cleaning this machine before I rode it again. I headed home, where I took my second shower of the day and flopped onto the bed to try and unravel my bizarre life.

It was dusk when I woke up. I yawned and made myself get out of bed. I padded down the stairs and looked in the fridge. I didn't see anything I wanted so I grabbed the Moose Tracks ice cream out of the freezer. I ate half the carton standing up, leaning against the counter.

I went to feed the outside animals. Then the dogs were hounding me, so I fed them and the cat, too. The rain had stopped. The evening was crisp and clear. The breeze had blown the damp air away into the night. I stood on the porch, hugging my sweatshirt around me, and watched the sky darkening while Annabelle entwined herself around my ankles.

I walked out to the paddock behind the barn, where Lucky was snarfing up hay. I hopped the fence and stood with him, rubbing a spot on his back just above his tail. He blew air at me and went back to his dinner. It was his way of telling me he liked being scratched. I told him about the fight with Meg and riding home all muddy. Lucky turned around, rubbed his face on my arm and let me pull the tangles out of his forelock with my fingers.

I headed back indoors and checked the clock. I wasn't scheduled to work at the Inn this evening, but I had a ton of unfinished work at the paper. The couch was calling my name but it seemed kind of pathetic to fall asleep watching TV. I grabbed my jacket off the hook and pulled on my boots and helmet. I picked up some rags and a soft brush and headed for the bike.

The mud on my bike was still too wet to be brushed off. I dragged the hose off the porch, attached it to the spigot, and pretended I had a high-pressure washer. That did the job, and I dried the bike with the towels. I put on my jacket and helmet. I threw my leg over the bike, forced myself into the darkness, and headed down the hill into town.

I was clicking along down the dirt road, about halfway to town, when I saw movement in the hay field to my right. I slowed a little and flicked my eyes to the right. Definitely something out there, but it was too dark to see what it was.

I glanced back at the road and then tried to focus on the movement. It was too big to be a dog. Too slight for a cow. Didn't move like a bear. The clouds cleared a little, and I took another look. Bells went off in my head. It was a fawn, a lone fawn. I shifted my vision back to the road, and in that instant, a doe appeared directly in front of me.

Five

I shoved the bike to the left, trying to swerve behind the doe as she bounded across the road in front of me. The bike missed the deer but lost traction. My tires started to slide out from underneath me on the gravel. I shoved right, trying to force the bike upright. It was too late. The dirt road was slick from the rain, and the bike was going down. I hit the engine cutoff switch, curled onto my side and pulled my left leg free of the bike as I hit the dirt. The bike slid for what seemed like forever, but it was probably only a couple of seconds.

I lay in the road for a moment staring into the dark sky. My left thigh felt like it was on fire. I hoisted myself up and gingerly moved around. Nothing seemed to be broken, but my leg hurt like hell, and I could feel warm blood seeping into my pants. The doe and her fawn were long gone. Well, at least I hadn't hit either of them.

It occurred to me that if a car came along now, I'd be flattened. I muscled my bike up off the road. I couldn't see it clearly, but I doubted there was any serious damage. Scratches, probably. I got back on, pointed it back up the hill, and motored home. I left the bike in the tractor shed and limped into the house to check out the damage to my leg.

I peeled off my helmet, jacket and boots in the kitchen and headed up to shower yet again. I couldn't seem to stay out of the mud. I clenched my teeth as I pulled off my jeans. My left leg was bleeding from my hip to my knee.

My boots had protected my calf, and the jacket had protected my shoulder and arm. I had a few abrasions on my side where my jacket rolled away from my skin.

I stood under the hot water and scrubbed the dirt out of my leg. I yelled like crazy as the gravel came away. I had a bunch of road rash and one pretty good gash in my leg. I must have slid over a sharp rock or piece of metal or something. The dogs whined at me through the door.

I turned off the water, dried myself off, and dabbed the blood off my leg. Band-Aids would be useless. I pulled on an oversized tee-shirt and went down to my mudroom. I rummaged through the cupboard until I found some gauze and neon blue vet wrap I keep around for the animals. I used them to fix up my leg. I had to roll the vet wrap around my leg, hips and waist to keep the gauze on. Wonderful. I grabbed a bottle of Motrin off the bathroom shelf, a yogurt smoothie out of the fridge and headed up to bed. It had been a very long day.

It was three in the morning when I realized I wasn't going to sleep. I gingerly got out of bed and crept downstairs. I was walking like a little old lady. Everything hurt. I wondered where the expression 'quiet of the night' had come from. My night was filled with the sound of snoring dogs. Four dogs can make a lot of noise when they sleep. Only Diesel woke and followed me down the stairs. He stood at the kitchen door, vibrating his stubby little boxer tail.

"Sorry, Bud. I'm not letting you out." I knew he wanted nothing more than to chase the creatures of the night. Woodchucks, not vampires. Last time I'd let him out at night, he'd treed some poor animal and barked until his voice echoed through the hills and woke the neighbors. Diesel remained at the door, his expression expectant until he realized I wasn't going to let him out. Then he sighed and collapsed on the doormat.

I rummaged through the fridge wondering what to do. I don't have many late night skills. I'm not an undercover novelist, and TV mostly bores me. I could read, but I didn't want to. Yesterday's sudoku puzzle? That could sometimes put me to sleep.

But I didn't really want to sleep. I wanted a revelation, a solution to my problems. I wanted the hand of God, or my fairy godmother, to tap me on the head and say "Bing, go out and play." *No. That's Bill Cosby.* What I needed was divine insight into the mind of a murderer.

I was on the couch when my alarm blared early the next morning. I couldn't shut it off from downstairs, so I groaned and rolled onto the floor. I hurt everywhere. I stumbled up the stairs, shut off the alarm, and headed into the bathroom. I pulled the vet wrap and gauze off my leg. I had to sit on the toilet and put my head between my knees. My leg looked disgusting, and it hurt like hell.

I talked myself into the shower again and cleaned up the best I could. If I kept bathing like this, I was going to turn into a giant prune. Then I re-wrapped my leg and pulled on some sweats and a big tee-shirt. I limped down to the kitchen and raided the fridge. I scrambled some eggs and ate them with toast. Then I fed the dogs and the cat.

When I sat down again, I noticed that there was blood on my sweats. Shit. I picked up the phone and dialed Max. He agreed to feed my animals for a couple of days and rang off. I sat there for a couple more minutes, bleeding and looking at the phone for inspiration. Who could I call? I didn't want to bug Meg again. Jim had to be in the office this morning. In fact, most of my friends worked days. It was still early, but anyone I called would end up missing work.

I called the office and left a message for Meg, telling her I'd be late to work. Then I shrugged myself into my scraped-up jacket and buckled on my boots. I rummaged through the mudroom and found my spare helmet. I'd send the old one into the manufacturer for replacement when I got a minute. For now, my spare would do.

I limped out of the house and pushed the bike out of the tractor shed. I gave it a quick once-over. It was scratched, but there wasn't any mechanical damage. The bike started right up, and I gingerly put my full weight on my left leg and swung my right leg over the bike. So far, so good.

I headed for Dartmouth Hitchcock Medical Center in Lebanon, New Hampshire. It would take me forty minutes to get there. There was a smaller, local hospital closer, but Hitchcock had the best trauma center. I rode carefully down the hill and made the pavement in one piece. I motored carefully down Route 14 toward town and decided I needed a cup of coffee. My leg was killing me.

As I stopped at the one stop sign in town, Jim pulled up on my right. He rolled down the window of his car, shaking his head at me. He closed his eyes for a moment, then opened them and looked at me slit-eyed. I could tell he was trying to maintain control.

"So what happened to you?"

"Dumped the bike avoiding a deer last night. It looks worse than it is."

"Well, that's good, because it looks as if you're going to bleed out through your thigh."

"How would you know? You're on my good side."

"I was in the law school parking lot and saw you drive by. I just about took out a parked car when I saw that leg. Where do you think you're going looking like that?"

"I was going to stop in at the paper and grab a coffee at the cafe. Then I'm off to Dartmouth Hitchcock. I think maybe I need to be stitched up."

"You think? Jeez, Bree. You can't ride your bike down there looking like that. Someone's going to see that leg and drive off the road. Park that thing, and I'll drive you. You should have called me."

"You'll be late to work. I didn't want you to get in trouble."

"I'm a partner. I don't get in trouble. I get someone to stand in for me. Get in."

I pulled the Kawasaki around and parked in a space on the side of the road. I hated to admit it, but I was glad for the ride. I opened the door to Jim's Lexus IS and looked down at my leg.

"I can't get in your car. I'll get blood all over."

"It's okay, Bree, get in."

I shook my head. "I can't. This car is worth more than my house. I can drive myself." I turned back toward my bike.

"Oh, good grief! Don't go anywhere, I'll be right back." Jim climbed out of the Lexus and strode down the street. A few minutes later, he came jogging back with an arm full of towels. "Here, I got these at the thrift store. You can bleed all over them." He threw a couple down on the seat and handed me the rest.

I slid into the car and relaxed into the seat. I didn't like to admit it, but I wasn't feeling my best. I was tired, and I hurt. I fell asleep about five minutes into the ride and didn't wake up until Jim stopped outside the emergency room.

"Do you want me to come in with you?"

"No, I know you need to get to work." Something about him puzzled me. "Why aren't you wearing a suit? You always wear a suit."

"Not always. We have staff meetings today, but no clients, so we're dressing down."

"You're wearing sneakers, jeans, a dress shirt and a suit jacket. That's not dressing down. You're cheating. Only half of you is dressed down."

"I'm not wearing a tie. That's all that counts. Now get your butt in the emergency room, or I'm going to have to do it for you. Call me when you're done, and I'll come get you."

I grunted and eased out of the car. I gave Jim a little wave and attempted a smile as he pulled away. Then I turned and trudged into the hospital. I checked in at the desk and a nurse whisked me away. I guess they didn't want me to bleed all over the waiting room.

It took a couple of hours to get me cleaned up, stitched up, medicated, and lectured. I didn't bother to tell the doctor that I knew exactly what I had done wrong. I just sat there and took the lecture while she pulled the sutures through my leg.

It didn't occur to me that I should have brought spare pants until I pulled my sweats back on. The left leg was stiff with dried blood. Gross. The blood had trickled down inside my boot, and that was disgusting, too. The boot was soggy, my sock was soggy, and my pants were disgusting. I didn't care about the sweats, but these were my favorite boots. I cussed in my head and gave the E.R. staff my most winning smile as I thanked them.

My mind was occupied with the chances for success if I Googled how to clean my boots. I limped out into the waiting room and immediately did a double-take. Meg was sitting there, reading a magazine.

"What are you doing here?"

"Nice to see you, too. Jim called me and told me you were here. He offered pick you up, but I was looking for an excuse not to work today, so I told him I'd come down." Meg gave me the once-over. "I want you to promise me that if you ever fall off that motorcycle again, you will call me immediately. Not after you've driven yourself to the hospital, not a day later when you are still bleeding. Jim told me he saw you riding that motorcycle with blood running down your leg, and he nearly lost his breakfast. I nearly passed out when he told me. Here," she handed me a bag. "I brought you a pair of jeans." She looked at my sweats and made a face. "You'd better put them on." She went back to her magazine.

I stood there with my mouth open for a couple of beats. I snapped it shut and headed for the ladies room. It was painful to pull the jeans up over the bandages, and I wished for something stretchy and baggy. Then I felt ungrateful, so I just sucked it up and zipped them. I tossed the blood-encrusted sweats into the trash. On the way out, I caught a look at myself in the mirror. Good God! I looked like a bag lady. I ran my hands through my hair, but that only made it worse, so I gave up and slouched out to Meg.

"Okay. Let's go to work."

*****

We reached town and parked on the street below the office. I limped up the stairs to the office and sat gingerly in my chair. I wasn't bleeding through my pants anymore, but I was still pretty uncomfortable. Someone had left a handwritten article on my desk; one glance at the writing told me it was Lucy Howe. She usually sent her articles in electronically. Either her computer was down, or she was looking for new ways to torment me.

I powered up my computer and looked at the stack of stuff I needed to get done. I couldn't seem to get started, so I limped down the stairs and up the street to the deli. I got myself a Coke and a sandwich. Meg had walked over to the post office to get our mail, and she joined me on the street.

"Anything but bills in there?"

"There are a couple of classified ads and some calendar items. Nothing earthshaking."

We climbed back up the stairs to the office. I pulled my chair over to Meg's desk and ate my sandwich while she opened the rest of the mail. There wasn't much of interest in the mail today, so I picked up Lucy's article.

It was about Vera's murder. Vera Post, head p.m. housekeeper at the exclusive five-star hotel, found dead, blah, blah, blah. The first thing that struck me was that Lucy had broken the ban on writing about Whispering Birches. The hotel guaranteed its clients there would be no publicity, and they could make breaking the silence pretty uncomfortable for anyone who challenged that. The second thing that struck me was the sentence: Bella Bree MacGowan, the *Royalton Star* employee who moonlights at Whispering Birches, discovered the body and is currently the only suspect.

Fabulous.

I looked over at Meg. "Have you seen Lucy's article?"

"No. She told me she was going to write about Vera. What's up?"

"She wrote about Vera's murder, including where she was found, and she says I'm the only suspect." My mouth felt tight. "Did you know about this?"

"Jeez, Bree, what do you think? You think I would say 'Yeah, go ahead, rat on my friend'? I thought she was writing about Vera's life. Hand that over, let me see what it says." Meg stood up and reached over for the article.

I handed it to her and limped to the window, agitated. The sun was shining on the trees, lighting the red, orange and yellow leaves. It was beautiful outside, warm for a fall day. There were a few small children running around on the green and climbing on the old cannon, their mothers watching. The moms were chatting together, and they all looked so happy.

Meg spoke from behind me. "It isn't that bad. We need to cut out all the references to the hotel, but I think we need to leave you in. It would look biased if we took out the references to you finding her."

"What about the part where I'm the only suspect?"

"Leave those in, too. Look, I'll typeset this if it bothers you. It won't take me too long."

"No, I'll do it. I should know what the whole thing says in case someone asks me about it." And I needed all the ammo I could get for when I saw Lucy next. As I took the pages back from Meg, I decided that Lucy had left it in rough draft on purpose. She was trying to get my panties in a twist. Well, she had succeeded.

I fumed while I typed. This would be a front-page article, which meant the larger papers might pick it up. Everyone in the Upper Valley would know I was a murder suspect. Maybe it was time to visit my younger brother in California. I didn't need any extra attention. I generated enough just living my life.

I calmed down when I moved on to set some ads that had come in. The process of taking a sketch made by someone who couldn't necessarily draw, and turning it into an ad, took all my concentration. I placed graphics, fiddled with font size, and did initial proofing before I sent ads over to Meg for the final proof. I was working on my third ad when the phone rang.

"Well, there you are," said a familiar voice.

"Hi, Jim." His voice made me smile. "What are you up to?"

"Looking for you, at the moment. What are you doing tonight?"

"Having my brain transplanted into a different body. How 'bout you?"

"I was wondering if you could stop by after work. I need to talk to you about something. Are you all right to ride your bike now?"

"I was never not okay to ride my bike," I lied, "but when you get that stubborn look in your eye, I know better than to expect you to be reasonable."

"Oh, really. And I suppose a reasonable person tries to ride a motorcycle to the hospital while her life blood is draining out of her leg?"

"See? You're doing it again. I bet you anything you've got that look on your face."

"Does that mean you're not coming over?"

"I'll be there around seven."

At six-thirty my eyes were vacant, staring unfocused at the computer screen while my brain was busy calculating the next time I could take a pain pill. Not until I got home. Riding under the influence of narcotics would only get me hurt worse. Not only was my leg smarting, but the other pieces of me were protesting about getting dumped on the road, too.

I shut down my computer and looked over at Meg. "I'm heading out. I'll see you tomorrow."

"See you," she looked up at me. "Are you sure you can ride that bike?"

"I'll be all right. I'm stopping at Jim's on the way home. That'll break it up a little."

"Not working that other job tonight?"

"No, I called them from the emergency room. I'm out sick for the next few days."

Jim lived in a log cabin that was up a long drive off Route 14. It was big and rambling with a vaulted ceiling in the living and dining rooms. It was a huge place for just one guy, so sometimes he rented rooms to a law student. He was between renters at the moment.

I banged on the door and then walked right in. Country people have the habit of wandering in and out of each other's homes. Everyone knows if they're going to have sex on the kitchen floor, they'd better lock the door, or they might get caught in the act. More than one transplanted flatlander has been flabbergasted to walk out of the shower and find his neighbor sitting in the kitchen brewing coffee and waiting for a chat.

Jim was standing at the kitchen sink filling his kettle. He set it on the stove as I walked in and came over to kiss me lightly on the mouth. I looked at him quizzically. Maybe he'd had a bad day. There were ways to loosen him up. My arms snaked around him, and I nuzzled my face into his neck. He relaxed a little. I nibbled his earlobe. His breathing changed as I pressed myself against him. His arms tightened around me, and he bent his head down and kissed me on the mouth. I let the tip of my tongue run along the edge of his lower lip.

He backed me up against the refrigerator and slid his hand into the waist of my jeans. My hands slid up under his shirt, and I let my fingers press into the soft skin of his back. Then I ran them down into the back of his pants. He pulled away.

"We can't do this right now. I need to talk to you.

"Now? Can't it wait until later? I'm nice and numb now, later I might not feel so good."

"It has to be now." He had a hangdog look on his face. "It wouldn't be fair to wait until later."

"So, what's up?" I asked, adjusting my shirt and sitting down at the island counter. I was getting a bad feeling about this. Maybe it was the way Jim was so obviously not looking at me.

"I've got some bad news. I don't really know how to say this, so I'll just say it, and then we can work it out after."

I nodded. I didn't trust my voice.

"The thing is, I can't see you for a while." He was looking studiously over my head. "I'm going to be really busy at work, and some other stuff has come up. It's not going to be forever, but I'm not sure when I'll be able to call you again."

"Okay." I made an effort to sound cheery and hopped off my stool. This was maybe the weirdest brush-off I'd ever gotten. It would have been better if he'd just said he was moving on and left it at that. I slid my jacket on and grabbed my helmet.

"Bree?" Jim started toward me.

"No, I'm fine." I held up a hand to stop him. "It's not like we were engaged or going steady or anything. We never even discussed whether we were exclusive or not."

"We were exclusive." Jim was quiet.

"But not anymore?"

"I can't ask that from you." He looked so miserable I almost felt sorry for him. "I don't know how long it will be before I'm free again."

"That's fine. You can look me up when you're available. See you later." I let myself out the door and closed it softly behind me. I stood outside in the cold air for a few minutes, thinking about crying. I decided it wasn't going to happen, walked over to my bike, got on, and rode home.

I went to feed my animals and realized Max had already done it. I'd forgotten that I'd asked him. I dragged myself into the house, swallowed a couple of pain pills, and took the dogs upstairs with me. I burrowed under the covers, and the dogs jumped up to lie on the bed. Annie snuggled up next to me and licked the tears off my face.

*****

I woke up to the phone ringing. It was still dark. I felt around on the bedside table and picked up the phone.

"Hey, did I wake you?" Nice voice. Not Jim. I couldn't place him.

"Who is this?"

"It's Rob. You know, your mechanic."

"Hi. Something wrong?"

"I heard you took a spill on your bike. Jordan Peevey saw you riding through town all covered in blood. I just wanted to be sure that you weren't bleeding to death over there."

"I'll be fine." It wasn't really a lie. The damage wouldn't be lasting. Not to my thigh, or to my heart. "It's not as bad as it looked, really. I'll be fine."

"Will you call me if you need anything?"

"Sure."

"Will you promise not to climb on the bike and try to drive yourself to the hospital again?"

"I'll think twice. That's the best I can offer."

"I guess I'll have to live with that. Sorry I woke you. Go back to sleep. And don't get up early tomorrow, it's Saturday."

I looked at the phone in my hand for a minute. I was used to news going through town like wildfire. There was nothing new in that. What was new was my mechanic calling to check on me.

Six

I spent Saturday doing as little as possible and nursing my thigh. Max fed the outside animals for me, and I took care of the dogs and Annabelle. After explaining to Ranger that he was too big to lie on the couch, I spent the early afternoon napping with Annie in my lap. Ranger, Hank and Diesel lay sprawled on the living room floor, while Annabelle curled in the big, overstuffed chair in the sun-filled room.

By midafternoon, I got tired of feeling sorry for myself and called Val. "How would I go about finding out the details of Vera's death?"

She was quiet for a moment. "Depends on if the O.I.C. is releasing information or not. Could be common knowledge, if it's he's talked to the press, but if he's trying to keep certain details quiet, it could be a while before the details are released to the public. What do you want to know?"

"Everything. Being at the top of the suspect list is bugging me."

"You could try Googling Vera's death. I can see if I can get any details from the investigation for you. Give me some time."

I rang off, booted up my laptop, and Googled Vera Post. Nothing. No details of the murder beyond what I already knew. No mention of a will. Nothing to indicate someone might have been on Inn property who shouldn't be there. I dropped my head into my hands.

Vera had been in the housekeeping closet attached to Gunnar Ericson's room. In a closet he shouldn't have been able to get into. Would Gunnar Ericson murder a housekeeper? I had no answers.

That brought me to why Gunnar was following me around. Surely, it wasn't typical for a mega-star to pursue a housekeeper. It wasn't as if there weren't any single women staying at the Inn, women who had status and money. Maybe he liked slumming. Or maybe he figured he could trust a housekeeper to keep quiet. We were required to sign contracts with confidentiality clauses.

I looked at the clock. Five on Saturday evening. I took a chance and called Tom at home.

"Hey, how do cops go about conducting an investigation?"

"Is this a question about investigative technique or about Vera's murder?"

"The murder. I want to know when she died. How she died. Did she have a will? Who had motive?"

"Bella." He was quiet for what seemed like forever. "Why do you want to know?"

"I want to clear my name. Being a murder suspect makes me feel slimy."

"Are you sure that isn't the pain pills you're taking?"

"I haven't taken any pain pills today. Come on, Tom, how would you feel if your name was on a short list of murder suspects?"

"It would suck."

"But you'd have access to tools to help you clear yourself of the charges. I've got nothing. I don't like sitting around here waiting for someone else to do it for me."

"I get the picture, Bella. I'll see what facts Brooks is willing to part with. Maybe there will be something to help you. But don't hold your breath. Hang on, Meg wants to talk to you."

Meg came on the line. "Why don't you come to lunch tomorrow? You need to get out of that house. I'll bet you slept half the day away."

"Okay, Mom."

* * * * *

I piddled away the next morning doing chores. At eleven I jumped in the shower and cleaned myself up. My leg still looked awful, but it wasn't hurting quite as much as it had the day before. I left it unwrapped and dried my hair before I pulled on jeans and a tee-shirt. I fussed over my eyes for a couple of minutes, swiping on shadow and mascara.

My heart dropped when I remembered I'd have to ride the bike again. It was a nice day, not too cold, but the thought of getting on the bike was depressing. There weren't any other options, so I pulled on my boots, grabbed my jacket and helmet, and headed out to the tractor shed.

My initial unease dropped away from me as I started down the road. The ride down to Meg's and Tom's was breathtaking. Autumn in Vermont never fails to amaze me. The countryside is dotted with little farms interspersed with the wild color of the woods. The air cooled as I dipped down to ride across the river and warmed again as I zipped up the hill on the other side. Heaven.

The table was set for eight when I walked into Meg's kitchen. I shucked my jacket and left my boots by the door. Meg was pulling one of her famous homemade pizzas out of the oven. When her tomatoes were ripe, she simmered the sauce for days and then canned it. She made the crusts fresh every Sunday.

"Hey, there." I plopped onto a stool at the counter. "Who's the eighth for lunch?"

"Beau. He and Tom are taking the kids to the Tunbridge Fair this afternoon. They want to watch the pig races again." Beau, Tom's younger brother, spent a lot of time hanging out with his nieces and nephews.

"I used to love the pig races. Now they just give me a headache," I said.

"I know. They're way too loud. It takes an entire day to get your hearing back. Are you going to the fair this year?"

"No. I always spend too much money when I go to the fair. I'm saving up for car repairs."

"How's your leg? Getting any better?" Meg set Parmesan cheese and chili pepper flakes on the table.

"A little stiff, mostly. Doesn't hurt too much. Have to pop ibuprofen every so often."

"I wish you'd sell that motorcycle. It makes me nervous when I know you're riding it."

"Can't. It'd break my dad's heart."

"Humph." She walked over to the stairs. "Cover your ears." She hollered, "Lunch!" The thunder of feet sounded overhead as they all came thudding down the stairs. Pete, the ten year old, came first, followed by Gemma, eight. Next came twelve-year-old Louise, and lastly, Jeremy.

"Bree!" Gemma threw herself into my lap. They milled around me, embracing me in a group hug. Three silky brown -haired heads tugging me in for kisses. Two pairs of brown eyes, and one of green, laughing at my protests of being squished. Jeremy stood apart from the others, but even he flashed me a welcoming smile. Tom and Beau clomped down the stairs, and we all sat down to eat.

"Hey, Bree," said Tom. "Did you ever get that car of yours inspected?"

"My car's at the shop now. That's why I'm freezing my butt off on the bike."

"Well, be careful on that thing, will you? I don't want to lose my best babysitter."

"What were you guys doing upstairs with the kids? They were so quiet, I didn't even know they were up there."

"Beau was showing them how Google Earth works. We were looking at satellite pictures of our house."

"If it kept all our kids quiet, it was magic." Meg plopped down in her chair.

Meals are a hectic affair at Meg's and Tom's. Food is passed around the table, and the talk comes from all directions at once. I pulled out my worst manners and joined right in, passing pizza in all directions and talking with my mouth full. Meg had salad and cookies on the table with the pizza. The kids ate everything in no particular order, but their parents didn't seem to care.

I enjoyed watching Tom and Beau together. Same wavy dark hair, same gray eyes, strong jaw and chin. Beau was taller and thinner, and more muscular, than Tom. A stonemason by trade, his job kept him fit. Tom held himself with more authority than Beau. I wasn't sure if that was because he was the elder or because he was a cop. They shared a sense of humor and kept us all laughing.

There had been times when I thought Beau was attracted to me, but I tried hard to keep him at arm's length. He was attractive and a great guy, but if things went wrong, and with me they always did, I was afraid it would get in the way of my friendship with Meg and Tom. His attention was focused on the kids today, so I could watch him across the table instead of pretending that I wasn't interested.

After lunch, Gemma, Pete, Sara and Jeremy scurried around looking for shoes and jackets. As the men pulled on their coats, there was a mad scuffle to see who would get out the door first. While Sara and Jeremy jostled at the door, Gemma slipped between them and skipped down the sidewalk, taunting the others. Within minutes, they were all belted into the car and on their way.

Meg cleared the plates from the table and put water on for tea. "Are you going to tell me what happened at Jim's last night?"

I sucked in my breath and let out a deep sigh. "He dumped me."

"What? He's crazy about you. I know he's crazy about you. How could he dump you?"

"Dunno. Just said he couldn't see me for a while. He was sort of cryptic, and I didn't really give him time to explain. I felt kind of blind-sided, so I just left. There didn't seem to be much reason for sticking around. I wasn't going to beg him not to dump me or anything."

"Do you want me to call and talk to him?"

"God, no! Then I'd really look pathetic. I'll just lick my wounds and lay low for a while. I'll hang out with Rob, when he's not with Lisa. It's not like I don't have stuff to do or anything. Anyway, if I act like I don't want him, he's more likely to want me back."

We finished cleaning the kitchen and headed into the living room. Meg almost never had control of the television, so when the kids were out of the house, she liked to sit and flick through the channels. She plopped on the couch and grabbed the remote. At my house, TV reception was worse than the cell phone reception. I only got three channels. I plopped right down on the couch next to her. TV with Meg was fun.

The first show we watched was on the do-it-yourself channel. A married couple was decorating on the cheap. They made a valance by rubber-banding fabric to a piece of cardboard.

Meg looked at me. "I bet I could rubber-band a newspaper together."

"I bet I could rubber-band a car together."

"I bet I could rubber-band a marriage together."

"You got me there, but I bet I could rubber-band a boyfriend together."

"Well, you got that half right." Meg grinned at me. "But it wouldn't be a rubber band."

I threw a pillow at her. "You are just rude."

"Hey, you just got dumped."

"Uh, yeah. I don't think you have to rub it in."

"No. I mean doesn't that call for margaritas?"

"I think it does."

"Well, then." Meg dragged herself off the couch and went into the kitchen. I flipped through the channels while the blender whirred in the background. Meg came back and set a couple of huge margarita glasses on the coffee table.

I tossed her the remote, and she flipped to a channel where a huge lady was parading a Bullmastiff around a show ring. Then a guy with flowing red hair pranced around with an Irish Setter. "Did you know," I said, "that somebody did some kind of study that showed that people really do look like their dogs?"

"What does that say about me, then? All my dogs are different."

"Maybe you started out like a poodle, and you'll end up like one of those wrinkly Chinese dogs."

Meg threw the pillow back at me and switched over to the NASCAR races.

"I can't watch this. It's making me dizzy."

"Have another margarita, that'll make you feel better." I got up, stumbled over the coffee table, shuffled into the kitchen, and poured myself a drink from the blender. "You want more?"

"Nah, I'm a light weight." She switched the TV to CMT. Tim McGraw was singing about being a real bad boy. "Too bad he's not single. I'd chase him around the bed a couple of times."

"You're drunk. You wouldn't take your eyes off Tom long enough to chase someone else. Jeez, you got panicked over flirting with Scott."

"Hey! You could go after Scott now. He'd take your mind off Jim, believe me."

"No, thanks. I think I'll go after that waiter down at the cafe in town. He has got the best eyes."

"Pfff." Meg snorted. "Eyes, nothing. He's got a nice ass, is what he's got."

The shows we watched got progressively more hilarious as the day went on. Gilligan's Island was playing, and Meg and I were giggling hysterically over Gilligan's pants when Tom walked in. Meg jumped up to give Tom a kiss and fell over the coffee table into a giggling heap on the floor.

I leaned my head over the back of the couch to look at Tom. "You could kiss me instead. I'm a lot better kisser than Meg."

"Am not," came a muffled cry from the floor, and Meg extricated herself from the blanket she'd had wrapped around her on the couch. Her hair was wildly on end from static.

"You're drunk."

"Yeah, it's a good thing we didn't go anywhere, huh?" I said.

Meg found her way across the room and threw herself at him. Tom caught and kissed her before setting her back on the couch. "You stay there. You're a hazard to yourself. It's a good thing the kids are out to dinner with Beau. You two are a mess."

"I need another drink. Can you get me one while you're up?" I smiled my most beguiling smile at Tom. "I'd make it worth your while." I felt flirty and wondered if I should undo the top button on my shirt. My faulty life skills had kicked in again. I knew it, but I couldn't stop myself.

Tom leaned over the couch and kissed me on the top of the head. "You are going to be hurting enough tomorrow as it is. I'm going to make you two something to eat, and then it's off to bed. There are only two days until the paper comes out. You girls are going to wish you didn't do this."

"We had to do this," said Meg. "Jim dumped Bree."

Tom shook his head and headed into the kitchen. I could hear him on the phone with Max, making sure my animals would get fed. Meg and I watched some more country videos, but my eyes were having trouble staying open. Tom brought us scrambled eggs, and after we had eaten, he helped me up the stairs to bed.

"You should take me home." I sat on the bed with my eyes closed. "You'll get in trouble for hair brushing, I mean harboring a fugitive."

"You're not going to be a fugitive, and if I take you home, you'll have to clean up your own barf. This is way more fun."

*****

My mouth was dry. I pried my tongue off the roof of my mouth and cracked open my eyes. *Dark.* I reached for the light and felt the world tilt. I dropped my hand without turning on the light. *Still drunk,* I thought. *Still drunk and very thirsty. And I have to pee.* I tried for the lamp again and managed to turn it on. *Yikes!* I squeezed my eyes shut.

Great. I have to pee, but I can't open my eyes. I cracked my eyes and levered myself up into a sitting position. So far, so good. I swung my legs over the edge of the bed and put my feet on the floor. *Cold!* I looked for my slippers and realized I wasn't home. I grunted and got to my feet. I made it out the door and to the top of the stairs. Didn't want to use the upstairs bathroom and wake one of the kids.

I looked down the stairs and realized there was a light on downstairs. Someone must have forgotten to turn it off. I inched myself carefully down the stairs and peered around the corner into the kitchen. No one there. I padded across the kitchen and into the downstairs bathroom.

When I was done, I headed for the kitchen sink and ran the cold water. I filled a plastic tumbler and turned toward the stairs. There was a man standing in the archway between the kitchen and living room. I gasped, startled, and the glass flew out of my hands and bounced on the floor. It took me three, full, very scared seconds to realize it was Beau.

"What are you doing here?" I sounded like I'd been inhaling helium.

"Well, I was going to spend the night, but there was somebody sleeping in my room. So I was trying to decide if I should sleep on the couch or go home."

"I'm sorry. I didn't know."

"That's all right." A slight smile played on his lips. "The view is worth the trouble."

I looked down. I was wearing my tee-shirt and panties. *Great.* I felt my face get hot. I looked around, grabbed

Tom's jacket off the back of a chair, and struggled to zip it over my tee-shirt. My fingers didn't want to do what I asked them. If I could just get it closed, it would just about cover the essentials.

"Bree. I've seen you in less than that down by the river."

"Yeah, well, that wasn't my underwear! I've got to clean up this mess." I waved at the pool of water at my feet. I opened a drawer next to the sink and pulled out a handful of dishtowels. I was pretty sure Meg didn't use her dishtowels on the floor, but I wasn't going to search around for something more appropriate. When I turned back around, Beau had the tumbler in his hand and was blotting the floor with some paper towels.

"Wow. How did you do that so fast?"

"I'm probably not as drunk as you, and I happen to be standing next to the paper towels. Let me get you some more water." He opened the freezer and grabbed a handful of ice, then refilled my glass.

"How'd you know I like ice in my water?"

"Jeez, Bree. I've known you forever. Come watch some TV with me, and we can decide if I should drive home or not."

He didn't hand me my glass but turned and walked into the living room. I thought for a moment about just going back to bed. But he had my water, so I followed him. I plopped down on the couch next to Beau as he clicked on the TV. I curled my feet up on the couch to keep them warm.

Beau reached over and traced his fingers along the stitches in my leg. It was healing pretty well, not so scabby anymore, but not exactly attractive.

"Did you do this falling off your bike?"

"Yeah." I let out a sigh. "Slid over something sharp. I'm not sure what it was; I didn't realize until later that I was cut like that. Thought it was just road rash."

"Tom told me you were trying to drive yourself to the hospital?"

"I didn't want to bug anybody. I waited until the next day. Guess I was hoping that I didn't need stitches." I shrugged and shivered.

"Here." He draped a blanket over us both. I took my water from him and drank it.

"Much better." I rested my head on the back of the couch and closed my eyes. Beau slid his arm around my shoulders, and I relaxed my head and rested it on his shoulder. I listened to him changing channels. The sound was on so low that I could barely hear. He pulled me in closer.

"You're not going to try and take advantage of my drunken state, are you?"

"You bet I am. I've been trying to get with you since sixth grade. I've always been attracted to older women."

"I'm only a year older than you are."

"A year and a half. It might as well have been ten years when I was twelve and you were fourteen."

"Well, yeah. I was about six inches taller than you."

"Well, now I'm about six inches taller than you. Does that mean our roles are reversed? Because I'd be willing to sacrifice myself, if you're feeling a need for my body."

"What I'm feeling a need for is another drink. One more, and I'll pass right out."

"Trying to make it easy for me? Perfect. Let me go get you a shot of something." He made as if to get up off the couch, and I yanked him back down.

"Oh, sit down. I'm not going to drink myself into a stupor for your sake." I closed my eyes again.

"Too bad." He flicked through the channels another minute, and then I felt his fingers gently bushed my bangs off my face. "How can you see with this mess in your face?"

"I can't see anyway, my eyes are closed."

He slid his hand through my hair and down the side of my neck. I felt myself relax a little more. He slid his thumb along my jaw and under my lower lip.

"Nice lips." He brushed his finger across my lower lip. "Hmmm." I was really very comfortable. Beau was warm, and I liked the feel of his finger on my mouth. He smelled faintly of soap and hay.

"Why do you smell like hay?"

"Because I spent the day sitting on bales." Beau's voice was quiet. "Why, do you like it?"

"Uh huh. The smell of hay reminds me of summer. Summer reminds me of warm nights, swimming in the river and looking at the stars with a boy."

"Sounds like a good memory." I felt his breath on my neck. "Lean forward."

"Why?"

"Just do it."

I leaned forward. He slid his arm off my shoulder and turned toward me. He tucked his right leg behind me.

"You're pushing me off the couch."

"Hush. Just cooperate." Beau took hold of my shoulders and turned me so that my back was to him. He massaged my shoulders and my neck, and I relaxed into the pressure. I bent my knees so I could rest my arms and head.

"Hmm. Too tense. That's not good for you. Not that you don't have reason. Tom told me that Lieutenant Brooks is riding your ass."

"Drunk people are not supposed to be tense," I muttered into my arms. "Wait." I raised my head. "You guys have been talking about me?"

"Tom keeps me updated. Let's see. Lately you dropped your bike and split your leg open. That idiot Jim Fisk dumped you, and Lieutenant Brooks can't wait to get his hands on you. Not that I blame him, but I think he's going about it the wrong way."

"He doesn't want to get his hands on me for the same reasons you do. He just wants to put me in jail. What'd I ever do to him? Jeez, my life is pitiful right now."

"I could make it seem much, much better. He slid his arms around me and pulled me to him, the warmth of his breath on my neck distracting me. I leaned my head back and he slid his lips along my jaw. I shivered.

"That's supposed to make you feel warmer, not colder." I could hear the amusement in his voice. "Let's try this instead." He tilted my head toward him and kissed me on the mouth. His lips were soft and warm and tasted sweet. I felt his tongue on my lips, and my mouth developed a mind of its own.

"I think we should go upstairs. It's more private." His breath was soft on my neck.

"I don't think this is a good idea," the smart part of my brain made a desperate attempt to reassert itself.

"Oh, no. You're not backing out on me now. Your mind might be saying no, no, but your body is saying yes, yes. A kiss never lies." His lips touched mine, and all thoughts of no left me. I twisted my body and rested my legs across his thigh so I was sitting sideways on his lap. Then I shrugged out of Tom's jacket and slid my hands under his shirt and around his waist, feeling the smooth heat of his skin.

Beau tugged at the back of my tee-shirt and slid his hands up underneath, against my skin, his left hand on my belly, the other on my back. My breath caught as he slid his thumb across my nipple and then cupped my breast. He leaned his head down and nudged the fabric of my shirt aside, running his tongue around my hardened nipple. I moaned.

Beau stood up, lifting me off the couch. Tom's jacket fell in a heap on the floor. Steering me through the living room, he carried me up the stairs to the spare room. The sheets were thrown back from when I'd wandered down the stairs. Setting me on my feet, Beaux slid my tee-shirt back up and over my head and dropped my panties on the floor. The room was cold, and Beaux wrapped his arms around me when I shivered.

"Get in bed," he whispered. I slid into the bed while he shed his shirt and jeans. The shade hadn't been drawn, and moonlight lit his body. He was perfect. As he slipped into bed, I ran my hand across his abs and then up his chest and down his arms. Hard muscle under smooth skin. He groaned as I ran my hand up the back of his neck and into his hair, and he bent to kiss me again.

Beau straddled me, teasing. I wrapped my arms around his shoulders and pulled myself up against him. His chest was warm and soft under my mouth. Sliding my hips out from under his weight, I wrapped my legs around his waist. Beau moaned deep in his throat and slipped into me.

The power of the moment peaked and faded. As I floated into sleep, it crossed my mind that I didn't feel especially guilty. Beau was right. I did feel much, much better.

Seven

I could tell that the sun was out, but I didn't want to open my eyes. I smelled bacon and coffee. Who could be cooking at my house? I cracked one eye. *No good.* I squeezed both eyes shut and rolled over. The room spun around me. *Whoa.* That was not the right thing to do. I willed myself back into unconsciousness.

When I woke up the second time, Tom was standing next to the bed with a cup of coffee. Oh, yeah, I was at Meg's. Oh, my God. I'd slept with Beau. I felt behind me to make sure he wasn't still in the bed with me.

"Wake up, Bella. Meg says it's time to get to work."

"Meg's up? How can she be up? She can't drink worth beans."

"Apparently, she didn't drink quite as much as you did. But she's in pretty bad shape too."

I groaned, sat up and steadied myself. When the room stopped spinning, I took the coffee. "Just give me a couple of minutes." I sat up and looked down at myself. I was wearing my tee-shirt and undies. Thank God. I had vague memories of Beau helping me pull my tee-shirt over my head. Before that? I remembered being put to bed before my late night excursion. "Hold on. Did you undress me?"

Tom grinned, and his eyes glinted. "There are definite perks to finding a couple of drunk women in your house. You can do almost anything with them."

I shot Tom a startled glance and opened my mouth to protest, but he cut me off.

"Don't worry. I was a gentleman and let you undress yourself. You, on the other hand, tried to seduce me."

"I did not!"

"No worries. Meg was significantly more fun than you were."

"Men."

Tom laughed and left the room. I drank some coffee and pulled myself out of bed. I struggled into the clothes that Tom had left on the foot of the bed. I made my way gingerly down the stairs and pulled on my hiking boots in the kitchen. Meg was sitting at the table with her head in her hands.

"Why do I drink? Everyone knows I can't handle it." She raised her head slowly. "You want some breakfast?"

"No. I'm going to walk into town to clear my head. I'll meet you at the office."

I walked the mile into town with my hands shoved into my pockets to keep them warm. The cold air helped to clear my head, and I felt a little better. I kicked myself for sleeping with Beau. Jesus Murphy. What did I think I was doing? This could go wrong on so many levels, it wasn't even funny.

As I passed the cafe on Chelsea Street, I saw my friend Val sitting at a table for two. I turned around to join her. She looked up and waved me over as I came in the door.

A group of local women sat at the big table at the back of the room. They might have been the same group of moms I'd seen out the window a few days before. A couple of them were staring at me but turned away when they noticed me looking. There was some whispering, and the words "murder" and "Vera" floated over to me. One of them glanced up at me. She forced a tight smile at me and turned away. They murmured together some more, huddled toward the center of the table.

I shrugged off my jacket, put it over the back of a chair, and sat down. I wondered what the town verdict was. Guilty, most likely.

I met Val in high school. She'd been a pretty cheerleader type with long, wavy, red hair, while I was an awkward, brown-haired thing covered in grease from my dad's garage. Somehow we struck up a friendship that outlasted all our boyfriends and survived the three miserable years she spent in law school.

Val smiled over at me. "Haven't seen you in a while. How's Ranger doing?" Val had discovered Ranger wandering by the river several months back, bone thin and covered in burdocks. We'd looked for an owner, as Irish Wolfhounds don't usually turn up stray; but no one ever came forward, so he stayed with me. Val lived in an apartment and couldn't have dogs.

"Ranger's great. One of the pack now. Annie totally cows him. You should drop by. He looks great, when he hasn't been running through the fields. That dog's a bur magnet."

"I'll come see him. He was such a pitiful baby. So how's Jim doing? Word is you're still together. That's got to be some kind record."

"Word is wrong. He dumped me a couple of days ago. He needs time or space or something. Isn't that what guys say when they want to screw somebody new?"

We were interrupted by the arrival of the Muffin Man, which is what we call the waiter behind his back. He serves us excellent muffins, and then we get an eyeful of his buns as he walks away. He squatted at the table, his baseball cap on backwards, long-lashed hazel eyes gazing into mine. "You ladies having the usual today?"

"What's fresh?" asked Val. I knew she was thinking he was.

"Raspberry, blueberry and apple cinnamon."

"I'll have apple cinnamon."

"Raspberry," I added.

"One coffee, one tea?"

I nodded. Val fanned herself as he walked away. "That boy is fine. He's the only reason I come in here. Eating muffins is hard on my wardrobe. I can't fit in my pants anymore."

"Why don't you ask him out?"

"I'm old enough to be his mother. And what would we talk about, skateboarding? He's barely out school."

"Hmm. I don't think talking would be the reason I'd ask the Muffin Man out."

"Hush, he's coming." He set our food on the table, shot us both a smile, and headed back to the kitchen. Val looked at me. "You don't think he heard us, do you? We really should grow up."

"Yep. Do you know, I don't even know his name?"

"Me neither. I think I'd better keep it that way. So, I heard about Vera. Is the paper right? The cops think you did it?"

"Apparently. My freaking fingerprints were all over the room where she died. I'm in there all the time. Guess that's enough to make me a suspect."

"Wow. I can't see it, myself. But then, I've seen you swerve to avoid running over frogs in the road. What does Tom think?"

"He knows I didn't do it, but I think Montpelier is putting the pressure on."

"If you need representation, call me. I can probably keep you out of jail for a while anyway." Val glanced at her watch, pulled a couple of bills out of her pocketbook and stood up. "I'd better get going. Got a client coming in."

"If you were a really good lawyer, you could keep me out of jail forever, guilty or not!" I grinned at her. She's actually a pretty decent lawyer.

Back at my desk, I booted up the computer. Pretty soon, I was knee deep in an ad that didn't work. No matter what I did, the balance didn't look right. I was thinking of starting fresh when Meg came in. Two seconds later, Scott walked in.

"Hey, girls. I brought you donuts from West Leb."

Meg looked up. "Glazed?" Her eyes lit up. If she had a tail, it would be wagging.

"Glazed, Boston cream, sprinkles and a couple of croissants. One chocolate, one almond." Scott set the box on Meg's desk and opened it. "I'll be right back." He ran down the stairs, and the lower door slammed.

Five minutes later he was back up the stairs, juggling three hot drink cups. He set one on my desk. "Coffee, right?"

I nodded but refused to be impressed.

"Tea for Meg." He set a cup on her desk and a second next to it. "Chai for me. Now I'm ready for a donut." He pulled a chair up to Meg's desk.

The pastries were calling my name. Loudly. But I didn't want Meg to get the idea that I approved of Scott bribing her with food. I sat stewing while Scott and Meg laughed quietly. Meg reached out and touched the back of Scott's hand. He didn't pull away. I got up and walked out of the office. I descended the stairs and paced the sidewalk in front of the launderette.

If I told Tom, I'd be betraying Meg. If I didn't tell Tom, I'd be betraying him. I lengthened my pacing to include the sidewalk in front of the market, video store and pizza joint. I'm sure people were watching me through the window, wondering if I'd finally lost my marbles.

Finally, I pulled out my phone and dialed Tom. He sounded surprised to hear my voice. "I think you should call Meg. Ask her to lunch or something."

"What's up, Bella? Is she having a bad day?"

"Do you remember what I told you before you took Meg to Crossroads?"

"Which part? You've got to give me a hint here."

"The part about what might happen if guys think Meg is available."

"What are you trying to tell me? Is Meg going out on me?"

"No, no, no. Meg is not going out on you. But she's being buttered up. Flattered. Treated nicely. Nothing over the line. Nothing beyond friendship. I just think you need to show Meg what a fabulous catch you are. Remind her why she married you."

"I'm on it."

"And Tom?"

"I'm listening."

"Don't tell her I called you. Don't accuse her of anything. Promise me."

"I understand. She can't know you called, and I can't act like a jealous husband. No threatening to pulverize anyone. Is there anyone I should be threatening to pulverize?"

"No! Just wow her with your charm."

"Wow her with my charm."

Five minutes later, while I was examining the glass snowflakes hanging in the market window, Scott came out of the building, climbed in his truck, and rattled away. I waited another few minutes, bought myself a soda, and climbed back up the stairs.

Meg was waiting for me. "Where have you been?"

"I went down to Hairlairious to get an appointment. My eyebrows need waxing."

"Tom called and asked me out to lunch. Want to come?"

"No. I've got too much to do. You go."

"I thought it was quite a coincidence that Tom called while Scott was here. You wouldn't have anything to do with that, would you?"

"Tom calls you all the time."

"Yeah, but did you have anything to do with him calling this time?"

"Why does it matter?"

"I don't know. Sometimes I'm not sure whose friend you really are, mine or Tom's."

"You are both my friends. You were both my friends before you even met. I can't choose between you any more than I could choose between my brothers."

"And you didn't stick your nose in my business?"

"Do you really want to know if I called your husband and finked on you? I can't stop you from ruining your life, if that's what you are intent on doing. But I can remind you of what you have. What you stand to lose."

"You didn't fink on me, but you did tell my husband to ask me out to lunch."

"I went downstairs to get a soda. I also happened to go into the hair salon. It's possible one or two other things might also have occurred to me while I was down there. I needed to be out of the way in case Scott decided to kiss you again."

"Scott is a friend. Just like Rob is your friend."

"I guess I can understand that." Privately, I was thinking that other than a jab to the shoulder now and then, I didn't touch Rob. And I certainly had never kissed him.

After Meg and I closed up shop, she gave me a ride back to her place so I could pick up my Kawasaki. When I got home, the dogs were doing their happy dance as I walked up from the tractor shed. They barked and chased around me like I'd been gone forever. Ranger took my sleeve gently in his mouth and led me to the house. The rest of the dogs made happy, growly sounds, legs bent in submission and delight, their tails wagging.

I fed the animals and spent a few minutes brushing Lucky. I checked my answering machine when I got inside. No messages. *Figures*. I grabbed a yogurt out of the fridge and ate it standing at the sink.

*****

It was unnaturally quiet when I woke. I lay listening to the hush. Then it hit me. I sat up in bed and looked out the window. Snow. Not a little snow, either. Eight inches on the porch roof, and it was still coming down hard. I groaned. No car. Cripes, how was I going to get to work?

I got up and pulled on my cold weather barn clothes. Long johns, sweats, wool socks, long-sleeve undershirt, hoodie, snow boots and barn coat. I banged down the stairs, stomped into the kitchen to start the coffee maker, and headed out the door. The snow packed into the tops of my boots as I trudged to the barn.

By the time I was halfway through my chores, I'd shed my coat and hoodie. With the animal chores done, I fired up the snow blower and cleared the snow out of the dooryard, from in front of the barn and tractor shed. I tucked the snow blower away and went back in the house, shaking the snow off my clothes on the porch.

My answering machine was blinking. I pushed the play button and was rewarded with Tom's voice. "Bella, Meg says to tell you not to ride that bike in this weather.

I'll bring the jeep up to get you around nine." The answering machine made its I'm-all-done-playing-messages noise and fell silent. I checked the clock for the time and hustled upstairs for a shower.

Tom beeped his horn right at nine. I poured the rest of my coffee down the drain, rinsed my cup, and went out to join him. The snow had stopped falling, but the sky hadn't lightened.

"I didn't know it was going to snow. How'd I miss that?"

"It was forecast on Sunday, but I think Sunday is going to be the lost vacation for you." Tom smiled at me. "There was a winter storm warning last night. You don't turn your TV on much do you?"

"I always fall asleep when I watch TV by myself. And I do so remember Sunday. I just don't remember seeing the weather forecast."

"Oh, really? Do you remember getting undressed?"

"Oh, sure, bring that up." I felt my face warming up. *Great.* I couldn't think of anything smart and snappy to say, so I was quiet the rest of the way into town. Tom dropped me at the paper with a wave.

Meg and I were well into Tuesday paste-up mode when Lucy Howe waltzed into the office. She planted herself in front of Meg's desk.

"I've got an addition to my article. Do you think we could get it in the paper? It would really spice things up."

"I don't know." Meg turned to me. "Bree, what do you think? Is there room?"

"Personally, I think that article is already spicy enough. Too bad you couldn't come up with any facts to put in it. It's all rumor and supposition." I'd watched my share of crime scene shows.

"You can keep your sour grapes out of this, Bree." Lucy turned her back on me. "I don't know why you keep her here. If I was in charge, we wouldn't have a murder suspect working for us."

Meg gave Lucy the beady eyeball. "Innocent until proven guilty. I don't for a minute believe that Bree killed anyone." She turned back to me. "Bree, do we have room to add to Lucy's piece?"

"It depends how long it is, but we could probably make it work." Inwardly, I was raging. Why couldn't I just freaking lie?

"And do we have time to type, proof and set it?"

"Probably." My teeth clenched. I was going to have to set the rest of that stinking article.

Lucy watched while I added paragraphs to her article. She could have sent it in electronically and saved me some trouble, but I think the whole point was to make me squirm. The additions were all about Jim Fisk's firm taking on a wrongful death suit that Vera's family wanted to file against Whispering Birches. No wonder Jim had to dump me. I'd probably end up named in that lawsuit.

Anger and adrenaline simmered in me for the rest of the day. I was hurt that I had to find out from Lucy Howe why I'd been dumped. I was angry that Jim made it appear as though he thought I was guilty. And Lucy just made me want to spit, sneaky little backstabbing Howe that she was.

It was after eleven when I finally sent the paper to the printer. I stood and stretched, rolling the kinks out of my neck. My stomach felt heavy, as though I'd swallowed a rock. My head ached. I couldn't help but think about how my life was about to change. Tomorrow, the whole doggone town was going to think I killed Vera, and there was nothing I could do about it.

I killed the lights, locked the door, and trudged down the stairs. I pulled my jacket tight as I stepped through the door at the bottom of the stairs. Snow was drifting through the night sky, reflecting the streetlights. I looked around. Where did I park my car? I stood puzzling for a minute. "Oh, yeah. It's in the shop." I was stranded.

There was nobody on the street, but I could hear laughter from the grill on the corner. I turned in that direction. Somebody at the bar could probably give me a ride home. I started down the street as a couple walked out of the restaurant into the night. They laughed, and the guy slid his arm around the woman's shoulder as they started to cross the street.

I watched, wishing I were laughing with someone. Then the guy turned and pointed to something down the street past where I stood in the shadows. They turned in my direction, their faces visible in the light. I reached out and steadied myself on the brick storefront. Jim Fisk was strolling down the middle of the street with his arm around Lucy Howe. The snow swirled around them as they chatted, bumping into each other and laughing.

I shrank into myself. *Don't let them see me,* I thought. *Please, don't let them look this way.* I didn't need to worry. They were too absorbed in each other to notice me standing next to the building. They turned away from me, and I hurried down the street.

I walked through the restaurant into the bar and found a small table on the far wall. I sat with my back to the room and rested my head in my hands. It was warm and noisy in the room, and I felt faintly sick. My thoughts jumped back and forth, trying to make sense of what I had seen. I didn't know what to think. I groaned out load.

"Hey, you feeling all right? Is your leg bothering you?"

I just about jumped out of my skin. I looked up to see Rob standing next to me, looking concerned.

"Sorry, I didn't mean to startle you. But you don't look like you're feeling very good."

"I'm fine." I scowled at the concerned look Rob was giving me. "No, really, I'm fine. Just had a hard day."

"Get the paper put to bed?"

"Yeah, that was the easy part."

"Wanna talk? Let me get you a beer." Rob walked away before I could protest. I didn't want a beer, and I didn't want to talk. The last thing I needed was to get drunk and start crying in public. What I wanted to do was to get mad. Once I was good and mad, I'd feel much better.

Rob set a beer in front of me and slid into a seat across from me. "So what's going on?"

"Just waiting to get angry

"Waiting to get angry? Why's that?"

"Because once I'm angry, I'll feel better. I need some righteous indignation to straighten me out."

"Um, do you want to tell me what we're talking about?"

"Not really." But I did anyway. "Did you see James Fisk and Lucy Howe in here earlier?"

"Yeah, they were over in the restaurant. Why?"

"Because I was wondering if they were as friendly in here as they were out on the street after they left."

"Oh. Don't know. I saw them in here when I walked in, but that's all. Are you and Jim still together?"

"No, he broke it off with me. I just didn't realize he was with Lucy."

"What a fool."

"Me?"

"No, not you. Jim."

"Why would you say that?"

"You're digging for compliments. Let's just say that given a choice between Lucy Howe and you, I wouldn't be dating Lucy Howe."

I felt myself flush red. I looked down at the table. "Oh. Thanks."

Max, was in the bar playing darts, so I hopped a ride home with him. When I got into the house, there was a message on my answering machine. Rob had neglected to tell me that my car was ready.

As I got ready for bed, it occurred to me that running into Jim and Lucy had one positive consequence. I felt a lot better about having slept with Beau Maverick.

*****

Wednesdays were a day off at the paper. There was always work to do, but Meg felt that we needed a day to clear our heads before starting the next paper. Often, Jim would take the afternoon off, and we would bum around. I no longer had a bumming partner. Meg liked to spend Wednesday cleaning house and catching up with her kids after school. The rest of the world worked on weekdays. At least today I had Vera's funeral to look forward to.

I begged a ride down the hill with Max. He dropped me at Rob's shop, and I tromped through the snow to the small door for customers. The big car door for vehicles was closed, and the shop was comfortably warm.

My car was sitting in the bay, brand new inspection sticker shining in the front window. Rob was standing at his workbench, bent over a work order, tapping his pen in beat to the song on the stereo. He had on jeans and an old sweatshirt. His black boots showed a hint of red sticking out from under his jeans. I'd seen the top of those boots. There's a red flame running up the sides. I smiled.

"Hey." I walked up to him. "How's it going?"

"Good." Rob looked into my eyes. "How are you doing today?"

"Oh, I'm fine. Thanks." I felt my cheeks heating up. "What do I owe you?"

"Three hundred fifty dollars." He pulled an invoice out of a pile. "I was able to get you a discount on the parts."

"Are you sure? I really don't want you to undercharge me."

"I'm sure. And you should always take advantage of undercharging. You've got to take into consideration you're probably being overcharged most of the time."

"But not by you."

He half shrugged and looked back down at his paperwork while I searched around in my bag for my checkbook. I had my fingers crossed that this check wouldn't bounce. The computer showed I had plenty of cash in my account, but there was always the worry that when the check went through, there wouldn't be enough to cover it.

"Deposit this right away, okay?"

"Yeah, sure. But it's fine, if you need to wait for your paycheck or something."

"No. Just put it in the bank today."

Eight

Rob drove my car out of his shop, jumped out, and held the door open for me. I climbed in and waved as he pulled another car into the bay and rolled down the big door. I eased out of the drive and pointed my car towards home.

My dressy clothes were jammed at the back of the closet. I laid them on the bed and surveyed the mess. How do you dress for a funeral? I had the sneaking suspicion that whatever I chose would be wrong. Some little detail would give offense, because I'm emotionally ill equipped for this kind of occasion. I decided on a black wool jumper my mom had given me, added black tights and a turtleneck. Slid my feet into low-heeled, black, fur-lined leather boots. If this wasn't somber enough, then screw it. It was the best I could do.

At the church, I sat toward the back, away from the other employees from the Inn. I zoned out during the sermon and stared at my feet while family and friends came forward to talk about Vera. Somehow, I couldn't reconcile the petty, vindictive woman I knew with the angelic Vera I was hearing about. The good mother. Friend to all. Caring supervisor. I had a distinct desire to throw up.

Dotty broke into tears before she even reached the front of the church. A male relative—her brother, I think—rushed forward and escorted her back to her pew. At last it was over, and we trooped to our cars. The casket was driven once around the green in final farewell, and we followed the hearse to the cemetery on Route 12.

I thought seriously about skipping the ashes-to-ashes part of the ceremony, but I knew my absence would be commented on. I definitely didn't need to give anyone anything more to talk about, so I went.

The wailing started as the coffin was lowered into the ground. I wasn't standing close enough to see who was crying, but I imagined it might be one of Vera's daughters. At last, flowers and earth were tossed onto the coffin, and I was free. I turned to walk back to my car, picking my way through the headstones. I don't like to step on dead people.

From the corner of my eye, I caught movement behind me, and a hand grabbed my shoulder. The impact whirled me around, face-to-face with Vera's oldest daughter. Her cheeks were red and showed traces of tears. The malice in her expression scared me.

"You came to gloat, didn't you?" Her voice was shrill and loud. I looked for a way to escape, but she had a death grip on my shoulder. "How dare you? You bitch!" She swung her free arm back and slapped me hard across the face.

I gasped and pulled away. Before I could flee, she attacked me with her fists, pummeling me and knocking me to the ground. I curled into a ball in the snow, trying to protect myself. She was sitting on me, pounding my ribs, my head, my hands. Then she was gone, her weight lifted away from me.

"Bree?"

I looked up to see Brian frowning down at me. Behind him, Steve Leftsky had Vera's daughter around the waist and was hauling her away. She was thrashing and swearing, but Steve held on. He was speaking quietly to her even as she was trying to turn her attack on him.

"Bree?" Brian spoke again. "You hurt?"

I struggled to sit up. "I'm fine. Nothing's broken."

"Why didn't you defend yourself?"

"She just buried her mom. If it were me, I'd probably go berserk, too." I stood up. I hurt, but not unbearably.

"You've got a nasty welt on your face."

"She must have been wearing a ring or something."

"Come on. I'll walk you to your car. We don't need anyone else thinking you're a punching bag."

I looked to see what Steve had done with my attacker. Mourners surrounded her. Steve was nearby keeping an eye on things, but he had let her go. I caught his gaze across the cemetery and gave him what I hoped was my you-did-good smile. I was glad he hadn't dragged her off in a police car.

*****

That evening, I was at the Inn doing my house-elf thing. Dotty was already back at work. Weird. I avoided my coworkers by standing at the farthest table, folding towels. My hands did the work automatically, which freed my mind to dwell on Vera, Jim, and the rest of my unhappy life.

Lucy and Jim were actually making complete sense to me. A lawyer and a reporter. The perfect match. Lucy could be a charming companion, and she knew how to find things out. Jim would lead Lucy straight to the news. Not that Jim would intentionally tattle on his clients, but Lucy had a way of being where she could overhear conversations.

Vera's death had me stumped, and I thought Lieutenant Brooks must be nuts. Not only did I not have anything to gain by killing Vera, I was losing. People in town had started to stare at me. Jim had stopped seeing me. Lucy Howe had written about it in the paper.

I shook my head and puffed out some air. I finished the guest towels and started in on a pile of rags. The rags were mostly worn-out towels that had been hacked into pieces and hemmed. I'd made a significant dent in the pile when Dotty came across the room to see me.

"The kitchen needs someone to come down and clean up some ash that blew out of the hearth. And they need more wood. Check the common rooms, and pick up the treats before you come back up the hill."

"Okay." This was a fairly normal request. At least she hadn't asked me to clean the office, as well.

"And Bree," Dotty called as I walked away. "Take a Jeep. We've got a busy night tonight, so I want you back as soon as possible."

"Yes, boss." I wondered if it was hard for her to be doing her sister's job.

I drove a Jeep down the steep hill to the main building and parked in the kitchen lot. I slid through the busy kitchen, avoiding being trampled by the servers and sous chefs who were starting to prepare for dinner. Knives were flashing over vegetables, butter was being whipped, glasses shined. The air smelled of roasting poultry, and I guessed duck was on the menu.

"Bree!" The kitchen manager snapped at me. "You're in the way. Move on through."

I slipped through the anteroom between the kitchen and the dining room. It was a quiet space that kept the kitchen noise from reaching the guests. The wine steward was decanting a bottle of merlot. I nodded hello and pushed through to the refectory, a large, high-vaulted room with wood beams in the ceiling and huge stone fireplaces at each end. The long walls held floor-to-ceiling windows. One side looked out over the terrace and the fields beyond. The other showcased a small, informal courtyard filled with fall color. Tables were scattered throughout the room.

Black powder dusted the hearth and floor around the nearest fireplace. When the wind came down the hill at just the right angle, it would force air down the chimney, sending sparks and soot into the room. A panel in the wall hid a camouflaged latch that popped open the door to a hidden cupboard. Inside the cupboard was the hose to a whole-house vacuum system that helped us keep the place clean. I flipped the switch to activate the suction, pulled the hose over to the fireplace, and sucked the soot away. I flipped off the suction, rolled the hose, and stowed it back behind the panel.

Turning around, I ran smack into Gunnar Ericson. He reached out and grabbed my shoulders before I could fall back into the fireplace. I tried to step back away from him, but he held on, forcing me to choose between rudely pulling away and standing still, face-to-face with a guest.

Both options were unacceptable. The first was downright rude. The second was against Inn policy. House elves shall not act as if they are of equal status to guests. I chose not to be rude and stood smiling at Gunnar. I didn't, however, speak to him, as that would be breaking the biggest rule: A staff member never speaks to a guest unless the guest speaks first. Gunnar smiled his movie star smile at me and tilted his head just slightly. I caught myself wondering if he had a normal smile for his mom and dad, or if they were subjected to the star treatment, as well.

"Before I let you go, you have to promise you won't go scooting off like last time."

Was it my imagination, or was his European accent getting thicker? "Okay." Another hotel rule: If a guest asks you to do something, do it.

Gunnar let go of my shoulders, and I took a step back. I wasn't particularly comfortable with this man in my comfort zone. Surely he'd learned to stay out of other people's personal space in kindergarten. I stood waiting to be released from his presence and repressed a shiver.

"You certainly are elusive. I had to bribe one of the kitchen staff to call me if they saw you around. I spent hours hanging around here waiting. Very boring."

"I only work part-time." I put on my best be-nice-to-the-guests smile. It apparently hadn't occurred to him to find out where I live or check for me in town. That was fine with me. I didn't want him showing up on my doorstep.

"You know, I'm going to keep asking until you accept, so you might as well say yes. I'd like you to have dinner with me in my cottage. Tomorrow night?"

I was spared rejecting Gunnar by the appearance of Brian. He whipped around the door from the kitchen, his eyes catching us standing by the unlit fire.

"There you are, Bree. Dotty is wondering where you are. Why didn't you bring a radio with you? She's frantic."

"Sorry. I didn't think of it. She could have called down to the kitchen, if she needed me. She knows where I am."

"Well, get back up the hill right now." Brian turned to Gunnar. "Mr. Ericson, is there something I can do to help you? I'm sorry to pull Bree away, but she's needed."

I scooted out the door.

Dotty wasn't really looking for me. Turns out the sous chef Ericson had bribed developed a conscience and told Brian I was cornered in the dining room. We still had at least thirty minutes until guests started vacating their rooms for dinner, so Dotty sent me down to the spa with clean linen.

I parked the Jeep in front of the pub, a big, log building with an open bar, huge TV, pool table and fireplace where guests could go to relax. It sat above the spa, and often the male guests would chug their favorite beer or hard liquor and watch the projection TV while their escorts were pampered below.

I took the path that ran alongside the building and schlepped the tubs of towels and robes down the stone stairs, past the door to the exercise room at the entrance of the spa. Janine, the receptionist for the spa, was sitting behind a desk just inside the door. A pert blond in her early twenties, her skin testified to regular spa treatments.

"Hey, Bree. Got towels for us? That's great. I thought the spa goddess ..." She tilted her head toward the door of one of the treatment rooms. "...was going to blow a gasket. She was stomping around here earlier, making all kinds of noise." Janine motioned me to come closer. "You should have seen it. She was in full tantrum, raving and stomping her feet, when a guest walked in. I thought she would choke!" Janine snorted. "Her face turned all red, and then its all, "Well, how are you today? What can we do for you?" Sweet as honey. And you know that guest had seen her having a fit. There's no way she could have missed it!" Janine laughed. "What I wouldn't give to see that lady report her highness to the boss!"

I backed away from Janine, smiling. "I've got to get this stuff put away before I get caught out here." Janine nodded, and I slipped into the changing rooms. I stacked towels and slid the rolled robes into cubbies. In the spa ladies' prep room, I stacked face clothes and towels and slippers for clients' use. Then I grabbed my empty bin and headed back out to the entrance to escape Janine.

"Hey, Bree?" She stopped me as I walked past the reception desk.

"Sorry, Janine. I've got to get back up the hill. Turn down will start any minute."

"Cool. Then it's time for me to get out of here. But wait a sec, I've got something good to tell you. The boss worked up a new whole day spa treatment for the guests, and they're trying it out on the office and dining room staff. She never thinks to ask the housekeeping staff, but I asked Brian, and he said of course the housekeeping staff could have appointments. You're pretty free on Wednesdays, aren't you? Do you want me to make you an appointment for next week?"

"Do you have room for two on that Wednesday? I'd love to be able to bring Meg Maverick. Could you swing that?"

"Oh, sure, the spa ladies don't know who works here, really. They are 'professionals' and don't hang out with the rest of us. They'd never know. And I don't think Brian would mind. He really likes you."

"We're just old friends. I'd really appreciate it if you'd fit Meg and me in. Meg's been really stressed lately, and it would be good for her."

"And you, too." Janine handed me an appointment card. "You found Vera dead." Janine shivered. "And now everybody talks about you behind your back."

Oh, great, like I needed to know that. "I gotta go now, Janine. Thanks." I waved the little card at her as I one-handed the laundry bin through the door. I headed back up the stone steps, planning to take a quick look in at the pub to see that everything was in order. Gunnar was standing at the back entrance blocking the door. He appeared to be talking to himself. As I started backing away, he turned toward me, and I saw that he was holding a cell phone. He scowled at me. I hot-footed it around the building and checked the pub via the other door.

*****

"Bree." Dotty called to me as I walked back into the laundry. "Brian wants to see you down in the office. Now." I hopped a ride back down the hill with one of the other girls. She was grim, no doubt figuring she'd be picking up the slack while I was with Brian.

Brian was sitting at his desk. I plopped into the chair opposite him. "So what's up?" I asked.

"Miles Brooks has been around asking about you again. That shit won't listen to anything I tell him. If you have any idea how to prove your innocence, this would be a great time to tell me."

I dropped my head and looked at my hands, which lay idle in my lap. Air puffed out between my lips. "I told them everything, Brian. There isn't anything else." I felt like I had a rock in my stomach, and I wanted to go home and crawl into bed forever.

"I want you to come with me to the cottage where Vera died. The police tape is down, and I think we'd better take a look and see if there is anything unusual about that closet."

"Why not take Dotty?" I really didn't want to go back there. "She must have an inventory sheet for that room."

"I tried taking Dotty down there. She burst into tears and ran out of the cottage. I don't think she's going to be any help. Come on."

My stomach started churning when we reached the door of the housekeeping closet, but once we were inside, I started feeling better. There was no sign that anyone had bled and died in this room. It looked the same as it had a hundred times before.

"I want you to look carefully and tell me if anything is out of place or missing. Lieutenant Brooks was asking if anything was unusual. Dotty's too distressed to tell me. It's up to you."

I looked around the room. The shelves were stocked with all the usual stuff. On one wall the towels, sheets, washcloths, candles, matches, extra duvet cover and extra feather bed lived. Light bulbs, coasters, treat plates, glasses and doilies sat on a shelf over the sink. Cleaning supplies on the bottom shelves. Extra pillows. Extra beverages for the refrigerator. The carafes that I'd been coming to retrieve when I'd found Vera. Everything seemed to be in place. Almost.

"Looks to me like everything's here. Except there isn't supposed to be an empty spot on the top shelf. I can't think of what goes there, but something does."

"You sure you can't remember?"

I closed my eyes and tried to picture the room, but the image wouldn't come to me. I opened my eyes and shook my head. "Nope, nothing."

We drove back up the hill and I joined the house-elf brigade.

* * * * *

I called Meg about our spa appointment the minute I made it home. Well, the minute after I fed the animals and gave Lucky his customary rubdown. Then I made myself a cup of tea. I sat on my comfy, overstuffed couch. My feet were tucked under Ranger, who had leaned on my legs and then collapsed, as his feet slipped out from under him on the hardwood floor. My feet were trapped under his warm body. Annie was on the couch with her head in my lap, Hank had his head on Ranger's flank and Diesel was practically sitting on Ranger's head, his nose on the couch against my other thigh. Annabelle was on the back of the couch, her tail occasionally flicking my head.

I was feeling dejected, despite the four-legged companionship. My life had taken this strange turn, and I couldn't see how to get it back on track. I didn't even know what *on track* was. I was working my butt off at two jobs that didn't really pay enough money to cover the bills. I couldn't keep a man interested. Thank God, the farm had been paid off before Grandma passed it on to me, but there were still taxes and upkeep. The animals cost me a small fortune to feed.

I pulled my thoughts back to Vera. Me. Jail. I still couldn't picture what belonged in the missing space in the housekeeping closet. It nagged at me. How ironic if I ended up in prison because of a faulty memory. Could they convict me? Yes. Innocent people got sent to jail all the time. Well, at least you were always hearing about them on the TV. D.N.A. evidence proves so-and-so is innocent after fifty years. Oh, boy.

The tea wasn't doing its job. My eyes were heavy, and my brain was numb. I pushed Diesel's head off my leg and pulled my feet out from under Ranger. I laid my head on the cushy arm of the couch and swung my legs up next to Annie. I'd get up in a minute, but for now, I just wanted to lie here.

* * * * *

I was breathing in something humid and stinky. It puffed onto my face with irritating regularity. "Go away." I didn't want to open my eyes, but the smell kept coming at me. I squinted reluctantly and found a Boxer snout centimeters from my face. As my eyes opened, Diesel's tail began to quiver. His eyes opened wider, and he wiggled from head to toe. Then he gave me a big sloppy Boxer kiss. I sat up wiping my face with my sleeve. I was still on the couch, only now the sun was streaming into the room. The other dogs were at the kitchen door making squeaking noises and wagging their tails. I guessed that Max must be out feeding the outside animals. I needed to let him know that I was healthy enough to do that again.

The answering machine was blinking when I walked into the kitchen. I punched the button so I could listen while I was making coffee. "Bree, Lucy told me you saw us together." It was Jim's voice on the phone. I stopped short as the message played on. "It's a misunderstanding, Bree. Call me."

I thought about him walking down the street with his arm around Lucy. A mistake on his part, maybe, but not a misunderstanding. I erased the message.

* * * * *

A little after noon, Meg raised her head from her work. "Do you think we could find anything out while we're at the spa next Wednesday? Could we snoop around a little? See if we could discover anything Brooks hadn't noticed."

"I doubt we'll find anything that Brooks hasn't, but who knows. The worst that could happen is I'll lose my job. I hate that job anyway."

"Then why do you stay?"

"I need the money to support my animal habit, and besides that, Brian asked me to. He said he needed people he could count on to actually show up at work. I was flattered. More the fool, me."

Meg laughed. "Guys could always get you to do what they wanted with a little flattery. You're way too easy."

"Okay, so I have a bad habit of doing favors for guys who are nice to me. At least I'm not doing favors for nasty guys. Or doing nasty favors for kinky guys. Or doing any favors for married guys."

"Enough, already." Meg paused a moment. "Scott said something that bothered me the other day."

I raised my eyebrows at her.

"He said Tom's friendship with you could be trouble. He said I should fire you. Why do you think he said that?"

"I don't know. What do you think?"

"If I knew that, I wouldn't be asking you."

Nine

I was fiddling with a tricky graphic, but I couldn't concentrate. There was a vague feeling niggling at the back of my brain. I couldn't quite put my finger on it, but the feeling that something wasn't right was distracting. I let my mind go blank, hoping that whatever was there would either go away or at least become concrete, so I could take care of it.

I leaned back in my chair and closed my eyes. Sleep immediately started to take over. I felt warm, and my mind started to drift into places unknown. I jerked myself back up in my chair and decided I'd better go get a soda.

The minute I walked into the deli, it came to me. Scott was right. By staying at the paper, I was putting Tom at risk. There would be talk that his friendship with me displayed bad judgment.

I bought my soda and went back to work. I sat at my desk a few minutes, thinking about my options. When it came down to it, I had no options. I looked at Meg. "I'm quitting the paper." She started to say something, but I interrupted her. "Don't make this harder than it needs to be. Scott's got one thing straight. It's not good for you or Tom for me to be here."

We went back to work, but the mood in the office was changed. Meg looked pained, and God knows what kind of expression I had on my face. I was disgusted with myself for not realizing I was putting Tom in a bad spot. I should have quit sooner.

"I'm going for a soda. Do you want anything?" Meg stood up and stretched.

"No, I was just down there. Sorry, I should have gotten you something."

"No, that's okay. I need to walk anyway."

I heard Meg banging down the stairs in her boots. I looked back to the ad I was creating and tried to concentrate. I reread my notes, trying to remember what I'd agreed to do, trying to force my brain back into work mode.

"Bella Bree MacGowan."

I was hearing my full name a little too often these days. I looked up to see Lieutenant Brooks standing at my desk. "Sorry." I let out a sigh. "I didn't hear you come in. I'm sort of in the middle of something." I didn't think this was the time to explain the mechanics of layout to him. He wasn't smiling, and somehow I didn't think he much cared how inconvenienced I was by his presence.

"Bella Bree MacGowan," he repeated. "I am authorized to detain you on the suspicion of murdering Vera Post. Will you come with me please." It wasn't a request.

Meg banged through the door right at that moment and stood looking at us. Then she moved to her desk and set down her purse. "Can I help you?" she asked the Lieutenant.

"He's arresting me, Meg."

"What!" She started to say something else, but Brooks interrupted her.

"Please come with me, Ms. MacGowan. I understand that you are friendly with a number of officers at the barracks, so I will refrain from using handcuffs. But understand that if you try to avoid coming with me, I will use force. Is that clear?"

It was all too clear. My heart was pounding, and my legs were shaking. I wondered if Tom or Steve knew what was happening. I wished one of them were here to help me. I heard Meg talking quickly into the phone. She was too quiet for me to hear what she was saying.

"Is that clear?" Lieutenant Brooks asked again.

"Yes, it's very clear." I stood and grabbed my jacket. Meg was off the phone. "Meg, I'm going to leave my purse and keys here. If you could take care of them, that would be great." Lieutenant Brooks took my elbow and steered me toward the door. "And call Max," I called to her as we stepped through the door. "Make sure that everyone gets fed. Please." I could hear the pleading in my voice and hated it. "And don't call my family!"

*****

It's weird how my brain works. Sitting in the back of the squad car on my way to the barracks, the solution to the closet mystery came to me. An image of the room popped into my head. There should have been a basket of large, solid glass balls in that blank space on the shelf where Vera died. We used them for decorating at Christmas.

I entertained the idea of telling Lieutenant Brooks but decided against it. I pulled my cell phone out of my jacket pocket and dialed Brian. I got his message machine. "Brian, it's Bree, I remembered what was missing from the closet. It's the big, glass balls we use to decorate the table at Christmas ..."

"Hey!" Lieutenant Brooks raised his voice from the front seat. "You do not have permission to use your cell phone. Hand that phone to me."

I hung up and handed him my cell phone. It didn't matter now anyway. There was no one else to call. At least, not yet. I thought I'd probably get my traditional one call from the station.

*****

Tom was deep in conversation with Lieutenant Brooks. I was sitting in the middle of a line of chairs against the wall. There weren't any other criminals waiting to be booked. I didn't know if I should be grateful that I didn't have to consort with scumbags or disappointed that there weren't any around to compare me to. I'd probably look pretty good sitting next to a drug dealer or a pedophile.

"Excuse me. Am I allowed a phone call? Because I'd like to call a lawyer."

Tom looked over at me distractedly. "Yeah, Bree, go ahead." He waved his hand at the phone and turned back to Lieutenant Brooks. Both of their faces were tight. I turned back to the phone and started to dial. Before I could finish, I heard a commotion behind the door.

Val burst into the room, hitting Lieutenant Brooks in the butt with the door. He wheeled around, hand on his holster.

"I can't believe you arrested Bree MacGowan!" Val pointed her finger at him. "Do you know her father was the fire chief here for twenty years? Do you know who her grandfather was? Are you so totally incompetent that you can't find the real murderer?" She turned to me. "Are you okay? I heard in town that a state trooper escorted you to a police car. Meg's in a panic. She says she'll be too busy helping you to finish the paper. She's worried that they'll send you to prison to wait trial, and you'll get raped or knifed." Val leaned in and spoke quietly. "She sent me over here to keep that from happening. I don't really think they'll hold you. The evidence doesn't appear to be very strong. Anyway, I'll try and get the judge to release you on bail."

"Listen, tell Meg not to worry about me and to focus on the paper, I'll be fine. Tell her that Tom will make sure that nothing horrible happens to me. Okay?" I took a deep breath. "I don't have money for bail, but maybe it won't come to that. I heard Tom say something about being responsible for me. The only person I'm likely to murder at the moment is Lieutenant Brooks, so it would be safer to have me out on the streets than here in the barracks."

Tom's and Brooks' discussion ended with Tom leaving and closing the door loudly. Val stood in front of Lieutenant Brooks, talking quietly but firmly into his face for a few moments, and then Brooks invited us to all sit down at the table.

I sat beside Val as they argued. My mind was drifting in and out of the conversation, and I was having trouble sitting still. I think shock had set in or the aftermath of too much adrenaline, whatever that's called. I wanted to cry, but I wouldn't let myself break down in public. If only I was at home in bed with four furry creatures to keep me warm.

"There is nowhere near enough evidence to detain Bree on these charges," Val was saying.

"I think we get to determine what constitutes sufficient evidence." Lieutenant Brooks had his feet planted shoulder width apart, unmoving.

"I think the judge gets to decide that." Val got right up in his face.

"Her fingerprints were all over the murder scene. According to our sources, she was after the deceased's job and had been spotted trying to sabotage Vera's work. They also had a huge fight in front of several other employees a couple of weeks back."

Val shook her head. "Everyone fights, fought, with Vera. She was an old cow. Of course Bree's fingerprints were on that room. She works there. She probably was in that room four out of every seven days for the last year."

They argued for so long that in the end, it was too late to bring my case before a judge. Brooks wanted to put me in a cell, but Tom insisted that I be allowed to stay in his office. Brooks wasn't happy about it, but I think somewhere in the back of his mind, he remembered that Tom was actually the captain.

I slept curled up on a couch in a little room that opened off of Tom's office. The room was meant to be a place for grieving relatives to sit in private, but I suspected that people besides me had used the couch as a bed. It was a quiet room with a couch and two armchairs on one side and a table with four chairs near the window on the other side. No exit except through Tom's office. The perfect place for a tryst.

I'm sure I looked a sight when Tom came in to get me the next morning. I hadn't slept well. My clothes were crumpled, and my hair had developed a bad case of static and was sticking up all over the place. I had raccoon eyes from my mascara. Other than that, and a bad case of morning breath, everything was hunky dory.

The judge sent me home after Tom testified that he'd be responsible for me. He didn't make me post bail. He agreed with Val that the evidence was slim, and one fingerprint on the wrist did not make a murderer. He looked at me over his glasses, though, and informed me that if I was not present at my court appearance, I'd be a felon.

Oh, boy.

It was mid-afternoon by the time Steve dropped me off at home. "Do you want me to stay, Bree? I think I could safely say it was in the line of duty."

"No, it's okay, Steve. I'll be all right. Really, I've got my dogs, and I'm not much in the mood for conversation right now anyway."

"Okay, call if you need anything." He bumped back down the road.

My dogs acted as if I'd been gone a month. Ranger stood on his back feet and put his paws on my shoulders, giving me a deep and mournful look and a big sloppy dog kiss. Hank, Diesel and Annie scolded me with growly voices and snuffled my clothes for clues about where I'd been.

I went upstairs, stood in the shower, and cried until the hot water ran out. Then I pulled myself together. There is something about a shot of freezing cold water at the end of a hot shower that'll snap a person right out of self-pity. I dressed, dried my hair, then headed downstairs.

I sat down with a cup coffee and a pen and piece of paper. I decided I would list all the people Vera could have pissed off. The more I thought about it, though, the more impossible it seemed. Ninety percent of the people who live in this town had had problems with Vera at one time or another.

Think. I tapped myself on the head with the pencil. Okay who had access to the housekeeping closet? That would be a substantially shorter list. Brian, the kitchen staff, the housekeeping staff, the owner of the hotel, and possibly the guests. There also was the possibility that someone could have snuck onto the property, avoiding the surveillance cameras. That would mean premeditation, skills like lock picking, and an intimate knowledge of the Inn. It seemed unlikely.

The keys to the closet were a sticking point. When they weren't signed out to a particular staff member, they were kept in a lock box. The shift manager had the one key to the lock box where Brian kept a spare.

Vera would have had a key. Could she have been with someone? Or maybe someone knocked on the door. She'd been bashed on the back of her head, so she had to have trusted her murderer enough to turn her back to him or her. Oh, hell, she never would have believed someone wanted to kill her. She waltzed around without a care in the world, assured of her own superiority.

I closed my eyes. My thoughts wouldn't settle on any one detail. I desperately wanted to sleep. *You think if you stay awake, you'll solve this mystery?* I asked myself. *That's foolish.* I let myself drift and found myself dreaming about skipping town. I was on a boat with Kenny Chesney, and it was warm. The sun was hot on my skin. Kenny was licking my neck.

Licking my neck? I woke up to find Annie's nose in my face. She wagged her tail and snuffled my neck some more. Then she jumped down off the chair and ran to the back door. I let the dogs out and dragged myself back upstairs to get ready for work at the Inn.

Dotty looked surprised when I walked into the laundry. She took a quick look around and hurried over to me.

"I didn't think you'd be in here today. I called Sally in to work your shift."

"Okay. I'll happily go home." I turned away.

"Wait. You called Brian on your way to jail. Are you okay? Do you need anything? I can't believe they are still trying to pin Vera's death on you."

"Well, apparently, it seems perfectly reasonable to them. I wanted to ask you about the Christmas decorations we used to keep in the housekeeping closet where Vera died." I watched Dotty's face. I didn't want to distress her, but she didn't seem fazed by the question

"Those big glass balls?"

"Yeah, those. When did you last see them?"

"I don't remember, why?"

"Because they're missing now. I wondered if they had anything to do with Vera. Maybe they're clues."

"Oh, Bree, I wish I could help you. But I don't know when I saw them last. And even if I did know, I don't see how they could help you. It's not like there would be fingerprints or anything. We keep them way up high, and they get polished after anyone handles them. I'm sure when we find them they will be perfectly clean. You really should let the police do the investigating. They are trained to do it right."

I went home to bed.

*****

I woke feeling disappointed that I hadn't dreamed of Kenny. I wondered if I could make myself drift off again, when I heard cooking noises in my kitchen. The dogs weren't barking. Must be someone they knew. Either that, or they're all dead. *Shut up,* I told myself. *That's just morbid, and I'm not letting you scare me.*

I pulled on some clothes went down the stairs into the kitchen. My big brother, J.W., was standing at the stove, cracking eggs into a skillet. "So, you're awake." He took a long look at me. "I hear from my sources that you are in a funk. Having been released from jail through the generosity of friends, you are repaying their faith in you by hiding in bed and sulking. That true?"

"No. That's not true." I made a face at him and sat down at my table. "I was making a list of possible suspects, and I fell asleep. "

"You skipped work. You never skip work."

"How did you know that I skipped work? Got spies at Whispering Birches?"

"Who names a place Whispering Birches? Whispering Pines, that's good. Whispering Meadows, that's okay. But Whispering Birches? It just doesn't sound right."

"You aren't answering my question."

"Don't change the subject. We are supposed to be talking about you, not that crazy hotel you work for."

"I didn't change the subject. You changed the subject, and I was just following along."

"Well, we need to figure out how to get your life back. Meg is worried. When Meg worries, Tom gets worked up. When Tom gets worked up, he calls me, and then I get worked up. I get worked up mostly because he calls me in the middle of the night. Five a.m. is too early for a man to be up." He looked down at me. "I could get you smuggled out of the country until this all blows over. I've got a friend in Montreal you could stay with. A really nice gal."

"I'm not leaving the country, and I am not staying with one of your million girl friends. 'Oh, J.W. is sooo fabulous.'" I did my best falsetto. "'He bought me a car and a little dog and screwed my brains out.'" I dropped the falsetto. "I did not kill Vera, I'm not going to start acting as if I did. If I sneak away in the night, everyone will assume I did kill her. I'm not giving them the satisfaction." *Besides,* I thought to myself, *who would take care of my animals?*

"Eat this." J.W. shoveled a pile of eggs onto a plate and set it in front of me. "You're going to need your strength. I hear things can get pretty rough in those women's prisons."

I threw my fork at him, but it missed and landed on the counter. The truth is, I'm afraid I will go to prison. It nags at the back of my mind, and I don't know what to do about it. That doesn't mean I want my older brother butting in, trying to make me feel better but ending up making me feel worse. I needed to take action and get the situation back under control. If only I knew what action to take.

I got another fork and shoveled some eggs into my mouth. "These are good. Just like I like 'em. You're a good brother."

"A lot of thanks I get for it." He sat down with his own plate of eggs. "What do you want me to tell Mom? She's been calling me every day since one of her local biddy friends called to tell her that you're a murder suspect."

"She didn't mention it to me. Sneaky. Tell her I'm fine. Tell her I didn't kill anybody. Tell her you came over here and found me dancing on tables." I sighed. *Get real.* "Tell her it will all be sorted out soon." *I hope.* "Tell her to make her old biddies keep their noses out of my business."

After J.W. left, Meg showed up with Beau and the kids. I felt my heart jump when Beaux got out of the car, and I told myself to stop it. *This guy is not for you, B.B.,* I told myself.

Beau smiled sheepishly. "I thought I'd come up and help Meg with the kids. Tom's up to his neck, as usual."

I saw Meg shoot us a look. I figured she was getting ideas, but there wasn't much I could do about that. I followed the herd into the barn.

We spent an hour visiting all the animals. Lucky got groomed and fussed over. The chickens were counted, and Meg had to settle a couple of arguments over which chicken had what name. The bunnies were petted. Annabelle, the cat, was held and kissed until she hid under the couch. The dogs pulled out their toys, and the kids stood in the front door yard tossing balls and rings in the snow.

Beau wandered around after us. He picked up Gemma, when she slipped on the ice in the yard, and broke up a tussle over who had named the green-tailed rooster. He pulled the sleds out of the back of Meg's S.U.V. and helped me pull Gemma and Pete to the top of the hill.

After an hour of hard sledding, we were all covered in snow. I had fallen off the toboggan into a drift and had wads of it packed down the back of my jacket. The kids were all rosy faced and tired. We trudged back to the house for hot chocolate and cookies. Luckily, Meg brought cookies, because I hadn't thought to make any.

We stood in the kitchen, warming our backsides in front of the wood stove. The kids were reliving their runs down the hill, and the adults studiously avoided talking about my jailbird status. When Gemma's fingers had stopped hurting from the cold, and everyone's feet were dry, Meg decided it was time to head home to make dinner.

"Hey, Meg," said Beau after we had loaded the sleds back into the car. "I'm going to stay here for a while, if you don't mind. I want to talk to Bree about something."

Meg raised her eyebrows, but she couldn't have been more surprised than I was. "How will you get home?" she asked. "Your car is at my house."

"I'll figure it out, don't worry."

"Okay, then, see you later." She shrugged. The kids packed into the car and waved until the car disappeared around a turn in the road.

"Want some coffee or something?" I asked Beau after we escorted the dogs back in the house. I opened the fridge. "I've got some beer in here, too, and soda."

"Nope. None of those things is what I want."

My heart began to beat a little faster.

"How you are doing? I hear it's been a tough couple of days." His voice was quiet and a little husky. He slid his arms around me. There was a fire starting in my belly.

"I'm okay. Not that I'd ever want to repeat the last few days. I never, ever, want to spend the night in Tom's office again. And I hope to never see the inside of the holding cells." I rested my head against his chest. Something about the maverick men made me feel safe and protected.

"Well, then." Beau spoke into my hair. "I think the next order of business is to help you forget all about that place." I backed away from his embrace. "It's not that I don't think you could make me forget. It's that I don't know if it's a good idea." I turned to the sink and ran water into a glass. He was making me thirsty. Well, at least I was going to blame it on him.

I felt him move close behind me. "No, I definitely think we need to work on erasing that memory. I hate to think of you sleeping in Tom's office. Especially when you should be sleeping with me." He lifted my hair and kissed me on the back of my neck, lingering there, just breathing a moment or two. "You smell nice. Like lavender."

"That's just my shampoo."

He slid his arms around me from behind. He was warm, and I felt my heart beat a little faster as he held me tight, our bodies pressed together. His hands slid up under my shirt in the front, and he ran them up until they heated the skin on my rib cage, just below my breasts. He breathed warmth onto my neck just under my ear. I felt a corresponding heat developing below my belly button.

What have I got to lose? I thought. I could go to prison tomorrow, and I would have passed up my last chance for sex. I turned in his embrace and wrapped my arms around his neck, lifting my face to kiss him at the spot where his jaw met his neck. He smelled like the outdoors and faintly of something like old spice. I tasted just a hint of salt on his neck. He must have worked up a sweat out sledding. We stood, arms wrapped around each other, breathing for a moment.

He lowered his head and kissed me on the mouth. His tongue slid along my lower lip and brushed against my teeth. He pushed me backward with his weight until I came to rest against the fridge, and his kiss became more urgent. His hands slid down my hips and pulled me to him. I slid my thigh between his legs. There wasn't a sliver of daylight between us anywhere. I ran my hands down his back and up under his shirt. His back was a solid mass of tight muscle under my fingers.

He released me and took my hand. "Which way is your room?"

"Through there." I nodded to the archway toward the living room. "Then up the stairs."

He pulled me up the stairs and along the hall to my room. It was full of cool afternoon shadows, but the room was warm. I'd had the heat turned up and the wood stove blazing downstairs, so the kids wouldn't be cold after sledding. Beau slid my tee over my head. He ran his hands along the skin below my bra and reached up to unhook it. He pulled me to him again and kissed my neck where it met my shoulder. I felt hot inside. Beau was kissing my neck, and I was getting heat down below. Go figure.

“Hey. Did I lose you there for a minute?”

“No. No. Go back to what you were doing. I'm pretty sure I can keep my brain in check.”

He kissed my neck again, and I told the stupid thoughts in my brain to shut up. I wanted to concentrate on that feeling.

His lips, tongue, and breath were on my neck. A sigh escaped me, and my knees started to buckle. I reached out and curled my fingers into his shirt so I wouldn't fall down. He slid his hands up under my breasts, held them for a moment, and then ran his thumbs across my nipples. I pressed myself into him, and he slid his thigh between my legs.

I fumbled with the buttons on his flannel shirt, but I couldn't get my hands to cooperate. My brain was totally flooded with the sensation of his hands on my body. Beau backed me to the bed until my knees met the edge, and I sat. He pulled off his flannel and then his tee-shirt ,exposing a tight stomach and muscled chest. He shucked his jeans and boxers.

I wouldn't have been surprised if my mouth was watering. Beau seemed totally unaware of how perfect his body was. Building houses with stone and brick had toned him into hard muscle. He was broad-shouldered and slim-hipped without an ounce of fat on him anywhere.

He reached and pulled my jeans down, sliding them off my hips. He bent and kissed me just below my belly button. I felt my skin burning. My brain was screaming, *Enough of this! Get to it!* I moaned involuntarily.

"Something wrong, Bree?" Beaux's voice was husky with desire.

"Oh, my God. You are torturing me. Finish pulling my pants off, and get up here."

"You're such a romantic." He laughed. He nuzzled his head between my thighs, and my breath caught in my throat.

"Beau. Beau, don't make me beg."

Beau raised his head and smiled at me. "What is it that you want, Bree?"

"Like you don't know." I slid down along the full length of his body until I was on the edge of the bed. I let my jeans fall to the floor and wrapped my legs up around him. Sometimes you just have to take matters into your own hands, or legs, in this case. I drew him down, and he lowered himself onto and into me. I sang the "Hallelujah Chorus" in my head.

We were lying in bed, drifting in the warmth; my back snuggled into his front, when I realized I'd done it again. I really should stop sleeping with Tom's brother. If only it didn't feel so damn good.

*****

I drove Beau down to Meg's later that evening. He'd offered to ask Max for a ride, but I wanted to see how things were coming on the paper, and Sunday evening seemed like a pretty safe time to be downtown.

Beau planted a warm kiss on my mouth, told me to take care of myself, jumped into his car, and headed out. I drove into town and parked as close as I could get to the office. I sat in the car for a moment, getting up nerve. The sidewalk was deserted, as I hoped it would be, so I jumped out of the car, slammed the door closed, beeped it locked, and ran through the door and up the stairs to the office.

I switched on the light and booted up my computer. A pile of letters were stacked on Meg's desk, and I walked over to take a look. Meg had taken my advice and contacted a local agency about replacing me. There was a mound of résumés for her to read. I looked through them, trying to see through the education and experience to the person underneath. Meg needed someone who was fast and self-motivated but also had a sense of humor and would be fun to work with.

I sorted through the letters, reading about past accomplishments and future plans. Then I ranked them. After tossing half of them in a reject pile, I put the best five on top of the remaining résumés. I wrote, "Try this one first" on a sticky note and stuck it on the top of the pile.

I went back over to my computer and pulled up the layout for the next paper. Meg was doing a fine job of keeping up with layout on her own. I walked back over to her desk and pulled a hefty stack of ads and articles to be set out of her in-box. Looked like she was placing stuff as she set it.

I brought the stack of stuff back over to my desk and started sorting. Some of this stuff was similar to ads I already had on my computer and could just make minor changes to. Some of it would need to be started from scratch. A fourth of the stack was articles or calendar items that would need to be keyboarded in. If I put my mind to it, I could finish in five or six hours. Another four, and I could probably get everything laid out.

I put the stack of stuff that need to be started from scratch in my in-box and started on the ads I had prototypes for. I have a simple but effective filing system on my computer, so if I recognized an ad, I could bring it up at a moment's notice. It was a lot faster than starting fresh on every ad.

When I looked up, it was midnight. I had finished the last of the easy stuff. I contemplated the stack of stuff left undone. I was tired. Too bad I hadn't brought some soda or coffee with me. I got up from my desk and walked over to the windows. I stretched and swung my arms around and tried to roll the tension out of my neck. I turned on the radio to keep me company and sat back down.

I was well into the second pile, concentrating hard on not making mistakes, when the door opened. I jumped and knocked a bunch of papers on the floor. Tom came through the door, and I let the air out of my lungs. "I thought I might find you up here."

"Why's that?" I bent over to retrieve the scattered papers.

"Because Meg doesn't usually leave the lights on." He smiled at me. "How are you doing? Anything I can help you with?"

"No, not unless you can convince Lieutenant Brooks of my innocence. But I think you already tried that, didn't you?"

"Yeah, I tried. He's not having any of it. I wouldn't worry, though." he smiled kindly. "There doesn't seem to be enough evidence for you to actually go to trial. In fact, there's almost no evidence against you at all. It makes me wonder what Brooks is up to."

"Can't you make him tell you?"

"He's in a different division. I do wish he'd talk to me, but I think he's afraid there's a conflict of interest. And he's right, there is." Tom reached out and touched my hair. "I promise this will blow over. You are not going to jail."

"Boy I'd really like that to be true. This is a nightmare." I started sorting through the papers I'd dropped, paper clipping stuff together.

Tom sat on the edge of my desk. "Bree, I wanted to ask you something. Miles told me that you made a phone call from the squad car. I was wondering if you'd tell me who you called."

"Sure. It was the funniest thing. A few days ago, Brian took me to the housekeeping closet where Vera died. He wanted to know if anything was out of place or unusual. He was trying to help me. I don't think he believes I killed

Vera either. There was an empty space in that closet, up on the top shelf, and I couldn't think of what belonged there.

"When I was in the squad car, I had a flash. I remembered that we kept these big glass balls up there in a basket. We use them at Christmas to decorate the mantle in that room. I called Brian to tell him that I'd remembered what was missing. That was the phone call I made."

Tom nodded. He was silent for a moment, eyebrows furrowed and his mouth set. "Did you tell Miles this?"

"No. I really didn't think he was interested in anything I had to say, and I was afraid he'd turn it against me somehow." I placed the papers in my inbox.

"I can see why you would feel that way. But I want you to tell him now. Okay? I'll pick you up and take you to the barracks tomorrow." The way Tom said it was a statement. I didn't think I really had a choice.

"Okay. But I'm going to be here late, so don't make it too early."

"No, I won't. I'll call you before I come."

Tom left me to finish setting ads, while I sulked about being taken back to the barracks in the morning.

Ten

It was a quiet ride to the barracks through swirling snow the next morning. I was trying to do the mature thing, but I really didn't want to give Brooks the information. *Don't be stupid,* I told myself. *If they find the balls, there might be a clue to the real murderer. I'll be off the hook. On the other hand, there might not be any prints at all, and as I'm the only one who knew the balls were missing Brooks is going to throw me in the slammer.*

"Earth to Bree," Tom's voice cut into my thoughts. "What's going on in that head of yours? I can see wheels turning, and your ears are going to start smoking any minute now."

"I just don't think that talking to Lieutenant Brooks about this is going to help me any. Everything I say seems to incriminate me more. If it were up to me, we'd be going anywhere except the barracks. Shit, my stomach hurts. Do you think I could be getting an ulcer?"

"Oh, stop your whining." He reached over and ruffled my hair. "You could keep this information to yourself, but then all kinds of bad things would happen. You could go to jail for withholding evidence. If you fall off that motorcycle and hit your head, there won't be anyone to come forward and tell us what you know. Give me a couple of minutes, and I could come up with one or two more reasons why this is a good idea, but we're here now, so you've got to suck it up and do the right thing."

Tom took me in to see Brooks. He was sitting in his office, talking quietly into the phone. He looked up when Tom stopped in the doorway and motioned us to the chairs in front of his desk. I sat fidgeting while Brooks talked, and Tom relaxed into his chair and closed his eyes. I wondered if this was deceptive. He was the superior in the room, after all.

It only took a couple of minutes for me to tell Brooks what I knew. He nodded and thanked me and let me go. I heard him thanking Tom as I scooted out the door. I was down the hall and practically out the door before Tom caught up with me.

"You trying to avoid getting bitten by a snake? I've never seen you move so fast."

"I don't much fancy getting spending another night in your office."

"Well, I can't blame you for that. Listen, I'm going to get Steve to take you home. Okay? He's at the end of a shift and headed that way anyway."

*****

Instead of heading back down the road, Steve turned off the cruiser's engine and followed me into my house.

"Want some coffee?" I asked.

"Not in a hurry? Thought you'd be fussing to get to the paper."

"No. Meg's got a replacement for me. All I'm doing is looking over her shoulder today. Giving her the benefit of my superior experience."

"You sound thrilled. Why don't you just stay here instead?"

"Because Meg's my best friend, and she wants me to be there." I set my coffee down on top of the newspaper. "Might as well get going."

"You didn't let me get any coffee."

"Missed your chance." I shrugged myself into my coat and grabbed my bag.

A knot formed in my stomach on the way to the paper. I hadn't recognized the name of the woman Meg hired to replace me, but that didn't mean she wouldn't remember me. I really didn't want to teach someone to do my job, but I especially didn't want to deal with someone who was sniggering behind my back.

I parked on the green and dragged my feet across the street. I bypassed the door that led up the stairs to the paper and headed into the café. I ordered a coffee and muffin to go from Muffin Man. I handed him some bills, and he looked me right in the eye and smiled. Not an I-know-you're-a-murderer smile. A hey-I-think-you're-great-and-I'm-sorry-you're-going-through-a-bunch-of-crap smile. I immediately felt better. I smiled back and headed up to the office. My feet were a lot happier now.

There was a pretty, young blond sitting at my desk. I had to remind myself that I'd quit. It wasn't my desk anymore. I'd made that choice. It didn't have anything to do with the girl who was sitting there. She focused her baby blues on me and smiled.

"Boy, am I glad you're here. I'm muddling along, but I'm sure I could get things done faster with a little direction." She stood and stuck out her hand. "I'm Deirdre," she said. "I just moved into the area."

"Bree." I shook her hand. "It seems like you already know who I am."

"Well, there's a picture of you and Meg on the wall. It wasn't hard to figure out."

I'd forgotten about that photo. Tom had taken it the day Meg published the first *Royalton Star.* I smiled at Deirdre.

"It pays to be observant." I walked over to stand behind her chair. "Let's see what you've been up to. Where's Meg, by the way?"

"She had to go home. Her youngest couldn't find her Brownie outfit? Something like that."

"Sounds about right. The paper is Meg's baby, but it will always come second to her family." I reached over Deirdre and clicked on the computer screen with the mouse. "What are you working on now?"

Deidre showed me the ads she'd been setting. I gave her a couple of tips, but there weren't any serious problems.

"Have you done this before?"

"Yeah, I worked on a *Parents' Monthly* in Florida. Same idea but one quarter of the deadlines. How do you decide where to place articles and ads in the *Royalton Star?*"

I pulled a binder off the shelf beside the desk and flipped it open. "This will tell you what page to place the different features on. The paper is pretty much the same page count every week, unless there's some wild news story in town. And sometimes we do a special insert. Like at Christmas, there's a special section for events and merchants that gets slipped into the center. The Calendar always starts four pages from the end, even in the event of extra pages. All that information is in this binder. If you ever have a question about layout, and Meg's not around, you can look it up in here."

"Okay. I think I'll keep that close." Deirdre put the binder on the desk next to her computer. "What about ad placement? Is that in the binder too?"

I explained my method for placing ads and showed her where to look on the proof sheets for special placement. Meg had already set a number of articles and ads, so I walked Deirdre through the process of adding content to the paper. She was a quick study, and within the hour, I had my feet up on the bookcase. Deirdre asked the occasional question, but she could have managed without me.

Meg walked in about noon. She dropped her bag on the floor and began shaking snow out of her hair. "Snowing again. There's a big commotion down in the café. I guess it got out that Gunnar Ericson is in the area. There's a gaggle of middle-aged women all giggling and gossiping. They're hoping he'll show up in town."

"If they knew Gunnar like I know Gunnar, they wouldn't be so thrilled. He's got a layer of slime. And he takes it for granted that he'll get what he wants. I detest that in a guy."

"I wouldn't mind meeting him," Deirdre piped in. "Even if he is nasty, it would be fun to have my picture taken with him. It might even make it into the tabloids or something. I'd like to be famous."

"I don't know." I looked over at her. "If fame is such a great thing, why do so many celebrities pay Whispering Birches a huge amount of money to get away from it? I don't think I'd survive a week with the press watching me."

"You do tend to get in trouble more often than the average bear," said Meg. "Most of us could probably manage to behave for a week!"

"Having people follow me around would drive me over the edge," I said. "I already feel like everyone in this town knows every stupid thing I've ever done."

"It would be worse if they knew you'd talked with Gunnar," said Meg. "Hmm, this reeks of good blackmail material. Either you do what I want, or I tell the whole town you know Gunnar Ericson."

"If you tell about Gunnar, I'll tell about Scott." I shot Meg the beady eyeball.

"Scott? Who's Scott?" asked Deirdre.

"It's an inside joke," I said. "Sorry, it wasn't very nice of me to say that in front of you. It's old news, but I like to tease Meg with it when she's getting on my nerves."

"Oh. Okay." Deirdre was disappointed, but Meg looked furious. She sent me an if-looks-could-kill glare and stomped over to her desk.

Deirdre had my job down cold, and my self-confidence had taken a beating, so I decided I'd go home. Meg wasn't acknowledging my existence, so I waved a hand in her direction and headed down the stairs. The air outside was cold, and it felt as if it might snow again. I patted my car on the hood. I was grateful I had it back.

At the edge of my property, I noticed that there were large birds roosting in my trees. Slowing down to take a second look, I realized they were chickens—my chickens, almost certainly. I pulled into the drive and drove down to the chicken house. I gazed at the tracks around the coop. Among the chicken scratches were the unmistakable prints of fox, more than one fox, which wasn't unusual.

I looked around for signs of kill, but there weren't any. No blood in the snow anywhere. For chickens, my birds were pretty smart. They must have headed for the trees at the first scent of predator. Getting them out of the trees would be a different matter. I went into the barn and scooped some grain into a bucket. Back out at the chicken house I shouted "Chick, chick, chick!" while I tossed grain on the ground. Pretty soon, the bolder birds flew down from the trees and flapped along the ground toward me. I watched the chickens squabble over the feed. The chaos at my feet made me think of my life. My fingerprints were on Vera. All over the room where she was found. Of course they were. I had been in there a thousand times. Why wasn't there anything to link anyone else to that room? Surely there were other fingerprints, other clues.

When I was satisfied that most of the chickens had returned, I put the grain bucket away and went to the house. The dogs were inside. They'd lain on their beds this morning when I left, and I'd taken that to mean that they didn't want to go out today. They wanted out now and almost bowled me over as the door opened.

It was still early, and I wasn't sure what I should do with myself. It had been a couple of years since I'd been home on a Tuesday. I decided laundry was probably in order and started sorting clothes. I had a bunch of clothes that were covered in mud, and I took them outside to shake them out over the edge of the porch.

The minute I was outside, the phone started to ring, so I dropped the basket on the porch floor and went back in to answer the phone.

"Bree?"

"You have a lot of nerve calling me, Jim."

"I've been hearing rumors. I'm just calling to see if you're okay."

"Never been better. Thanks for asking." I went to hang up the phone and heard him calling out.

"What is it, Jim? I've got work to do."

"I miss you. And I'm sorry how everything has turned out."

"I've got to go." Before he could say any more, I hung up. "Bastard!" I stomped back outside to find that Ranger and Hank had dragged the clothes from the laundry basket into the yard. Ranger was tossing a sock into the air and catching it in his mouth. Hank was rolling on a pair of jeans. I swore at the dogs. Ranger dropped the sock into my hand and then looked at me hopefully. He thought I was going to play with him.

"No such luck, buddy." I collected the rest of the laundry, dragging the jeans out from under Hank. He looked at me with his best hey-you're-ruining-my-fun expression, and I carted the laundry back into the house. The mud could wait until some other time. I threw a load of un-muddy clothes into the washer and threw myself down on the couch.

I didn't know what to do. I didn't want to spend the rest of the day watching TV. I didn't want to work on one of the hundred chores that needed doing. I didn't want to do anything. I closed my eyes and willed myself to sleep. My eyes popped open. Nope, couldn't sleep.

I thought about the Christmas balls that had gone missing. Twelve days of Christmas, twelve solid glass ornaments the size of a softball. I called Tom at work.

"How many Christmas balls did you find when you searched the grounds at Whispering Birches?" I wondered if they'd found them all.

"I don't know if they found them yet, Bree. I'm not sure Brooks has sent anyone to look for them. But I can find out, if you want."

"Would you, please?" I asked, and we rang off. Damn that Brooks. He was so pig-headed he wouldn't follow up a lead I gave him. And why couldn't I leave well enough alone? Did I really think I was going to find anything out? I shook my head at my own stupidity.

After I finished feeding the animals, there was a message from Meg. The paper was finished, and did I want to come to dinner. Conflicting emotions ran through me. I was glad for Meg that the paper was done, but on the other hand, how had it gotten done so fast? Was the new typesetter Superwoman? I didn't want her to be better at my job than I was.

I returned Meg's call. "I thought you were mad at me."

"I got over it. Do you want to come for dinner?"

"Sure." I didn't have any food in the house anyway.

I filled the day with laundry and target practice. If my dogs didn't keep the foxes away, then I would. I fed my animals early, throwing a few extra carrots into Lucky's bucket, and headed down the hill. I fought the feelings of inadequacy all the way to Meg's. I swore to myself I wouldn't say anything.

"Hey." I walked into Meg's kitchen. "How did you get the paper done so early? We almost never got the paper done before nine."

"Well, Deirdre knows her stuff." She smiled. "But I also worked straight through the weekend and late every night. Tom had to take over getting the kids fed and to bed. Rest assured, as good as she is, Deirdre will never take your place in my heart."

"Humph. How long were you planning on dragging that out?"

"Way longer than I did, that's for sure. But when I saw the look on your face, I took mercy on you. Just because I'm such a good friend."

"A good friend doesn't think of ways to torture people." I smacked Meg on the arm.

"A good friend doesn't get accused of murder and leave people in the lurch."

"It's not like I found that body on purpose. If I had it to do all over again, I would have stayed home sick that day."

Meg laughed. "Yeah, I bet. Here, help me set the table." She handed me a stack of plates.

I started placing the plates on the table and realized that there were too many. I went to put one away.

"We're going to need that. Beau is eating with us tonight." She shot me a look. I wondered what she knew. Did Beau tell Tom and Meg? Did they guess? I put a totally unconcerned look on my face.

"Oh? That's nice."

"You must think I'm totally blind." She shot me a slitty-eyed look.

"I don't know what you're talking about. I'm not about to screw up my relationship with you and Tom over some boy. Besides, Beau is too young for me."

"Oh, give me a break. What is he, a year and a half younger than you?"

"I am not seeing anyone exclusively. I'm operating under the assumption that all single men are scum, and all married men are out of bounds." I stuck my tongue out at Meg. "So that means Beau is scum, unless he was to marry me. Which he can't, because I'm not marrying any scummy single man."

Meg laughed. "I'd hate to be inside that brain of yours. You are a mass of contradictions. Be nice to Beau today."

"I'm always nice to Beau." I doubted my smoke screen was working, but I wasn't about to spill the beans, especially as having sex a couple of times didn't exactly count as having a relationship. What was I going to say? *Hey, Tom, I'm shagging your brother.* I don't think so.

"Hey, Meg. I'm sorry I messed things up yesterday."

"Forget it. You were right. It's my own fault. I should never have told you about Scott."

I shot her a look. Was she serious?

Meg laughed. "Like I wouldn't tell you everything."

We finished setting the table, and Meg pulled a gigantic casserole dish out of the oven. I stepped over and sniffed.

"Enchilada casserole?"

Meg nodded.

"Pasta or tortillas?"

"Pasta on one end, tortillas on the other. That way, everyone is happy. Even you."

"Is there ice cream?"

"Only if you eat your dinner."

"Then I'm happy."

"What are you happy about?" Tom wandered in from the other room.

"Ice cream," I said.

"Oh, I thought it might be because Beau's coming to dinner."

"What is it with you two? I'm not involved with anyone at the moment. Jeez. What would be the point, when I'm about to be hauled off to jail?"

"Well, poor Beau's going to be disappointed," said Tom. "I'm pretty sure he was hoping for some pre-incarceration sex."

"You lie." I was hoping it was true.

"What does he lie about?" Beau came in through the mudroom. "Besides everything."

"Bree is pretending…" Tom started.

"We are not discussing this!" I shouted Tom down. "This conversation ends right now, or I'm going home."

"Okay, that's it. If Bree goes, I go," Beau said.

Tom shot Meg an I-told-you-so look, and I rolled my eyes. Nothing about my life was private anymore.

Meg called the kids to dinner, and we sat down at the table. Dishes went flying around the table, and food was consumed at an alarming rate. Beau was beside me, and his knee kept brushing against mine. I tried to ignore it. I didn't want to get distracted and miss out on eating, but every time I felt the touch of his body, a tingle shot through me.

I was doing a pretty good job of not thinking about sex with Beau, which was hard to do when he was so close. He leaned toward me and slid his arm across my back to tap Jeremy on the shoulder.

"Hey, Jer, how are things going at school this semester? I heard a rumor that you have a girlfriend."

Meg's eyebrows shot up, and she looked pointedly at Jeremy. The corners of Beau's mouth twitched, and he straightened up, but he didn't take his arm off my shoulder. Now the electricity was running all through my body.

"W… Where'd you hear that?" Jeremy stuttered at Beau. "I don't know any girls who would go out with me."

"Me neither, Jer. Me neither," Beau said. He laughed. "Ain't life a bi.., uh pain?"

"You are such a bad liar." Jeremy smiled around me at Beau. "Everybody knows you've got it bad for Bree. The whole town is talking about what will happen if Bree goes to jail, and you're reduced to dating Lucy Howe like Jim."

I smacked my forehead with my palm.

"Doesn't anyone have anything better to talk about than my life? I didn't know every detail was common knowledge."

"Sweetheart," said Beau, "There is nothing more interesting than what's going on in your life. Every woman in this town is dying to be you. Or if not to be you, at least to be as wanted as you."

"Ewww." Meg said. "I think we'd better change the subject."

"Yeah, why don't we talk about me instead?" Beau pulled me close. "I'm likely to die of unrequited love at any moment. We could write my eulogy. That way it'd be all ready to go when I fade away of a broken heart."

"If you haven't died of a broken heart yet, it's not likely to happen now," Tom said. "You're closer to having your dreams come true than at any other time in your life."

"If they haven't already," said Meg pointedly, raising an eyebrow in my direction.

"What are you guys talking about?" asked Gemma. She looked around the table.

"Romance," Pete said. "Bree is pretending that she doesn't like Beau to throw Mom and Dad off the trail."

My mouth hung open. Since when did Pete become so perceptive?

"Maybe she really doesn't like Uncle Beau," said Louise. "She doesn't have to be pretending."

"Oh, she likes Uncle Beau, all right. She's just afraid that something will go wrong, and it will ruin her friendship with Mom and Dad."

"How do you know?" Louise asked Pete. "I've never heard Bree say anything like that."

"Ryan heard his mom say that she heard Bree say that to Val in the coffee shop the other day. Anyway, Ryan's mom was talking to Ryan's dad at dinner, and Ryan told me 'cause Beau's my uncle."

"Our uncle." said Gemma.

"Uh, I think I need to go." I slipped out from underneath Beau's arm and stood up.

"Oh, don't be such a spoilsport." Beau grabbed my hand. "If it wasn't for you, half the women in this town wouldn't have anything to talk about besides their kids. I know you want to keep everything casual. I'm a big boy.

If that were a problem for me, I wouldn't hang around. You can sit down and eat your dinner."

I took a stab at pulling away, but Beau had a lock grip on my arm. I could make a scene and leave, but then Jeremy would tell Ryan, who would tell his mom, who would tell anyone who would listen. Then the whole town would know I had a crush on Beau. So I sat.

"Bree," asked Gemma, "how come you don't like it when people talk about you?"

"I like to pretend that my life is private." I looked her in the eye. "I do lots of stupid stuff. It makes me feel bad when everybody knows."

"Well, I won't tell anyone, Bree," she said, "and I don't think you're stupid. I'm glad Uncle Beau wants to romance you. I think he should marry you, and then you'd be family, too."

"I'm already family, Sweetie. Your mom adopted me."

"Like our cat." Louise smiled.

"Yeah. Like a cat."

Eleven

Beau stood shoulder-to-shoulder with me, scanning the shelves in the video store. I'd suggested a movie after our dinner with Meg's family, but he was on call at the volunteer fire department tonight. We'd compromised on a DVD, and he had offered to let me pick the movie.

"How about 'Enchanted April?'" I asked. "It's one of my favorites."

"Cool. Let's rent it. It'll give me insight into how you think."

"My taste in movies, maybe, but how I think? I'm not buying it."

"Humor me," he said. "I'm trying to be nice here."

Trying to get me into bed again, more like it. But I didn't say it out loud. I wasn't sure how I was feeling about that possibility. We rented the movie and jumped in the truck to head back to Beau's house.

Plopping down on his couch, I took in Beau's surroundings while he loaded the movie into the DVD player. It was a small house, at least from what I could see of it. The living, dining and kitchen areas were all one room. Along one side, the floor-to-ceiling windows looked out onto a deck spotted with rectangles of light spilling from the windows. The place was sparsely furnished but comfortable. No rugs on the floor. An overstuffed couch and chair, dining room table with four chairs. A fireplace filled the wall at the side opposite the kitchen. Nothing on the mantle.

No dogs or cats. Hardly any signs of human habitation. Beau lowered himself onto the couch next to me and pushed the play button on the remote.

"You don't have any animals," I said.

"No, I'm out of town too much for that."

"I'd never guess a mason would have to go out of town to get work."

"Oh, I'm in demand. Travel all over. Apparently, there's a shortage of good stonemasons. I'm leaving tomorrow for a job in California. I'll be gone a couple of weeks."

"What are you building?" I asked.

"A fireplace and chimney for a couple in Grass Valley. I'm going to face the lower part of their house with stone and put in a patio, too."

"Will you do all that by yourself?"

"No, I've hired a local contractor and his team. They'll do most of the grunt work, and I'll oversee it. Certain stuff, I always do myself, like the fireplace. So I'll build the fireplace myself with maybe one guy helping me. While I'm doing that, the local guy can work on the patio with his team. You're missing your movie."

It was raining in London on the screen. Lottie was stalking Rose through the church sale.

"I love this movie," I said.

"Why?" Beau slid his arm around my shoulder and pulled me to him.

"Because it's about transformation. These women transform their lives by doing something out of the ordinary. By taking chances. Lottie is totally unappreciated by her husband, and it's affected her self-esteem. But in Italy, she blooms. I'm not telling you any more, or you'll fall asleep instead of watching it with me."

"I have no intention of falling asleep. Quite the contrary." He kissed me on the neck.

"Hey," I said. "If you start that, we'll miss the whole movie. You said this was a date, not a make-out session."

"Making out is part of a date," he said. "I won't rush you, though. I don't want to ruin your favorite movie." He ran his fingers through the hair at the base of my neck.

On the screen, Lottie and Rose were turning Mrs. Fisher down. I was starting to think the movie wasn't that important. Beau's body was warm next to mine, and I had this visceral memory of the last time we were alone together. I leaned into him and closed my eyes.

The scanner sitting next to the toaster went off, and Beau swore. He disentangled himself from me and strode into the kitchen area. His legs were long and strong. His backside was inspiring. I remembered what it felt like to run my hands down the warm skin on Beau's back and over his butt. It was still raining in London, but now I really didn't care.

"Shit!" Beau listened to the radio squawk and turned to me. "There's a fire." He pulled on boots and picked up his fire gear. "I've got to go. Stay. Watch your movie. I'll be back before long."

*****

I opened my eyes to find Beau bending over me. He gathered me in his arms and carried me up the stairs.

"Where was the fire?"

"Just an old barn down by the flats." He lowered me onto his quilt and pulled off my sneakers.

"No one hurt?"

"Naw. "

Beau yanked off my socks and unzipped my jeans. "Do you want me to sleep downstairs?" He grabbed the bottoms of my pant legs and slid them off.

"Pete said you wanted to romance me. I'd hate to miss that."

"You seem kind of sleepy for romance." He looked around his room. "What do you want to sleep in?"

"Sleepy sex is the best." I reached around to unhook my bra. "I don't sleep in jammies, if that's what you're worried about."

"I thought we were talking about romance, not sex." But his voice caught in his throat as my bra slipped down my arms. His eyes softened. His demeanor changed from all business to something else entirely. Beau sat down on the bed and ran a finger from my lips over my chin. He traced my skin lightly. Down my neck, between my breasts and over my belly until his finger snagged on the top of my panties.

"You sure you want me to stay with you? I'll have to leave before morning. I have a plane to catch."

"Are you kidding? This is my last chance until you get back. I might be in jail by then."

"Doubtful." He turned and unlaced his boots. They dropped to the floor with a thud. Then he shucked his jeans.

"You're not wearing underwear. I'm shocked." The thought that he'd been sitting next to me all evening without his skivvies on flashed into my brain. Electricity shot straight down my spine. I wasn't sleepy anymore.

"I was doing laundry. If I waited for them to dry, I would have been late to dinner." He pulled his shirt over his head.

"You were commando all evening, and you didn't tell me?"

"I didn't want to brag." He eased himself down onto the bed beside me. "Do you like it?"

"No. Not at all." I reached my arm around his neck and pulled him to me. "Girls are totally turned off by that kind of thing. Didn't you know?" I kissed him. He smelled faintly of campfire. Oh, yeah, that would be the burning barn. He slid his tongue between my lips and along the edge of my teeth. He broke off the kiss and gathered me up in his arms, twisting his body until he was sitting on the edge of the bed. I straddled him, kissing his neck and ear.

Beau spread small kisses down my neck, and his tongue lingered in the hollow above my shoulder blade. I shivered and started to slide off his lap.

"Where are you going?" Beau held me to him.

"I still have my undies on."

"No matter." He reached down and slid the silky material to the side. He arched his back and was inside me. "Oh, my God. I feel like such a tramp! I've never done it with my underwear on before."

"Is that a bad thing? Or do you like feeling like a tramp?" His laugh was breathless as he plunged into me again.

I was overwhelmed by a wave of passion, and speech was lost to me. I latched onto Beau's shoulder with my teeth and gripped his back with my fingers. We slid off the bed onto the floor with a thump. I was laughing, and he disentangled himself from me.

"Don't go. I'm sorry I laughed."

"I'm not going anywhere. Just going to wipe that grin off your face." He kissed my belly and ran his tongue toward my mound. He ran his mouth over the silky panties and nipped gently with his teeth.

Fire ran through me, and the laughter died. Now I was gasping, so far over the edge and needing him inside me.

"Beau." It came out as a whisper.

He knew what I needed. He slid the underwear away and thrust himself into me. We came together in a rush of release. We lay together on the floor until I felt a chill shiver through me.

Beau pulled the covers back from the bed and lifted me up. He slid between the sheets with me, and we lay together. His touch was hot and his breathing ragged. I nestled my head into his shoulder and felt his heart beating beneath me.

"Want to do that again?" I smiled into his neck.

"Are you trying to kill me?"

"No. I just don't want you to forget me while you're in California. I hear girls are wild out there. I might not measure up."

"I have no intention of finding out. I'm on rocky ground already, and I don't plan on screwing things up."

"On rocky ground?"

"Yeah. The girl I'm crazy about doesn't want to date me because she's friends with my brother. I have to be very careful, if I don't want to screw this up."

I rubbed my face against his skin. He was smooth and warm. I kissed his neck and closed my eyes. He's crazy about me. Cool. I felt myself drifting.

He woke me as he slid out from underneath my head.

"You going?" I missed his warmth.

He bent and kissed me. "Got a plane to catch." He gathered up his clothes.

I struggled to wake up. "I'll walk you out."

He kissed me again and gently pushed me back onto the bed. "I can let myself out. I want you to be able to go back to sleep. I'll call you from California."

I reached up and threaded my fingers in his hair. "I'm going to miss you. Can't think why."

Beau slid away from me. "Promise me something?"

"Uh huh."

"Don't get back together with Jim while I'm gone." He rested a finger on my lips.

"I think I can safely promise that." I smiled at him. "Kiss me again."

Beau kissed me one last time and left.

I closed my eyes, but I couldn't go back to sleep. Images of Beau kept running through my mind. After rolling over and plumping the pillow a couple of times, I gave it up for a bad job and drove home.

Twelve

I woke to knocking. The knocking turned to banging. "Go away," I muttered into my pillow. "I'm not ready to go to jail." The banging continued for a minute more. I heard the door slam shut, and a moment later, footsteps on the stairs. I sat up, blinking.

"Who's there?" I called out. I wished my voice sounded just a little steadier.

"It's me, Bree," Meg called as she came through my bedroom door.

"What are you doing here?" I asked.

"I came to make sure you hadn't offed yourself." She showed me her *duh* face. "It's Wednesday. We're having a spa treatment in about twenty minutes, remember? You made me set aside the whole dang day. So get your bony behind out of that bed. I don't want to be late."

"I don't want to go anywhere today. I'm tired." I stuck my head back under the pillow.

Meg grabbed the pillow. "Okay, so you had a rough couple of days. So what? You going to ruin the opportunity to be a star for a day? Don't be so selfish. You know I can't show up there without you."

"I could call. It would be all right."

"But no fun." She grabbed my foot and pulled. "I don't want to go by myself. Uff! Have you been putting on weight? You're heavy." She looked up to see me hanging onto the headboard. "Okay, now its war." She tickled my feet.

"Stop! Stop. Okay, I give. I'm getting up." I wrapped the sheet around me, tumbled out of bed and headed for the shower.

*****

We hit the spa and shed our clothes in the dressing room, then slid into robes and slippers. They'd placed two spa tubs in the same room, so we could chat while we were having hydro treatment. The water bubbled around me, smelling of lavender and something else I couldn't put my finger on. Lemon, maybe? I relaxed into the cushioned surface of the tub, sliding lower and lower in the water.

"Trying to drown your troubles?" Meg asked me. I had submerged myself so that only the top half of my head was visible.

"Yes." I raised my head out of the water. "Don't interrupt me. If I can deprive my brain of just enough oxygen, then maybe I will forget this whole crazy mess I'm in. I slept in the damn barracks the other night. The only reason I wasn't in a cell is that your husband took pity on me. This has gotten so far out of control that I can't cope." I sank back under the water.

"Yes, but..." started Meg.

"Don't you 'yes, but' me," I rose out of the water again. "I'm sacred shitless that I'm never going to recover from this mess."

"Yes, but," Meg shot me a smile. "We are going to scope things out while we're here, aren't we? I'll bet we can find something that will get you off the hook."

"What you think we are going to find is beyond me. Brian and I already checked out the housekeeping closet. I'm sure Dotty knows something, but she won't talk. Brooks has this thing about putting me in cuffs."

"I can't help but think there has to be some evidence of what happened. Some clue. If Tom were running this investigation, I wouldn't worry about them missing anything. But he's not. Brooks seems so focused on you that he's blind to anything else." Meg shook her head, sending droplets of water through the air.

"Don't most investigators believe that the simplest explanation is usually the right one? I found her, therefore I killed her. Can we stop talking about this now? It's giving me a headache."

The new treatments were developed from local products: maple and honey scrubs, milk baths, and fresh cream moisturizers. After our lavender soak, our attendants showed Meg and me into separate rooms. I shed my robe again and climbed up onto the massage table. I lay on my front and pulled up the flannel sheet. Mimi, one of the spa attendants, came in with small granite bricks that were mined and cut in central Vermont. She heated them with steam and set them down my spine. The air smelled of Maple Syrup. An image of maple cookies floated in my head.

"You're going to have to feed people." My voice was muffled by towel around my face. "The smell of maple is making me hungry. I can't stop thinking about food. Maple cookies, maple candy, maple sausage, maple pancakes."

Mimi laughed. "I'll tell Nancy you said that. I'm about to use an astringent on your back. You might feel some tingling. Then I'm going to use one of our new moisturizers on you. After that, I'll you roll over and do your face. Okay?"

"Sounds good." The heat of the stones was making me sleepy. They were heavy and pushed me into the table. I'm a human pancake, I thought. A maple pancake. I was thinking of food again. I had to get my mind off eating. I thought of Beau instead, but he was gone now. I couldn't decide if it had been a good idea or a bad idea to sleep with him. Lord, my brain was hurting.

Mimi removed the stones, flipped me over, and went to work on my face. My eyes watered from the astringent. When she used the scrub, I wondered how many layers of skin were coming off. Mimi applied the moisturizer, and the tingling stopped. She ran the silky stuff down my neck and arms. She pulled a towel out of a cabinet and placed it across my eyes. It was damp and warm.

"Nice."

"I'm done. Let's get you turned back over. Your masseur will be in shortly. Just relax until he gets here."

After my massage, I dozed for a while with cucumbers on my eyes until Nancy came in to wake me up and guide me back to the changing room, where I found Meg. I was as relaxed as I'd ever been. Devon had pummeled me into a mass of custard pudding. I could barely even walk. Meg was already in the dressing room, sitting on an upholstered bench with a bemused look on her face.

"I don't feel like looking for clues now," she said. "I'm so relaxed, you could pour me into a glass and drink me."

"That's okay. We probably wouldn't find anything, anyway." I sat next to her on the bench. "Let's go home. I don't want to ruin this feeling."

We dressed and meandered out into the reception area. Gunnar Ericson was talking with the receptionist. "I just couldn't believe it," Janine was saying. She looked up and saw us. "Oh!" She stopped in mid-sentence.

Gunnar turned to look at us. "Well, hello ladies." He smiled his million-dollar smile. "Ms. MacGowan, won't you introduce me to your friend?"

Meg was standing there open-mouthed, eyes wide. I wished he would stop it with the smile already.

"Mr. Ericson, this is Meg Maverick. Meg, meet Mr. Ericson."

"Call me Gunnar." He took Meg's hand and kissed it.

Meg visibly swooned. "Pleased to meet you," she squeaked.

I did a mental eye roll. "Well, we'd better be going. I've got to get Meg home to her husband. He's a police captain. Tom get's very upset when I keep Meg out too long. He's possessive."

"Oh, he is not!" Meg gave me the eye. "I was wondering, Mr. Ericson ..."

"Gunnar." He interrupted her firmly.

"Gunnar. I was wondering if I could have an autograph?" She reached for a slip of paper in her purse.

"Oh, I can do better than that. Come back to my room, and I'll give you an autographed photo of myself. How would you like that?"

Meg gave me a pleading look. Then she narrowed her eyes at me, and I could almost hear her begging me not to ruin this for her.

"Do you mind if I talk to Bree for a moment?" Meg asked Gunnar.

"Take all the time you like."

Meg dragged me back into the dressing room. "Bree, please. This could be our chance to see if something is wrong in his room. We might find something. And I really want a picture. Please, Bree, you meet celebrities all the time, but this might be my one chance."

"First of all, that room has already been searched by Brook's team, and I was in the closet with Brian, so I'm not sure what kind of clues we'd find now. If Gunnar was involved, there might be something in his room, I guess, but I have my doubts. I can't imagine Vera being a threat to Gunnar Ericson. Secondly, if I get caught socializing with a guest, I'll get fired. So maybe it would be better if you went by yourself."

"I can't go by myself," Meg wailed. "What would I say? And Tom would have a fit. I can't be in a strange man's hotel room by myself. What if he tries something? Please, Bree. I need you to go with me."

I puffed out a huge breath of air. I didn't think Gunnar would try anything, but then again, he'd been chasing me around since he'd been here, and he could just as easily come on to Meg. "Okay. If it will make you happy, I'll go with you." Yeah, why should I stop doing stupid stuff now? I'd done worse things than this with less forethought. We walked back out to the reception area.

"I guess that would be okay." I said to Gunnar. "I'm not technically working today. But just for a minute, I really can't afford to get fired."

"Oh, I won't let Brian fire you. That would be too unfair. Well, then." He gestured for us to precede him out the door. "Come with me."

We followed him out of the spa and up the stairs next to the pub. He had his Lexus parked in the no-parking zone directly in front of the path from the road to the spa. Not that that was unusual. Most of the wealthy people who came to Whispering Birches felt they could do whatever they liked. They paid enough to be here, so maybe they were right.

Gunnar opened the front passenger door for Meg, and she slid into the big leather seat. Then he opened the rear door, and I ducked into the car. I was way out of my comfort zone. Not only was I totally unaccustomed to this kind of treatment, I could lose my job for this. I smiled grimly at Gunnar as he shut the door, while Meg gushed about the car from the front seat.

"Is this a Mercedes?" she asked. "I've never been in a car with leather seats."

I groaned to myself. We were sitting in a Lexus.

"Wow, look at all these knobs," Meg was gesturing to the dash.

"That's just the stereo," said Gunnar. "It's like a home entertainment center. Are you girls buckled in?"

Gunnar was staying in the Spring Meadows Room, a small cabin that sat in a small depression between two hillocks, out of sight of any of the other cottages. He pulled into the covered carport, opened the doors, and escorted us to the door. I'd forgotten he'd been moved out of the room where Vera died. We wouldn't be finding any clues in this room.

Gunnar ushered us into the room ahead of him. Meg started at the sight of a bronze, life-sized statue of a moose in the entry of the cottage. The hotel was full of stuff like that, but I'd forgotten Meg hadn't been in many of the rooms.

"It hides the wood for the fireplace," I told her. "It rolls forward when you push on its hind leg."

Gunnar tossed his jacket on the moose and motioned us into the living area.

Opulent couches and overstuffed chairs sat artfully on one side of the room. They had been set so that you could see both the fireplace and the hidden, flat-screen TV from one seating area, and out the window overlooking a meadow with a stream running through it from the other. Gunnar motioned us to take a seat, but I walked over to look out the floor-to-ceiling window. I didn't like being in this room.

"Let me just get a photo for you," he said to Meg. "It's in the other room." The minute he left, Meg started rifling through the papers on the coffee table.

"Meg!" I hissed at her. "Stop that. You'll get caught."

"He'll just think I'm nosey," she whispered back. She moved over to look through the items on his bar.

"Meg!" I glared at her. "This isn't the cottage Vera died in. We moved Gunnar out of there. You're aren't going to find anything."

"Unless he was involved." Meg was looking for another spot to search. I shook my head at her. "Stop," I said. "He's coming."

Gunnar returned with a briefcase and made a big show of extracting a photo and signing it for her. She took it from him and smiled.

"Thank you so much," she said, simpering at him. "It's very kind of you to go out of your way."

"On the contrary," Gunnar turned around and reached into his briefcase again. "You have saved me a great deal of trouble." He turned back and pointed a gun at her.

Shit. All of a sudden, I didn't care so much about getting fired. It was way better than getting dead. I must be the queen of getting into stupid situations. Only this time, I'd dragged Meg into it with me.

"You," Gunnar said to me. "Get over here and sit next to her. And don't do anything stupid, or I'll shoot your friend. Her husband could be the king of Siam, and I wouldn't give a shit, so don't start going on about him being a cop."

I looked at him intently. Gunnar's European accent had disappeared. He sounded vaguely like he came from ... Chicago? Despite that, I still couldn't see him as Vera's killer. Why? What could Vera have done, seen, or heard that would make it necessary for a man like Gunnar to kill her? Why was he threatening us, for that matter? What could have we done or seen? It would be much easier just to pay any of us off. Or threaten us. My head was hurting again.

"Move," he said and rotated the gun in my direction.

I moved. I sat next to Meg on the couch while Gunnar paced for a few minutes. He pulled his cell phone out of his pocket and scowled at it. I would put money on his not getting service in this cottage. I never had service anywhere on Whispering Birches property.

"Okay, change of plan," he said. "Both of you into the bedroom."

We scooted into the bedroom. A huge bed dominated the room. The top of the mattress was probably four feet off the ground. A footstool sat on the floor beside the bed so you could climb up. The headboard was huge, running from the mattress top to the ceiling. It was solid wood, engraved with intricate designs in florals and swirls. Delicately detailed cutouts had been carved out of the wood so that we could see the fabulous gold wallpaper behind the headboard.

Besides the fabulous bed, there was a dresser carved in the same motif, with cut-outs along the bottom. A fireplace faced the bed with a flat screen TV hanging above the mantel. The floor-to-ceiling windows faced the meadow. Through the door to the bathroom, we could see a stone shower stall, and out the door to the main living area, I could see that stupid metal moose.

“Take off your shoes.” He shook the gun at us. “Now.” Meg looked shell-shocked. Her hands were shaking, and she had trouble getting her shoes untied. I was wearing my favorite cowboy boots, soft black leather. If Gunnar damaged my boots, I was going to kill him. They cost me two weeks’ pay. I slid them off my feet.

"Give me your bags, coats, shoes, belts, everything." Gunnar looked at Meg, who had started shaking her head. "I'm not taking my clothes off," she said. She shot him a defiant look.

His smile was creepy. "You can keep your shirt and pants," he said. Meg and I handed our stuff to Gunnar. He stowed them in a duffle and then pulled out what turned out to be a bunch of large zip ties.

"If you move I'll kill your friend," he said to Meg. He tossed one of the ties at me. "It's handcuffs," he said. "Put that on your left wrist." I looked at the cuff and looped the plastic around my wrist and threaded the end through the 'lock.' Gunnar stuck his gun in the back of his pants and grabbed my left arm. He tightened the cuff on my wrist and slid a second tie around the bedpost through one of the decorative cutouts. Then he looped it through the cuff on my wrist.

Meg was staring at me, horrified. She looked ready to run, but I knew she wouldn't put me at risk. I wanted to yell at her to get out, but I didn't. She couldn't outrun Gunnar in the snow without shoes.

Gunnar approached her. "Same thing," he said to her. "You move, she dies." He handcuffed her to the footboard. "You make any noise, I'll kill you. Do anything to attract attention, and I'll kill you. I think I'd enjoy that." He showed us his teeth and left the room.

Well, here I was on Gunnar Ericson's bed. There wasn't a woman in America who hadn't dreamed of this. Of course, most of them would have left the handcuffs out of the fantasy. The reality wasn't nearly as fun. I couldn't get comfortable with my arm cuffed to the headboard, and I wasn't really sure why we were cuffed to the bed. I could be wrong, but it didn't seem to be a sexual thing. Did Gunnar kill Vera?

I could hear Gunnar moving around in the other room. There was a knock at the door. My heart leapt, and I strained to hear what was going on. The door opened, and a husky, male voice spoke in an undertone. I couldn't understand what he was saying.

"I think they know." Gunnar's voice was clear.

"Well, if they didn't before, they do now." The husky voice was audible now. "I don't see what the big deal is, Gunnar. It hurts me that you date women and keep me hidden away. It's not like it's the 1950s anymore."

"That's not the half of it, and you know it, Joseph. My fans are all female. If my little habit comes out, my popularity will come crashing down. Do you want to end up on the street? You wouldn't be nearly as attractive without my credit card."

"I think he's gay," Meg said in a stage whisper.

"You think?" I rolled my eyes.

"These women are nothing to worry about, Joseph," said Gunnar in the other room. "Nothing at all. I've asked that no one enter my room. Now it's time to go to dinner." The door clicked shut and the cottage fell silent.

I slumped against the headboard, my head leaning against the scrollwork. Meg climbed up and lay across the foot of the bed, her arms angled out so she could rest her head on the mattress.

How in the world was I going to get Meg out of this? *Think. What do I know about this cabin, this room, this bed? This bed.* I closed my eyes and pictured how they had gotten the huge headboard into the room. I hadn't been there, but Brian had told me about it. It was designed to come apart so that it would fit in the door. It was brought into the room in two pieces, assembled on the floor, and then raised and attached to the rest of the frame.

I opened my eyes and examined the wood. The carving was intricate, and the join wasn't obvious. My arm was shackled a couple of feet above the mattress. It was just possible that I was attached to the connecting point of the post. I swiveled around, stretching my arm as far as it would go, and braced my feet in a couple of the holes.

I slid my butt closer to the head of the bed, my legs bent. The cuff cut into my wrist, making me suck in my breath. I anchored my feet in the cutouts, and then I pushed upward with everything I had. Nothing. My wrist was bleeding, but the bed hadn't moved. I shoved upward again with everything I had, pushing my back down into the mattress, the cuff slicing into me. The headboard didn't move.

"Crap, crap, crap!" I said.

"What are you doing?" Meg asked.

I looked down the bed to see Meg staring at me. "I think this headboard came in two pieces," I said. "I'm trying to pry them apart."

She shimmied up the bed, extending her arm above her head. Gunnar had left a lot more slack in her cuff than in mine, but she was still stretched way out. "I'm not tall enough. I don't have a lot of leverage, but I can help." Meg slotted her heels into the wood. There was hardly any bend in her knees at all.

"Get ready," I said, "on three. One, two, three!" We both pressed upwards with our feet. There was a creaking sound but no movement.

"Wait," I said. "Maybe we need to loosen the glue or whatever is holding the two pieces together. Try shoving against it like this." I put my feet flat on the surface of the headboard above where I thought the join was and pushed it back and forth with all the strength in my legs. Meg did the same. There was a splintering noise, and we shifted our feet back into the slots where I thought the join must be. We shoved upwards again. The headboard came loose and crashed down on top of us.

"Ow," cried Meg. "I think my kneecap just shattered."

I was seeing stars from the headboard bashing me in the head. "That wasn't the smartest idea I ever had," I said. I slid the zip tie up over the broken end of the headboard and wiggled out from underneath it. I pushed the broken wood off Meg and let it crash to the floor. I rubbed my head where the newel post had clobbered me.

"My wrist is bleeding," I said. "I'm going to rinse it off in the bathroom." In the bathroom, I held my hand under the cold water until it was numb. Then I dried off on one of the pristine towels. I looked at the bloodstained towel and sighed. With my luck, I'd be the one to have to clean it.

I came back to Meg and sat on the bed. Something Gunnar said hit me. "He's got a secret. Not that he's gay, something more."

"What do you mean?" asked Meg.

"Do you remember what he said before they left? Something about a habit?" I scrunched my face up, trying to remember. "I'm going to search the room."

Thirteen

"Look for something to cut me free while you're at it, will you?" Meg was sitting on the edge of the bed, rubbing her knee.

I started rifling through the drawers in the dresser. Nothing but fancy underwear and socks. I checked the closet. I went through the pockets of the clothes hanging there. I pulled the suitcases out of another closet. I knelt on the floor and started unzipping cases.

I found a pocketknife in one of the cases and cut the nylon tie off Meg's wrist. She rubbed at the red line it made on her skin. "I wonder if his briefcase is still in the other room," she said. I looked at her.

"You're brilliant," I said.

I dashed into the living room and grabbed Gunnar's briefcase off the bar, where he had left it. I brought it back into the bedroom and set it on the bed. I snapped it open. It was full of papers. The first layer contained fan photos like the one he had signed for Meg. I pulled those out and tossed them on the bed. Under those was what looked like a script.

"Doesn't look like he's read any of that yet," said Meg. "It's totally untouched. I'm losing all respect for this guy."

"Well, then, this will really blow you out of the water," I said. I held a folder I had dug out of the bottom of the case. I placed in front of Meg and flipped it open, and her eyes just about fell out of her head. She closed it fast.

"I can't look at this," Meg said, opening the file again. "These are just boys. Teenagers. They can't be old enough for this to be legal."

"No. It's not legal," I said. I didn't need to look at the pictures in the folder anymore. The images were already burned into my brain. "I'm pretty sure he's a pedophile. And into bondage. And probably gay, but who cares about that?"

"Well, he is supposed to be a heartthrob," said Meg. "Every stay-at-home mom in America is in love with him, and half the workingwomen I know TiVo his show. Being gay might hurt that."

"Not as much as this stuff will," I said. My stomach started churning, and I ran into the bathroom.

"You all right?" Meg asked as I came back into the bedroom.

"Yeah, I'm fine. That just hit me the wrong way." I went to a cabinet and pulled a couple of pairs of hotel slippers from a drawer. "Not snow boots, but better than nothing. I'm walking to the next cottage," I said as I slipped them on. "If I have to, I'll walk all the way to the main house. It's not really that far. Less than a mile." I smiled at her. "Maybe I'll run into the turndown crew on the way. I'll be back as soon as I can."

"Are you kidding? I'm coming with you."

I heard footsteps on the porch outside the cottage and looked back at Meg. The door clicked open. Meg's eyes widened. I looked around at the mess I had made. The headboard cracked and lying on the far side of the bed. Clothes hanging out of all the drawers. Gunnar's suitcases on the floor. There was no time to make this room seem normal.

"Pretend you're still cuffed to the bed," I whispered. "And remember the hind leg of the moose."

"What are...?" Meg started to ask, but I signaled her to be quiet and dodged behind the door. We heard Gunnar swear in the other room. He strode through the door to the bedroom.

"Where the fuck is my briefcase?" He burst into the room. He stopped short, taking in the disheveled room and staring at the half headboard where I used to be.

This is it, I told myself. *Now or never.* I took a deep breath and launched myself at him. I hit him in the middle of his back, and we both went down on the edge of the bed. I was on top of him, trying to hold him down, but he shook me off, and I stumbled to the floor. I realized I didn't know where his gun was. It hadn't been in the briefcase. *Shit.*

I scrambled to my feet. We stood facing each other. I didn't know why he didn't take me. He was big and buff. I knew I was no match for him. I saw a quick movement behind him, and he yelled and flew forward into me. I guessed from his language that Meg had connected with a kidney. I thrust my knee at him but missed the mark and hit him in the thigh. Hardly a takedown blow.

Gunnar grabbed me around the waist and hoisted me up over his shoulder. My hands were trapped under my body. I kicked at Gunnar, but he had my legs snugged against his body. He carried me out through the living room. I looked around frantically, but I didn't see anything that could help me. Gunnar's gun was sitting on the coffee table in front of the fireplace. Great. I was hoping it had disappeared. But no, now I had to face the possibility of being shot.

I had a last look at the bronze moose, and we were outside. He carted me over to his car. I heard a lock click, and the next thing I knew, I was in the trunk of his Lexus.

"Hey," I said. "You didn't have to dump me in here. That hurt."

He slammed the lid on me, and I was in the dark. A couple of minutes later, I heard footsteps. Then the trunk opened.

"Where is she?"

"What are you talking about?"

"That woman who was with you. Where is she hiding?"

"I don't know." I was hoping that by now Meg had found the other door out of the box we loaded the wood into. If she was fast, she could be halfway to the next cottage.

I saw a movement behind Gunnar, and then Meg was on his back, her arm around his neck, trying to choke him. In one fluid motion, he flipped her off his back. She landed on top of me in the trunk. The air was pushed out of my lungs, and everything went black again as the lid slammed. I heard Gunnar walking away as we scooted around until we were side-by-side, spooning like lovers. It was better than having Meg on top of me.

"You should have run for help." I felt like howling.

"I couldn't leave you with that maniac. What if something happened?"

"Well, now we'll find out." I shifted my legs, trying to un-cramp them.

"How do you like this Lexus now?" I asked. "Comfy?"

"Oh, stop grousing. I don't want the last words I hear to be grumbling. Any way for us to get out of this?"

"It depends on if he remembers to bring his gun."

The car door slammed, and a moment later we were bumping down the road.

"If he doesn't have the gun, we could overpower him when he opens the trunk," I said. "But I don't think we can count on that."

"Oh, my God!" Meg said. "What if he never opens the trunk? What if he leaves us in here to starve? Or what if he drives us over a cliff or something?"

"He won't do that." I hoped. "Because this is his car, and he won't want anyone to associate us with it. Don't cars like this have latches on the inside of the trunk? Maybe we could pop the trunk while he's driving and jump out when he stops."

"What's this?" I could hear her fumbling around. The latch clicked and the trunk flew open. "I did it!"

"I wished you'd warned me first. I'm not ready."

Gunnar slammed on the brakes, and I slid deeper into the trunk. Meg was up on her knees, struggling to get a leg over the edge of the trunk. She got one leg out and fell onto the road. I heard her hit and some muffled curses.

"Run!" I yelled. "Get up and run!"

She was on her feet looking a little dazed in the evening sunlight. "Run!" I struggled to scoot to the edge of the trunk and rose to my knees. There was a shot from behind me. *Meg!* I screamed in my head, but my throat was so constricted, no sound would come out. I looked down the road to where Meg was running for all she was worth. Another shot rang out.

"Stop, or I'll shoot your friend," Gunnar's voice came from beside the car.

Meg stopped running. She put her hands in the air and turned around. She walked slowly back to the car. I prayed for someone to drive by. The problem with living in the boonies is that when you need someone around, there isn't anybody.

"Back in." Gunnar lifted Meg and dropped her back in the trunk. At least this time, I had the sense to move back so she didn't land on me.

"See this?" Gunnar held up his gun. "You try a stunt like that again, and I'll shoot you both. Understand?"

We nodded, and Meg lowered herself back down into the trunk. Gunnar reached in and found the latch to the trunk. He snapped the handle off, slammed the trunk shut, and we were on our way again.

We rode in silence for a while. I kept spinning scenarios through my head, but none of them were more than fantasy. We had nothing on a man with a gun. I thought about my dogs, and tears swam in my eyes. *You took care of that, Bree,* I told myself. They'll be okay. But I wanted nothing more than a big old sloppy dog kiss. *Now you're just feeling sorry for yourself. Hold it together.*

"Bree? What are we going to do?"

"I don't know. We'll just have to keep our eyes open and look for a chance to run. I want you to promise you'll try and get away. Even if Gunnar threatens to shoot me. Even if he does shoot me. Okay?"

"Bree." Meg was crying. "I can't. How could I leave you?"

"If I get shot, my only chance of surviving is if you can get help. So I need you to leave me and run. And I'll do the same if I have the chance." But I didn't know if I'd really be able to leave Meg if she was shot. How could I take the chance that she would die alone? What if she died because I wasn't there to stop the bleeding? Being accused of murder seemed like such a small deal now.

When the car finally stopped and the trunk opened again, it was dark outside. Gunnar lifted first Meg, and then me, out of the trunk. I had trouble standing for a moment. My legs were cramped and didn't want to hold me up. I leaned against the car and looked around. We were in Quechee. More specifically we were in the visitor parking of Quechee Gorge, below the Quechee dam. The gorge is like a mini grand canyon, a ravine cut deep into the earth by the river.

A bridge crosses the river at Highway 4. It was a summer tourist attraction, but this time of year, few people felt like braving the weather to stand over the bridge and gaze down into the gulch. The leaves had fallen off the trees. The landscape was barren and the water a cold grey.

"What are we doing here?" I asked.

"This is where you will have an unfortunate accident," said Gunnar. "You will fall into the gorge, and your friend will die trying to save you. Tragic, really."

"Like you could ever get away with that!" Meg exclaimed. "No one within a hundred-mile radius would believe that Bree and I would be at the gorge this time of year. That's just stupid!"

Gunnar hit Meg across the face. "I don't take kindly to being called stupid. It won't matter anyway. Even if it does seem strange, there won't be anyone to link you to me, so who cares what they think."

"What do you mean, no one can link you to us?" Meg was crying and rubbing her face. I was behind Gunnar shaking my head no, but she didn't see me. "We all walked out of the spa right in front of Janine."

I winced. We'd just placed Janine in danger. Meg seemed to realize it, too. She sucked in air and bit her lip.

"Of course, she probably won't remember," she said lamely.

Gunnar let out a deep sigh. "Okay," he said. "Back in the trunk."

"You're not going to kill us now?" That seemed like a good thing, but I sure didn't want to get stuck back in that trunk.

"You can't die until I'm sure that Janine didn't tell anyone else." He said. He turned and unlocked the trunk. He was facing away from me, gesturing Meg to come over so he could put her in the trunk. I shook my head at her. She hesitated just a moment, but that was all I needed. I ran at Gunnar and pushed him with all the strength I could muster. He was taken by surprise and lost his balance. He tumbled right into the trunk of the car, and I slammed the lid.

Meg looked at me in surprise for a couple of seconds, and then she started whooping and dancing all around. Pretty soon we were jumping up and down, laughing and shouting, "We did it. We did it!" Gunnar was pounding on the inside of the trunk and swearing at us. There was a shot, and a bullet came whizzing out of the trunk. I swear I could feel it part my hair.

Meg and I stopped jumping. We stared at each other, dumbstruck. "He still has the gun," said Meg.

"Yeah," I said. "I was going to drive the car to the Barracks, but I think maybe it's better if we find a pay phone and call Tom. With my luck, he'd shoot me through the trunk while we're going down the road." We grabbed our shoes and jackets out of the back seat, and scooted away from the car. My feet were freezing, and Meg was shivering. I was glad Gunnar had brought our stuff with him. The thought of hiking down the snowy road without shoes wasn't very appealing.

Meg set off to find a pay phone, and I stayed to keep an eye on the car. I didn't trust my luck enough to leave Gunnar and walk away. He'd probably find a way to get out, or some good-hearted soul would let him out, and he'd get away.

I stood far from the car just in case Gunnar decided to stop yelling and start shooting again. He was still screaming obscenities and threatening to kill me, if I didn't let him out. He had to have a pretty low opinion of me, if he thought I was dumb enough to set him free.

Eventually, he stopped yelling and started banging. I wondered what he was trying to do. I knew from experience that you couldn't get enough bend in your legs to kick up at the trunk. I smiled, betting he was sorry he had broken the inside release lever. I leaned against a tree, wondering when Meg would make it back. Just when I decided to sit down on my coat for a while, there were shots from the trunk, and the lid popped open. Gunnar sat up, holding his ears.

"Shit. Shit that hurt," he yelled, and he climbed out of the trunk.

Damn. I was back to having to defend myself from a crazy with a gun. Where was Meg, when I needed her? I was on my feet, ducking behind the tree, when Gunnar started firing at me. Two bullets went sailing past and lodged in trees beyond me. Lucky me. This guy obviously hadn't spent a lot of time on a shooting range.

I heard a click, and then Gunnar started swearing again. No bullets? I peeked out from behind the tree. He had thrown the gun on the ground and was kicking it. He must have forgotten me momentarily. I didn't have any illusions that that would last for very long. I debated the virtues of running away. For three, fabulous seconds I kidded myself that I could outrun Gunnar. Then I came to my senses and dashed out from behind the tree. I ran full tilt into Gunnar, who was still swearing and kicking at the gun.

I threw my shoulder forward and hit him where I hoped a vital organ would be. Of course, anatomy wasn't my strong point, so I was really just hoping to hit something vulnerable. We both went down. Gunnar fell hard, and I fell on top of him. He tried to roll out from underneath me while I tried to stay on top.

We were both jockeying for control, when I heard someone running. *Please be someone who can help,* I thought. "Help!" I shouted, and then I remembered that people almost never responded to cries for help. I think I saw that on a TV program sometime. "Rape!" *No, wait. People don't respond to that either.* "Fire!" I yelled. *Yeah, that was it. Fire was the thing that got people's attention.* "Fire!"

The gun was on the ground next to us, and I saw Gunnar reach for it. I grabbed his arm, trying to keep him from getting hold of it, but I was too late. He started to swing the gun, and I figured he was going to clock me in the head with it. But there was a sickening thud, and his gun hand dropped back to the earth. Meg was standing over him, and a good-size rock was next to his head.

"Did you drop that rock on his head?"

She nodded. "I couldn't find a working phone," she said in a rush. "I went everywhere, but no one is open, and the phone at the info center hasn't got the part you talk into. Do you want to tell me why anyone would steal the talking part from a phone? What in the world would they do with it?" Meg looked anxiously down at Gunnar. "I saw you two rolling around on the ground, and I just picked up the rock and dropped it on him. I didn't kill him, did I?"

"He's breathing," I said. "But we've got to figure out what to do with him before he wakes up. I'll keep an eye on him. Why don't you see if there is anything in the car we can use to tie him up."

A minute later, Meg was back with a couple of sets of nylon handcuffs. "I thought we could do his feet, too," she said, "so he can't run away."

We rolled Gunnar over on his side and got his hands cuffed behind his back. He started groaning just as we got his ankles bound. He struggled to get up for a couple of minutes, then gave it up, lying on the ground glaring at me. I could see the wheels turning in his head.

"There is no effing way you are going to get away with this," he said. "I'm a mega-star. No one will take your word over mine. I suggest you bitches let me go before you find yourselves in over your heads."

"You mean farther over our heads than when you were going to push us off the bridge?" I glared at him. "Because personally, I think being in trouble is better than being dead. I'm in trouble all the time. Doesn't faze me." I looked at Meg. "Let's get him in the car."

Meg and I each grabbed an arm and dragged Gunnar over to the car. He resisted the whole way, trying to wriggle out of our grasp and digging his heels into the dirt. We tried to lift him into the trunk, but we weren't strong enough to get him up and over its lip. We set him back down on the ground, and I leaned against the tail of the car, panting.

"How are we getting this sucker into the car? We could probably get him in the back seat, but I don't think he'd stay there."

"Why didn't we move the car closer to where he was lying? I'm dying here." Meg wiped the sweat off her face with her sleeve "Maybe we could lean him up against the trunk and push him in."

"We'd have to knock him out again. He's never going to cooperate."

"Would you stop talking like I'm a sack of potatoes?" Gunnar said. "It's insulting."

Meg and I looked at him. When I looked back up at Meg, her eyes were slits, and her face was red. She looked like she was going to blow a gasket.

"Calm down," I said. "You're going to give yourself an aneurism. Look at him, he has no idea what he said. He figures we should treat him like a human being, even though he was going to murder us fifteen minutes ago."

Meg took a couple of deep breaths. "Okay, I'm better now. How about we put him in the back seat and use another handcuff to attach him to the car. Then he won't be able to run away."

"And what if I won't let you put me in the car?"

"Then I'll run you over with it. And I'll be sure to run a tire over that pretty face of yours." I was getting cranky. I hadn't eaten anything in hours, my adrenaline levels were sky high, and frankly, I was sick and tired of the whole situation. "And if that doesn't work, I'll tow you over to one of those trees, cuff you to it and leave you there. Then I'll go find a phone, call the cops and tell them you're two miles down the road. By the time they find you, you'll be an icicle."

Gunnar looked at me through narrowed eyes. He must have decided I was serious, because I could see him sink in on himself. "Okay," he said. He puffed out a sigh. "I'll let you put me in the car. You can secure me to something. But I'm telling you, if you take me to the police, I'll deny everything."

"Deny away," I said. Meg and I pulled Gunnar to his feet and put him in the back seat of the car. The trouble was that with his hands cuffed behind his back, we couldn't secure him to anything. I pulled the knife out of my pocket.

"We need to cuff his hands in front."

"How the hell are we going to do that without him killing us?"

I shrugged. Eventually, we attached a new handcuff to his right arm and secured it to the handhold on the back of the driver's seat. Then we cut the tie that was holding his hands behind his back. We ran another cuff around the handle on the back of the driver's seat and slipped it through the link on his left wrist. Gunnar glared at us the whole time, but Meg was looking pretty pleased with herself.

There was a state police barracks in Hartland, but my hunch was that Gunnar was involved in Vera's murder, and in any case, I wanted to be around cops who knew me. "See if you can find a cell phone in his pocket," I said to Meg. "I want to call ahead and tell them we're coming."

Meg dug around and came up with a cell. She flipped it open, dialed the police barracks, and said a few words. She snapped it shut. "Steve Leftsky is going to meet us." She said. "Drive around to the receiving door at the back of the building."

Thirty minutes later, I turned into the Bethel barracks, the trunk lid bouncing up and down. Meg and I had just gotten out of the car when Steve came out the back door. Meg walked around the car and opened the passenger door, where Gunnar was sitting. Steve's eyes flicked from me, to Meg, to Gunnar. He took in the cuffs hanging from my wrist and the webbing circling Gunnar's wrists and ankles. I could see him struggling to keep his composure. There was a smile twitching at the corners of his mouth as he turned away. I saw his uniform expand as he took a deep breath, but he couldn't beat it. His shoulders started to rock with mirth, and pretty soon he was laughing out loud, bending over and gasping. It took him a few minutes to compose himself. I crossed my arms, put my best offended expression on my face, and waited.

I glanced over at Meg, leaning on the car. She had the same highly offended look that I imagined was on my face. Gunnar looked outraged. If he hadn't been cuffed to the car, I figured he would have tackled Steve and taken him out.

"Gee, Bree," Steve said. "I didn't know you were into bondage."

Meg's eyes narrowed. She pushed herself off the car and got right into Steve's face.

"Listen," she said. "I've had a very bad day. I've been kidnapped at gunpoint and had my shoes taken away from me. I was handcuffed to a bed, and the G.D. headboard fell on me. I got stuffed in a trunk, escaped from the trunk and was shot at. I was put back in a trunk. Then this nice man was going to toss me over Quechee Dam. I am not in a good mood. So if you say one thing about this to anyone, I'll shoot you. Then I'll tell my husband it was an accident. Better still, I'll say Gunnar did it, because I am good and tired of being jerked around." Meg burst into tears.

Steve looked uncomfortable and patted her shoulder. He grabbed his radio and called into the barracks for Tom and Lieutenant Brooks. Then he called for a camera and a set of cuff cutters. Then he called in for everyone to hurry it up.

"We're going to have to take photos before we take those cuffs off you," he said to Gunnar and me. "I promise you, they won't get in the paper. But I can't promise you that other officers won't see them." He was looking at me over Meg's head. I could tell he was feeling bad about laughing at us.

Tom and Lieutenant Brooks ran out the door with a third officer behind them holding a lumpy bag and what looked like box cutters.

Steve approached me with the cutter, and I held out my hand. Lieutenant Brooks glanced at Steve and shook his head. He nodded to the metal cuffs hanging on Steve's belt.

"Sorry," Steve said as he clicked the cuffs on me and slid away to Gunnar.

"Are you kidding me? I've been kidnapped, cuffed, and shot at. I can't believe you're cutting the cuffs off Gunnar and putting them on me."

"Don't forget having that headboard come down on your head," chimed in Meg. "That had to hurt like anything."

"We've already investigated Gunnar for Vera's murder," Brooks said. "He has an alibi."

I felt the world swimming around me. I tried to reach behind me to steady myself on the car, but the cuffs stopped me. I sat down hard on the ground. My ears were roaring, but I could vaguely hear Meg saying something about Gunnar's briefcase. The world started to steady again. I took a couple of deep breaths. Steve squatted down beside me.

"You okay?" he asked.

"Have you cut Gunnar's cuffs yet?"

He shook his head.

"Well, don't do it until you've taken a look at his briefcase. There's a folder in the bottom."

Steve nodded. "Tom's already gone to look for it."

There was a scuffle at the car. I looked over. Gunnar was standing outside the car holding the manila folder over his head. His right arm was still attached to the back of the driver's seat, and it was preventing him from moving from the car. Brooks and Tom were flanking Gunnar, trying to retrieve the folder from him. But Gunnar was taller and able to keep the folder out of their reach.

"What does he think he's doing?" I asked. "He's attached to the car. He can't get away or anything."

"It's my private property." Gunnar was shouting. "You have no right to go through my private property."

"I'm holding you on charges of attempted kidnapping," said Tom. "And as such, it won't be long before we have a search warrant. It would serve you well to cooperate at this point."

Gunnar was mincing around, his ankles still shackled together. He wasn't giving up that easily. "Do you know who I am?" he screeched. "I'll have your jobs for this." Tom shook his head and grinned at Brooks.

"Whoa." Steve grabbed my attention. "Your wrist is a mess." He turned my arm over, examining the gashes. "I'm taking this off. We can re-cuff you later, if we need to, but for now, you need medical treatment."

"Wait," I said. "I don't want you to get in trouble."

"Don't sweat the small stuff," Steve said. "I can easily justify removing these. You could get infected." He unlocked the metal cuffs.

I rubbed my wrist, but that hurt. It had bled and scabbed where the cuff had sliced into me. Other places, it was just raw. Steve helped me to my feet.

"Come on," he said. "I'll take you and Meg in to get fixed up. Let the big boys deal with the movie star."

I looked back at the car just in time to see Gunnar lose his balance and fall. He was tangled in the seatbelt and cuffs, but he still clutched the folder to his chest. Once they got a gander at that folder, he'd be done for. Add kidnapping and attempted murder to that. I wondered briefly how they'd explain his disappearance from his TV show. *Who cares?* I thought as I followed Steve into the building. *America needs a better heartthrob.*

Steve took us to the staff room and pulled out the first aid kit. The antiseptic stung like hell, but I felt a lot better when he rolled on the gauze and taped it in place. Tom came in to take Meg home. He dropped a hand on my shoulder.

"Sorry, Bella. You'll have to stay. We found those Christmas balls in the trees at Whispering Birches while we were looking for you. You need to stay until they're dusted for fingerprints."

"You were looking for us?"

"Janine got worried when she left work and your car was still at the spa. She told Brian, and he called us."

Meg started to protest leaving me behind, but Tom gave the slightest shake of his head, and she shut her mouth. He gestured for me to sit in the waiting area. I sat in an orange plastic chair against the far wall. I didn't think they could keep me overnight again, but maybe I was wrong. I was out on bail. Well, not on bail, on my own recognizance. Tom's recognizance? The question was, if they found more evidence, could they put me back in jail before my court date?

I didn't know the answer to that question. I thought about calling Val, but she had made such a scene last time, I decided I'd wait until I knew whether or not I actually needed her lawyerly skills. I rested my head against the wall behind me and closed my eyes. My mind was drifting back over the day. Very bizarre. I'd been kidnapped and had gotten free. Twice. Surreal.

Several hookers were waiting with me. They were all wearing short red dresses. *Where did they come from?* I couldn't think of a town anywhere near that hosted a population of street girls. A blond in spiky heels nodded to me. "MacGowan," she said, "wake up."

"Wake up?" I said. "I'm not asleep."

"Bree, you're talking in your sleep. Wake up."

There was a hand on my shoulder. I opened my eyes to see Steve standing over me. I looked around. "Where did the hookers go?" I asked.

"I don't think we've had a hooker in here in the last ten years," said Steve. "You must have been dreaming. Come on, I'm taking you to get something to eat."

Why am I dreaming about hookers? I wondered. Surely that was odd. Then I remembered my day and thought maybe it wasn't so strange after all.

Steve took me over to the deli, and we grabbed a couple of sandwiches and some chips. We sat at a little round table in the window. The room was warm, and Steve was good company, but I felt depressed.

"What are they waiting for?" I asked Steve. "Am I going to be arrested again? I'd really like to go home."

"They are checking potential murder weapons for fingerprints," said Steve. "It will take a little time to do all eleven of them. If your prints aren't on them, I think you'll be able to go home."

"And if they are on them?" I asked.

"You'll probably have to go before the judge again."

"Oh, joy," I said. The last time I appeared before that judge, I'd felt about ten-years-old.

Steve brought me back to the barracks and left me in the waiting room. I closed my eyes, but no more hookers appeared. I was still sitting in the chair the next morning when Steve came to tell me I could go home.

"No fingerprints?" I stood up. My body hurt all over, and I nearly sat back down.

Steve steadied me. "Oh, there were fingerprints, all right. Yours, Vera's, Dotty's, and probably everybody else who works in that place. Lots of yours. But no blood. Kind of hard to convince the judge that we've got the murder weapon, when there's no blood. Brooks has to release you, but he's not happy about it, so watch yourself."

My car was in the lot. I looked at Steve. "Did you bring that here?"

"No. That was Brooks. He had Tom take him to get it last night."

Brooks? I shook my head and slid into the car. Steve handed me the keys, and I raised a hand as I pulled out of the lot. Brooks? That guy was a bundle of contradictions.

Fourteen

I was in the barn grooming Max's Haflinger. Haflingers are classified as ponies, because they don't grow to be tall enough to be horses. But when most people see a Haflinger, they don't think pony. What they think is "Holy cow, that's a big horse." Rosie is average size for her breed. The highest point on her back is about five feet off the ground. Her hooves are the size of lunch plates, she's bigger around than my propane tank, and she weighs more than eight hundred pounds.

Besides being big, Rosie is sweet tempered, well trained, and beautiful. She's the color of golden straw with a white blaze down her face, two white socks, and mane and tail the color of snow shot through with gold. Rosie's gentle and affectionate, and she likes to rest her muzzle in the space between my neck and shoulder and blow softly. She's warm and comforting to be around. Her huge presence is like a windbreak between me and the outside world. She makes me feel safe. She's my favorite pony in the world, next to Lucky.

So now, although technically she belongs to Max, and I don't need to mess with her, I was in her stall brushing the sawdust and dirt out of her coat. A touch to her shoulder, and she stepped lightly away from me, giving me the space I needed to reach down and brush her belly. A touch on her rump, and she stepped forward and let me brush out her tail.

I had just finished rubbing her face with a soft cloth when I heard a noise in the barn. I straightened up, stretched the kinks out of my back, and glanced into the aisle to see which of the dogs had wandered into the barn. I gave a start; there was a man in the barn. My double-take made Rosie jump a little and give me a dirty look. She'd been relaxing, enjoying the rubdown with her eyes half closed. She knew there was a man in the barn. What was wrong with me that he'd taken me by surprise? One day I'd have to explain to Rosie about the inferiority of human senses.

This guy was not dressed for a barn. He was wearing nice slacks and fancy leather boots with a stacked heel. He had compulsively short hair that would never need brushing to look neat and was wearing a pristine white turtleneck, a big mistake in the country. He had a leather sport coat unbuttoned over the turtleneck. *Fancy pants, and no mistake.* I wondered if he'd lost his way and how he'd figured out to look in the barn. He looked like he'd never been on a farm in his life.

"Can I help you with something?" I asked. I banged the brush against the side of the stall; I'd forgotten to bring in a currycomb to clean the brush with.

"I'm looking for Bree MacGowan," he said. He looked annoyed.

"I'm Bree MacGowan," I said. A month ago, I would have cracked a joke or made some off-the-wall remark. Now, I got nervous when strangers appeared. "Can I help you with something?" I asked. *God, I hope not.*

"No," he said. "I just wanted to see your face."

"My face?"

"I wanted to see the face that ruined Gunnar's life," he said.

Gunnar Ericson? This guy was connected with Gunnar? And then the light went on in my head, and I knew I had heard this voice before. This must be Joseph. A little more butch and a little less whining than when I'd been trapped in Gunnar's room, but Joseph all the same.

"Gunnar ruined his own life," I said. "If he didn't want to go to jail, he should have left me alone."

"Women are all the same. Always hanging around, groping him. It's disgusting. I wish he had thrown you into that canyon."

"I think you should leave." My stomach was churning. I brushed Rosie, trying to hide the shaking in my hands.

"Leave? Not until Gunnar's out of jail."

"I can't get Gunnar out of jail." I slid my hand into my back pocket and slipped out my cell phone, using Rosie to cover me. I kept my eyes focused on Joseph but felt the keys and hit what I hoped was 911.

"You will get Gunnar out of jail. It's easy. Just drop the charges. Drop the charges, and you'll never see me again." A smarmy smile played around the edges of his mouth.

I could hear a voice coming from my cell now. I dropped my brush on the floor. "Oh, help." I set the phone carefully on the floor away from Rosie's feet as I picked up the brush. "Call Captain Maverick," I said as I straightened. I looked into Joseph's eyes, knowing that I could lie with the best of them and praying that the 911 dispatcher caught on. "Call Tom Maverick. He might be able to help you get Gunnar released."

"Why would I call Maverick, when I've got you? Everyone knows he'll do whatever you ask. One of the perks of sleeping with his brother." A smile lit his face. "I'll bet you're doing him, too. That would explain the favoritism."

My phone chose that moment to beep. *Shit.* My battery was low. Joseph was at the door to the stall immediately. His eyes scanned the floor.

"What was that noise?"

"I didn't hear anything." I pushed Rosie over, hoping she would mask the sound of the phone.

Joseph was scanning the floor. The phone beeped again, and he slid the stall door open. He saw the phone and stepped through the door, sliding it closed behind him. I kept Rosie between us, and as Joseph went to the phone and picked it up, I slid open the door, stepped through it, and slammed it shut. I took a spare snap hook and clipped it through the latch so Joseph couldn't open the door.

I ran for the house with everything I had, slipping in the snow and mud. I splashed through slush and spattered myself. The dogs ran out of the house as I ran in, tracking mud across the kitchen to the phone. I dialed 911 and explained what had happened to the dispatcher. I heard the dogs barking as I ran back to the barn.

"Good dogs!" I called as I trotted up to where they stood guard. They were jumping at the stall, their paws thudding on the wood. Annie was scratching at the bottom of the door, trying to dig her way through the concrete. I looked over the gate and saw Joseph plastered to the far wall. He had a look of terror on his face. Rosie had her muzzle resting on the middle of his chest. It looked like she was leaning into him just a little. She was probably wondering why he wasn't scratching her ears. He saw me and started pleading.

"Get this horse off of me! It's huge. My ribs are cracking. I can feel them caving in..." his panicked raving went on.

"Good girl, Rosie," I said to the horse.

*****

"Why hasn't she moved?" Tom asked, gesturing to Rosie. He and Brooks had arrived with two other cars, sirens blaring.

"I told her to stay," I said. "Max trained her for his grandkids. She does all kinds of different things. She'll stand like that for hours, if you ask her to. And she fetches balls like a dog." I nodded my head in Joseph's direction. "I could probably get her to sit on him, if I wanted to."

Joseph was looking green. He had long since stopped begging me to get him out of the stall, and now I think he was just praying I wouldn't ask Rosie to sit. Tom gestured the two uniformed guys into the stall with Rosie and Joseph, then smiled at me.

"You can call her off now," he said. "What was he doing in there anyway? I wouldn't think a guy who's afraid of horses would willingly lock himself in a stall with one."

"He went in after my cell phone, and I locked him in. After I let the dogs out of the house, I doubt he would have come out if he could have."

"Doesn't know your dogs, then," said Tom. He turned his head to Joseph "You'd have been safer with the dogs," Tom told him. "They might lick you to death, I suppose, but that'd be better than having your chest compressed."

"Rosie." I saw her ears flick in my direction and knew I had her attention. "Back now." The pony shifted her weight back away from Joseph and took two careful steps backward. "Good girl, Rosie," I said. "I'll come back and give you a good rub later."

The uniforms pulled Joseph roughly out of the stall, and Tom put cuffs on him. Joseph kept glancing nervously at the dogs. His behavior was making Hank nervous, and he started to growl.

"I should be pressing charges against her!" Joseph spat the word in my direction. "Look at me! My clothes are ruined. I've been practically squashed to death by a monster horse."

"Pony," I said. I glanced over at Hank, who had started to slink toward Joseph. "Hank! Lie down," I snapped, and Hank sank back to the floor.

"What?" Joseph looked at me like I was from outer space.

"Rosie is a pony, not a horse," I explained.

"Well she's the frickin' pony from hell," he said to me. Joseph turned back to Tom. "It wasn't like I was going to hurt her or anything. I just wanted to get Gunnar released. I figured if she could get him put in jail, she could get him out."

Brooks took a good look at Joseph. "Where are you from?" he asked. "You have absolutely no idea how the legal system works, do you?"

"I'm a writer for *The Unfaithful*," said Joseph. He looked at Brooks in contempt. "In my world, the legal system does what I say it does."

"Well, fortunately, that not the way it works in the real world," said Brooks. He nodded to Steve. "Put him in the squad car. I'm tired of listening to him talk." Brooks walked over to me and wiped some mud off my face.

"You okay, Ms. MacGowan?" he asked.

"Yeah, I'm fine." I said. Fine, but completely confused. Lieutenant Brooks was being nice to me. Go figure.

"I'm going out to question Dolly, again. I was wondering if I could persuade you to come with me?"

"Sure, I guess," I said. "Can I have a couple of minutes to get cleaned up?"

"Actually, if you don't mind, it would serve my purpose better if you went like that."

"What purpose would that be?" I asked.

"I'll fill you in on the way over there." He turned his attention to Tom. "If it's okay with you, I'm going to take Ms. MacGowan over to Dotty Walker's house. I think Bree might be the persuasion we're looking for."

"Persuade away," said Tom. "I'll take a look around and make sure the animals are secure."

I followed Lieutenant Brooks out to his car. I could see Joseph sitting in the back of one of the other cars. Brooks opened the passenger side door for me.

"You called me Bree?"

"Must have slipped out." He started the car.

We turned left out of my dooryard and bounced up the hill, heading up and over to North Road. Brooks briefly explained to me what he needed me to do, and about a mile from Dotty's place, he stopped the car. I got out of the front seat and held my hands behind my back for Brooks to cuff me.

"No," he said. "Let me cuff them in the front. I'm pretty sure Mrs. Walker is not going to realize that you should be cuffed behind your back, and it will be a lot less uncomfortable for you if I cuff your hands in the front."

I wasn't sure where the new and improved Lieutenant Brooks came from, and frankly, I wasn't entirely comfortable with him. I was getting used to stinging words and insults.

He helped me into the back seat of the car, and we made our way to Dotty's single-wide sitting in a small clearing in the back woods. Dotty came out of her trailer as we approached and looked at the car in puzzlement. Brooks brought the car to a stop and got out, leaving his door open.

He went and talked to Dotty for a few minutes. I could hear their voices but couldn't distinguish what they were saying. Brooks walked Dotty up to the car, and Dotty looked down on me with confusion on her face. Brooks stood behind her, dead serious. When I glanced up at him, he gave a barely perceptible shake of his head. He was warning me to keep quiet. I was shivering; the snow and ice had melted, leaving me a soggy mess. I looked down at my feet. A puddle was forming around them from the water dripping off my pant leg.

"But what happened to her?" Dotty asked. "She's all covered in mud." She turned to look at Brooks.

"Did some wrestling around in the snow and mud outside her barn," he said. "Put up quite a fight. You should see the other guy."

Dotty turned and stared back through the window at me. She looked shocked, disbelieving. I had a flash of insight. *She knows I didn't kill Vera.* The question then became, does she know who did?

"But didn't she tell you she was innocent?"

"Of course she says she's innocent. All guilty people say they're innocent. Don't you watch cop shows on TV?" Lieutenant Brooks had his cop face on. I almost felt sorry for Dotty. I knew what it was like to deal with Brooks when he was in cop mode.

"But she couldn't have killed Vera," cried Dotty. "How can you arrest her? She couldn't have done it."

"Do you have any facts to back that statement?" asked Brooks.

Dotty shook her head. She turned away and walked back to her trailer. I looked down at my hands, frustrated. Our plan to get Dotty to talk hadn't worked.

"Don't be too disappointed," said Brooks as he slid into the drivers seat. "Sometimes it takes a while for conscience to kick in. It's possible she'll change her mind and talk."

I watched Dotty open the door to her trailer. Something glittered beside the steps. It was a little gazing ball sitting in one of those metal holders. I'd seen them down at Pier One. The balls sat on metal stands shaped like dragonflies or frogs. Maybe flowers. There was something about Dotty's that didn't seem right. The gazing ball was the wrong size for the stand. Dotty looked back and saw me staring. Her head was tilted as she watched me. I caught her gaze, and she closed the door.

"That was weird."

Lieutenant Brooks looked back at me. "What was weird?"

"Dotty had a strange look on her face. She was watching me as she closed her door."

"Dotty doesn't exactly strike me as having an elevator that goes all the way to the top." He started the car and pulled away from the house.

Lieutenant Brooks stopped the car once we were out of sight of Dotty's and removed my cuffs. I moved back into the front seat and stared out the windshield. I wasn't sure what I had expected Dotty to do, but she didn't do anything. Didn't say anything. I couldn't help being disappointed.

When we got back to my farmhouse, the others had cleared out. The dogs were sitting on the porch waiting for their dinner, and I could see Annabelle stretched out in the window over the kitchen sink. What would happen if I fell in love with a man who didn't like animals? *That won't happen,* I told myself. *It's not worth worrying about.*

"You look tired," Brooks said. "You should take it easy for a while. And I'd appreciate it if you kept a low profile for a few days, just in case Dotty has a change of mind. If she thinks you're in jail, it'll eat at her some."

"I was planning to lay low for a while anyway. I'm getting a lot of negative attention. Thanks for rescuing me from that dickweed Joseph, Lieutenant Brooks."

"You didn't need rescuing, just a mop-up crew." Brooks smiled at me. "And you can call me Miles. We've spent too much time together for you to keep calling me Lieutenant Brooks."

"I'm not sure I could get used to Miles. I always think of you as Brooks."

"Well, then, call me Brooks, and leave off the Lieutenant part, okay?"

"I'll think about it." I slid out of the car. "Maybe when I've stopped being mad at you for treating me like a scumbag."

"Fair enough." Brooks flashed me a smile and pulled out of my drive.

I stripped off in the kitchen. Another set of clothes that needed to be dried and de-mudded before they went in the wash. If I didn't get to the laundry soon, I'd be all out of clothes. I dropped these in the laundry room and padded upstairs to the shower.

The water pounded on my back, and I watched the dirty water swirl down the drain. I wondered how much dirt could go down there before my pipes would be permanently plugged. My thoughts drifted over the day. Not one of the finest ever. How strange that Lieutenant Brooks was being nice to me. Had it impressed him that I'd brought Gunnar in? Or was it finding Joseph squashed between Rosie and the wall that had put him in such a good mood?

Too bad Dotty didn't jump for the bait. She sure had looked strange standing there inside her door. She was watching me. What had I seen? Oh, yeah, the odd gazing ball. Dotty had gotten a stand that was too small for it. Or maybe not.

I stepped out of the shower and dried off. I wrapped a towel around me and went in search of my phone. I was tempted to call Tom first to see if he'd discovered how many Christmas balls had been found. But I decided I might as well take advantage of Lieutenant Brooks being nice to me. Who knew how long that would last? I dialed his number.

"Did anybody count how many Christmas balls were found?"

"I've got the number written down somewhere. Why? Do you think it's important?"

I wouldn't be asking, if I didn't think it was important, but this probably wasn't the right moment to point that out. "Yes, I think it's important. There were twelve glass balls in that basket. If any are missing, it's significant."

Papers shuffled on the other end of the line. "Eleven. We found eleven. I'll send someone out to look for the other one."

"Don't bother. I think I know where it is."

"You are not to go after that ball by yourself. You hear me? Stay put, and I'll pick you up in thirty minutes."

"Okay. I'm waiting."

I threw on jeans and a long-sleeved tee-shirt. Then I pulled on my cowboy boots. Courage for my feet. I was actually glad Brooks was coming with me. I would have asked Tom or Steve, but Brooks would do just as well. Better even. He couldn't accuse me of tampering with evidence, if he was there when we found it.

I was waiting at the kitchen window when Brooks' patrol car pulled up. I pulled on my jacket and chased the dogs out of the house. I slid into the passenger seat. It was clean. He must have wiped out the mud before he came.

"Where to?" Brooks lifted a hand off the wheel and pointed his finger up, then down, the road.

"Left. We're going back to Dotty's." I explained about the gazing ball that didn't fit its stand right and reminded Brooks about the strange look Dotty gave me. We were bumping along the road, and Brooks was nodding at me.

Dotty's car was missing when we pulled up. I jumped out of the car as we stopped, but I could see before I reached the door that the ball was gone. The iron stand the ball had been sitting in was shaped like a beetle. The ball would have been the beetle's shell. I searched in the snow at the base of the wrought iron stand without much hope I would find what I was looking for.

"It's not here?" Brooks was looking over my shoulder.

"No. Dotty must have noticed me looking at it. That would explain the look on her face. Crap!"

Brooks smiled. "Let's make sure Dotty's not home." He banged on the door.

I looked at my watch. "She'll be at work now. She starts mid-afternoon. She probably was getting ready to go when we showed up earlier."

We hopped back in the car and made for Whispering Birches. We drove right up to the laundry building, bypassing the parking lot. There were a couple of Jeeps parked under the portico. Brooks locked his car, and we whooshed in through the automatic doors. Dotty was talking to one of the girls and looked up when we came in. Her eyes narrowed, and she darted into the back room.

"There's a way out of the building through there." I pointed after Dotty.

Brooks was already on the move; he skirted a tall table and jogged after Dotty. A Jeep roared to life in the portico. Man, that Dotty moved fast. I turned and raced out the front. Dotty was tearing up the hill, gravel flying out from under her tires. Brooks dashed around the corner of the building.

"She blocked the door in the back. I had to shove my way through. Come on." He ran for his car. He had his cruiser rolling before I was completely in the car. I buckled myself in as Brooks turned the car and headed up the opposite drive. The other Jeep was blocking the way and prevented us from following Dotty.

Brooks talked into his radio, giving instructions to dispatch. He sounded calm, unhurried, but he was driving full out. Whipping around corners, spraying gravel at every turn. Flying over the hills. He took us down the road toward Pomfret.

"Why this way?"

"We would have met up with her, if she'd turned up the hill. I'm pretty sure she's heading toward Woodstock." He hesitated for a split second when we came to Midway Road, but he passed it by and took us out to Route 12 in Barnard. He turned to me. "I'm thinking she's taking the paved roads, where she can make better time. But I've called in all possibilities, so the roads should be blocked regardless of which way she goes."

We were tearing down Route 12. The engine was whining, and the trees were flashing by me. I had my eyes glued to the road in front of us, trying to catch sight of the Jeep. "She probably won't get too far. We never fill those Jeeps more that half full."

"Why's that?"

"They're always going in the shop with fouled plugs and dead batteries. We aren't supposed to drive more than 25 mph at the Inn. The gunk never gets blown out. They're always at the dealer's and come back out of gas. So we don't fill them all the way up." I clutched the dash as

Brooks practically launched the car over a hill. There ahead of us was a Jeep.

"Is that her?" I couldn't make out the plate.

"Gotta be. No one else would be stupid enough to drive like that on this road."

Brooks increased his speed, and we came up on Dotty's tail. He clicked on the rooftop flashers and the siren, but she didn't slow. I don't think she even glanced back. We roared down the road in tandem, turning left and right with the road as if we were one car. I prayed that Dotty wouldn't slam on her brakes, or we'd fly right up her butt.

We took a wide, sweeping turn to the right and were almost in Woodstock. The road straightened out, and we could see flashing lights a ways down the road. Brooks' roadblock. Dotty had seen it. She was on her brakes and swerving. Brooks backed off, giving himself room to maneuver. Then the Jeep was spinning. I would almost swear that she did it on purpose. The Jeep came almost to a stop facing us. Then the engine roared, and she was racing toward us.

Fifteen

Brooks hit the brakes and swerved out of her path as Dotty sped past us. Then the Jeep was off the road, bumping through a pasture. It came to a stop, and Dotty was off and running on foot. Brooks spun the car so that we were facing the way we came. He pulled over, and before we were fully stopped, I was out the door. I jumped a ditch and ran toward Dotty. The slick soles on my boots were slipping in the snow. I was trying to avoid cow patties and ankle-twisting holes.

There was a crash behind me, and I looked over my shoulder to see a police car stuck in Brooks' driver-side door. He'd have to climb over the console to exit the car. I tripped and landed on my knees in the snow. I scrambled to my feet and wiped my hands on my jeans. *Cold.* I was up and running again. My breathing was coming in gasps, and I had a stitch in my side, but I kept going. I was going to catch Dotty Walker if it was the last thing I did.

I was gaining. Dotty had slowed to a walk and was holding her side. She turned, registered my presence, and started jogging again. My cowboy boots, while great at making me feel brave, were pitiful for running in. The soles slid over the earth, and the heels caught on clumps of earth. There was enough snow that I couldn't really tell what I was running over. The ground wasn't frozen, and with every other step, I sank into the muddy earth.

I glanced behind me. The cops were pulling Brooks out of his car. I hoped he wasn't injured and turned back to

Dotty. I was close enough to hear her swearing. I pushed myself to run faster. Sweat ran down my breastbone.

"You stay away from me, Bree MacGowan! I've got a gun. I'll shoot you if you get too close."

I thought that was unlikely. She was in her work clothes, blue tee-shirt over black pants. There were plenty of bulges, but I didn't think any of them was a gun. She was breathing hard.

"Give it up, Dotty. You can't get away." Who did I think I was kidding? I was barely gaining on her now. The stitch in my side was needling me at every breath.

"Stay back. I swear I'll hurt you." Dotty pulled something from her pants pocket and waved it at me. She had a pair of scissors. I shook my head. They were probably the scissors we used to trim flowers at the Inn. The blade was only about two-inches long.

"What are you going to do with those? Trim my hair? Come on, Dotty, I'm tired of chasing you through this field. I want to go home."

"Then stop chasing me. Are you a cop or something now? Are they paying you to chase me around this field, or are you stupid enough to do it for free?"

That was a low blow, especially as it was true. I gritted my teeth and forced my legs to move faster. I could almost touch her. I reached out to grab her shirt, but she spun away.

"Come on, Dotty. Give. It. Up." I was about ready to give it up myself. My breath was coming in gasps. I lunged with everything I had and got my arms around her legs. She crashed to the ground, kicking and yelling.

"God damn it, Bree. Why do you have to stick your nose in everything? You could have left well enough alone. But no. B.B. MacGowan has to get involved."

"Get real. If you hadn't left me to take the fall, I wouldn't have been involved." I pushed myself up and sat in the snow. I would have to walk Dotty out of here now, and I didn't think she was going to cooperate.

"It's not like you would have gone to jail, you stupid woman! There was no evidence against you! If you'd just waited it out, you would have been okay."

"Stupid woman? You have the nerve to call me a stupid woman? You ruined my whole, entire life." I stood up. "You're the stupid woman." I pointed my finger at her.

Dotty hauled herself up off the ground. She slapped my hand. "Don't you point that finger at me. I would have gotten away with it, if it weren't for you. I'm smart. I did everything right. You screwed it all up for me, you and that snoopy cop!" She lifted the hand that was holding the scissors and drove them into my arm.

"Shit!" I tried to grab the handles, but Dotty pulled the scissors back out of my arm. Adrenaline rushed through my body. I grabbed the hand with the scissors, bent at the waist, and head-butted her right in the stomach.

All the air whooshed out of Dotty, and she sat down hard. I twisted the scissors out of her fingers and threw them as far as I could. Dotty was on the ground, struggling to catch her breath. I looked over to where Brooks had been. He and a handful of cops were running across the field.

I grabbed Dotty by the arm and yanked her off the ground. We started across the field toward the cops. By the time I reached them, the adrenaline had subsided, and my arm was hurting. My sleeve felt warm and sticky, but I wasn't looking. I didn't want to lose my lunch on top of everything else.

"Thanks for your help." I gave Brooks the beady eyeball and walked past him. "You can have your murderer now. I let all the air out of her for you."

Brooks motioned for a uniform to take Dotty and turned and fell in step with me. "I think you should stop for a minute and let me put something on that wound."

"I'm fine. I just want to go home now. I've had kind of a lousy day."

"Ms. MacGowan, if you don't stop walking, I'm going to have to arrest you."

"What are you arresting me for this time? Apprehending a murderer without a license? Subduing a wild woman with flower scissors? Can't you just let me be?" I stopped moving. I felt lightheaded now that I was still. I thought maybe I was swaying a little.

An officer ran up with a little white box. He opened it for Brooks, who took out a pair of scissors and cut the sleeve off my shirt. I still wasn't looking. I gasped when he swabbed my arm.

"Jeez! That hurts!" I tried to pull away.

"Hang on. That was the worst of it. I just need to put a dressing on it now." He plastered a huge bandage over the hole in my arm. "Okay. Now at least you won't bleed to death before we get to the road."

I could hear sirens. I started walking toward the road again, wondering why more cops were coming. Surely they had plenty of men to subdue Dotty.

"Wait." Brooks put a hand on my good shoulder. He motioned to the cop with the first aid kit, and they scooped me up in a two-handed seat. They started toward the road. The siren was getting loader.

"You can put me down. I'm not going to bleed to death between here and the road."

"If you could see the color of your face, you wouldn't say that. You're a lovely shade of pale green."

I didn't want to admit it, but I wasn't feeling so good. An ambulance rushed up the road and stopped next to the crunched cop cars. The paramedics piled out of the truck and looked in the windows. Brooks whistled, and they looked up to see us. One of them opened the back and grabbed a stretcher, and they barreled through the snow to meet us.

"I am not getting on that stretcher! I can walk."

"I'm sorry, but we need to keep you as still as possible." He looked at Brooks. "How'd she get this wound?"

Brooks was standing beside me. "She was stabbed with a pair of scissors, which I'm going to have a devil of a time finding, because she pitched them." He walked beside me to the ambulance. The paramedics pulled a rolling stretcher out of the back of the ambulance, unfolded it, and set me on it. Brooks touched my cheek with the back of his fingers. "If I'd known she was carrying those scissors, I never would have let you run after her like that. I'm sorry."

"I'm just glad it wasn't a gun. That's what she said she had." I smiled at him. "You probably couldn't have stopped me anyway."

"I believe that. You'll be okay now? I need to go find those scissors and help bring Dotty to the station."

"I'm fine. Just a little cold."

Brooks motioned to the attendants, and they lifted me into the ambulance. "She says she's cold. Make sure she's got a blanket." The doors closed, and I was strapped to the gurney. I closed my eyes. I was shivering, but I thought I could probably sleep. Someone draped a heated blanket over me. Heaven.

"Bree? Wake up, Bree." A woman was looking down at me.

"Oomph." My mouth was dry. My arm hurt. "Hospital?"

"Hospital." The woman nodded. "I'm sorry to wake you. I understand you had a pretty rough day."

My brain registered the white coat. *Doctor.* "You could say that." I looked around. I was in the emergency room. "How long have I been here?"

"Long enough for us to stick an I.V. in you and check all your vital signs."

"I slept through all that?"

"They gave you some pain meds in the ambulance. Knocked you out a little." She smiled. "What I'm going to do now is going to hurt more. I was afraid you'd wake up fighting if I tried to examine this wound while you were sleeping."

"Great." Jeez, couldn't they just knock me out again? She pulled the dressing off my arm and poked around in the wound. I sucked in my breath and curled my fingers into the sheet. She let up, and I let my breath out.

"The next time someone stabs you, leave the object in the wound. It will do less damage. You're going to have to go into surgery. I'm not going to be able to repair this while you're conscious." She leaned her head out of the room and motioned to someone down the hall.

"Surgery? Are you sure you can't just put a couple of stitches in it and let me go? I'm not thrilled about surgery." People had started flooding into the room. It suddenly seemed very small.

"I need to stop the bleeding. I need you to be still. If you were to jerk your arm while I'm working in there we could do a lot of damage." A nurse was injecting something into the I.V. line.

"Don't I have to sign papers before you can do surgery?" Panic was building in my gut. I felt like the world was running out of control.

A nurse bent over me. "Your brother signed the papers. He's filling out forms at the nurses' desk. Would you like to see him before we take you out of here?"

I nodded. My brother was here? I wouldn't have been surprised to find that it wasn't my brother at all, but Steve or Tom. But the door slid back, and J.W. was standing there.

"Can't keep yourself out of trouble for five minutes, can you? Meg will be here when you wake up. Mom and Dad are driving up tomorrow."

"Not Mom and Dad. Can't you keep them from coming? I'm not dying or anything. It's just a little hole in my arm."

"And a tremendous amount of blood loss," my nurse amended.

"Still, it's no reason ..."

"It's time to go, Bree." The doctor interrupted me. "Let your family come. It will make them feel better."

A nurse opened a valve on my I.V., and a moment later, I didn't have a care in the world.

*****

It was quiet when I opened my eyes. The sun streamed through the window, coming to rest on Brooks sitting in a chair against the wall. He had his eyes closed. The shadow of a black beard graced his face, making him look slightly disreputable. Mostly, he looked tired.

"Have you been there all night?" My voice was hoarse.

Brooks opened his eyes. A smile played on his lips. "No, I haven't been here all night. I had to finish my shift first."

"You should go home and get some rest." I couldn't believe I was actually feeling sorry for him.

"I wanted to be sure you were recovering. I shouldn't have let the situation progress. You had no business chasing after a murderer." He stood up and dragged the chair over to my bed.

"You couldn't have stopped me. I was so mad at Dotty. You would have had to cuff me to the car to keep me from going after her."

"That's what I should have done. You wouldn't have been so involved if I hadn't led you to believe you were the prime suspect."

"I wasn't?"

"In the beginning, maybe. You'd be surprised how many murderers get tired of waiting for their victim to be discovered and go and discover the body themselves. It's some kind of neurosis. I told that reporter you weren't our main suspect before that article ran. She twisted my words. I told your boss that on the phone the other day."

"Lucy knew I didn't murder Vera?" I raised my eyebrows at him. "When did you decide I hadn't done it?"

"After I arrested you. I wasn't sure before that. After that, I knew. And then you brought in Gunnar, and after that, you fought off Joseph. I was thinking you should have been a cop. Maverick tells me that MacGowans are pretty resilient. If you're typical, I'd have to agree with him."

"Oh, sure, now you flatter me."

"I'd like to flatter you a lot more, but I understand you're seeing someone."

"Hmm. I have been seeing someone. I'm not sure we're exclusive, though. I need to work that out."

"It's not Jim Fisk, is it?"

"Jim Fisk was before. He dumped me at the first sign of trouble."

"He's not right for you anyway." He picked up my hand.

"You're the second man to say that."

"Must be right then. Can I ask you for coffee sometime?"

"Sure, I'm always up for coffee. But I have to warn you, I have a habit of spilling drinks on guys."

"You spill drinks on guys?"

"I talk with my hands, and next thing you know, someone's drink is all over the table."

I'll keep that in mind." He had his hands clasped over mine. "I'm glad you're going to be okay. I can't tell you how bad I felt when you came across the field with blood running down your sleeve."

"I wasn't too happy about that myself. But no worries. I'm fine. I don't seem to have it in me to hold a grudge against you, so maybe coffee will work out okay. Who knows? Maybe I'll be able to keep my hands in check, and you won't end up covered in it."

He left to get cleaned up and go back to work. The doctor came in on rounds and told me I'd probably get to go home today. J.W., Tom and Meg wandered in shortly after my breakfast. I was lamenting the lack of bacon when Jim waltzed in. He shook hands with J.W. and Tom.

"What in the world possessed you that you would go tearing after that madwoman? There isn't one sane person in that family. But you didn't hear that from me. Her nephew just admitted that he was planning to burn down your house because he thought you had killed his aunt."

"Her nephew? How old is he?"

"Fourteen. I don't know what the cops are going to do with him. Probably put the fear of God into him and let him go. He's usually a pretty good kid. They say he was distraught."

"A distraught fourteen-year-old was going to burn down my house." I shook my head. I didn't even know what to make of that.

I closed my eyes. Jim took that as a sign I was tired and left to go to work. Meg sat in the chair next to my bed that Brooks had vacated earlier. "I really wish you'd stay home and live the quiet life. You are giving me grey hair. How is your arm?"

"It's okay. They've got me on some pretty good painkillers. Did you know that Lieutenant Brooks told Lucy that I wasn't the main suspect, and she went ahead and wrote that I was anyway?"

Meg nodded. "Miles called and told me that when the paper came out. I meant to tell you, but that's the day we took that ride with Gunnar. I kind of forgot."

"Lucy Howe better watch her back. What she did is lower than pond scum."

"I'll fire her. Then you can write the article telling about how you weren't a suspect and all the other stuff that happened. You could mention she isn't working for the paper anymore, because she's lower than pond scum."

"Nothing would make me happier." I looked over at Tom. "So did you guys ever find the other glass ball that Dotty had? It disappeared out of her garden."

"Miles found it in her car. She left it parked in the lot when she took off with the Jeep. The ball has Vera's blood and Dotty's prints on it. Pretty damning evidence. How'd you know?"

"I had a hunch, that's all. I didn't know it was Dotty, but I had the feeling she knew who did it, and I was right. She did know."

Tom came over and stood next to Meg. "I need to tell Bella something, Hon. Do you mind if I commandeer your chair for a couple of minutes?"

"Go ahead. I'll go down to the cafeteria and find some bacon for Bree to eat."

Tom sat down next to me. "Now, Bree, I don't want you to be upset, but they are letting Gunnar go."

"What? How can that be? There are photos. He's in some of those photos with young men. Very young men."

"He had us check it out. Those guys all look young, but they're not. The agency Gunnar used to shoot those specializes in men who look very young. They keep meticulous records, so their clients don't end up in jail."

"There's an agency that caters to this kind of thing? That's disgusting."

"I agree, but as they are all adults, it's legal."

"But what about the kidnapping charge. How is he getting out of that?"

"Well, it's your word and Meg's against his. He's charming, famous and attractive. The D.A. feels that no jury will convict. His lawyer will say that you stowed away in his trunk and decided to claim kidnapping to escape embarrassment."

"Shit. What about Joseph?"

"Public nuisance charges might stick on him. But Gunnar will hire a big city lawyer for Joseph, so I doubt he'll even get fined. They'll both probably be back in California, free as birds, before the end of the week."

J.W. looked up from his magazine. "Did you ever find out why he kidnapped you? Obviously, it didn't have to do with Vera's murder."

"He thought I'd heard him on the phone booking a session with some boys, although apparently, they aren't really boys at all. Anyway, he thought I knew, and he was afraid I'd leak it and destroy his fan base. What he was going to say if anyone found out he kidnapped and killed Meg and me, I don't know."

* * * * *

Meg was sitting with me, flicking through the channels on TV. I had been discharged, but we had to wait for the nurse to come with the papers. Meg had ransacked my house for clean clothes, and I was wearing mud- and blood-free jeans and an oversized tee-shirt. Meg figured that my usual stretchy tee-shirt would hurt to wear.

The door opened. I shifted my gaze away from an "Ellen" rerun in hopes that the nurse had arrived. Lucy Howe waltzed in, carrying an enormous fruit basket wrapped in green cellophane.

"I guess you're innocent after all." She set the basket on the table, effectively blocking my view of "Ellen." She sat in the chair next to my bed and pulled a notebook out of her purse. "Why don't you let me write an article to set the record straight? It only seems fair."

"You want to write a retraction?"

"Well, not a retraction exactly. More like a here's what happened since we last talked. An update."

"I don't think so."

"Well, I'm going to write it whether you talk to me or not. There are plenty of other people I can get the details from. I don't need your input. I was just offering to be nice."

"You amaze me. You never change."

"Hard to argue with perfection, don't you think? Now, why don't you tell me how you figured out Dotty was the murderer?"

I glanced over at Meg. I was intending to give her my can-you-believe-this look, but Meg's face had turned a brilliant red. Her eyes were slits. If she had been a cartoon, steam would have been billowing out of her ears.

"Lucy." Meg's voice was tight. "If you want to keep writing for me, I suggest you leave. Now."

"But what about the story, Meg? You're going to have to run this story." Lucy sounded incredulous.

"Yes, I will run the story. But you won't be writing it."

"Who else is there? I'm the best reporter you have."

"I'm giving it to Bree to write."

"You're giving it to Bree? Bree's not a reporter."

"She is now. And if you don't get out of here, I'll give her your job."

Lucy threw up her hands. "I'm out of here. Sorry I disturbed you. Apparently, you haven't been getting enough sleep or something." She gathered her bag and scooted out of the room.

I looked at Meg. "You really want me to write the article? I thought you were kidding."

"You write at least as well as Lucy. Better when you put your mind to it. I'm surprised you never asked me to let you contribute."

"It never occurred to me."

"Well, you'd better start working on it. If you do a good job, I'll give you a staff writing position, and Deirdre can do paste-up. It's time you moved on to something that challenges you."

"Paste-up challenges me."

"Get real, Bree. You can do paste-up in your sleep."

Sixteen

Meg and I were alone at the paper. I had too many distractions at home, so I dragged a table out of storage and hauled it to the paper along with my laptop. Tom helped me cart it up the stairs, and I placed it in front of the window, so I could spy on the town while I worked. I knocked out a rough draft of my article and made notes about the incident with Gunnar.

An eraser bounced off the table and landed in my lap. I looked over my shoulder to where Meg was sitting. "Hey, that was a good shot," she said.

"Trying to get my attention?"

"Yeah. My barn is almost finished. Another week at most, probably less. I won't be hanging around with Scott anymore."

"Where's his next job?"

"All the way over in Goshen. And he lives in Barnard. I doubt we'll see him over this way."

"How are you feeling about that?" I knew how I felt about it, but I was keeping it to myself.

"It's probably for the best. Who am I kidding? Scott made me feel young, attractive. Funny. Now I feel sick to my stomach about the whole thing. I liked the way I felt when I was with Scott, but I'm not willing to give up my marriage for it. But I feel kind of addicted. Don't be surprised if I'm cranky for a while."

"Like you're not cranky every day. I'm surprised Deirdre puts up with it. Where is Deirdre today, anyway?

She didn't quit did she?" I was afraid I would be back typesetting any minute now.

"No, she didn't quit. She has a dentist appointment today. Don't worry. I'm not making you back into a typesetter."

"I wasn't worried about it," I lied. "I'm a good typesetter." I pictured myself getting a swift kick in the butt. What was I doing? Trying to lie my way out of being a reporter? *Yikes.*

Feet pounded up the stairs, and Rob burst into the office. He stopped inside the door and scanned the room. He waved a hand at Meg and headed over to me.

"Hey, is it true you got stabbed?" Rob reached out as if to touch my arm.

I jerked back from his touch. "Don't touch it! It hurts."

"Wow. That's wild. How'd that happen?" He pulled a chair over to my desk.

"I got stupid and chased Dotty across a field. There were cops all over the place, but somehow I felt the need to get myself stabbed." I shook my head.

"I take it you're not recommending apprehending criminals as a hobby?"

"Not in the least. It sounds way cooler than it is."

"I'll keep that in mind." He smiled at me. "Listen, I've got a couple of tickets to the motorcycle races at Loudon for a week Saturday. Would you like to come?"

"Won't Lisa get her knickers in a twist if you take me to the races?"

"Nah, she's not into motorcycles. She begged off."

"Yeah, I'd love to go to the races. Maybe by then I'll be off the pain pills."

"Does that matter?"

"Kind of sad to go watch the races and not be able to drink a beer."

Rob laughed. "It's a date, then. This is off subject, but did you ever find out why Dotty killed her sister?"

"No, never did."

"Motive," Meg said. "You need to find out."

"You expect me to interview a woman who stabbed me in the arm with scissors? You've got to be kidding."

"Do it before they let her out on bail. At least then you'll be supervised," said Meg.

"And she won't have access to any sharp instruments. They don't let inmates have pencils, do they? I'd hate for you to get stabbed with a pencil. The lead might break off in your arm." Rob was laughing.

"Very funny. Great. Just what I always wanted to do. Confront a psychotic killer." Maybe I should go back to typesetting, after all. No one ever tried to kill me for misplacing an ad.

*****

"You want to do what? Are you nuts?" Tom was clearly not thrilled about me interviewing Dotty.

"Listen, your wife assigned this to me. Did I ask to be a reporter? No. But if I'm going to do the job, I have to be able to interview creepoids. So give me a break, and let me in to see Dotty."

"Her lawyer will never consent to this." Tom shook his head. "But I can ask, if you want me to."

"I do." Once I've taken hold of a thing, it's hard to get me to let go.

*****

A couple of days later, I found myself in a little room sitting across from Dotty. She was wearing an ugly orange jump suit, and her hands were cuffed. A female officer stood at the door, and Steve Leftsky was sitting next to me.

Those were Tom's conditions. If Dotty went for me, I'd have double back-up. The truth was, now that I was sitting here, I had no idea how to start. Hey, Dotty, why'd you kill your sister? seemed kind of rude.

"So Dotty, how are you doing?" *Lame. Really lame.*

"Other than being charged with killing my sister? Oh, just fine. How 'bout you? Is your arm healing okay?"

"Yeah, I'm okay. Do you know why I'm here?" I examined her face. I found it hard to believe she would confess any wrongdoing to me.

"I do. My lawyer advised me against talking to you. But maybe if I get a lot of press, they'll change the venue. I could really drag this out. Not that it matters. I think I'm going to plead guilty anyway."

"So you admit you did it?" I couldn't bring myself to say the word kill or murder.

"It would be stupid of me to deny it after concealing the murder weapon, running from the cops, and stabbing you in the arm. Sorry about that, by the way. It was a heat-of-the-moment thing."

"Sure, I can understand that." *Just don't try and get too close to me again.* "But why did you do it?"

"Why did I stab you? No. You mean, why did I kill Vera. I would have thought that would be perfectly clear. She's been bullying me my whole life."

"So why didn't you change jobs or move. That would have been a lot less drastic."

"I didn't really mean to kill her. We were in a housekeeping closet, and she was up on a stepstool trying to find something she had hidden behind those hideous Christmas balls. It was the usual thing. She was telling me how stupid I was, how I never did anything right, and then the basket tipped, and those heavy, glass balls started bouncing off her head. She fell. She was lying on the floor holding her head and yelling at me. She called me a stupid bitch. I'm not sure what happened next. One minute she was lying on the floor, swearing at me, and the next minute, I was whacking her on the head with a sparkly glass ball. It was worth it. She stopped yelling and got real quiet. Her head was bleeding." Dotty ran her sleeve across her face. Her eyes were glazed, and there was a layer of sweat on her upper lip.

"But why did you hide the balls? If you'd left them, it might have looked like an accident."

"My fingerprints were on that ball with Vera's blood. I put on cleaning gloves and threw most of the balls into the woods. If they were found, so what? No prints. They weren't all there, but if someone noticed that, they'd just think it was lost in the woods. I threw the basket in the fireplace and made sure it burned. But I had to get rid of the ball I hit her with. I've seen all those 'CSI' shows. I know that even if I cleaned the ball, there could be traces of blood. So I tossed my gazing ball in the pond and put the Christmas ball on the stand. It wasn't right, though. You noticed it right away. It was too big for the stand. I guess Vera was right about me, I don't do things right."

"Why didn't you just toss the Christmas ball in the pond?" That's what I would have done.

"Didn't you know? They float. They're not solid all the way through. We floated them in a bathtub one year for a celebration. The bath was full of flowers and those floating balls. We lit candles and set them on the ledge around the tub. We had to take the balls out of the bath before the woman used it. I don't remember who did that. It wasn't Vera. She never did stuff like that."

"Can I ask you one more thing?"

"Sure."

"Did you tell your nephew to set fire to my house?"

"God, no."

Rats. Now I still had to worry about someone coming by in the night and crisping me while I slept.

"No. That was Vera's son Sid. He read in the paper how you were a suspect. He got real mad that you were out of jail and running around free. So he talked his cousin into helping him. Didn't think it was right. He came over and told me about it. I told him not to be foolish, and I'd whip him if he tried anything like that."

"How old is Sid's cousin?" Relief washed over me. No late-night crisping for me.

"Oh, he's thirty-two. Ought to know better by now."

Dotty was led away without making any attempt to stab me with a pencil or any other object. I was feeling distinctly creepy. I couldn't sense any remorse or any other feelings, for that matter, around the death of her sister. I shivered and followed Steve out of the room.

"Well, that was interesting," said Steve. "Remind me to do something nice for my sister."

"Why? You worried she'll smack you in the head with a ball if you don't?" We headed down the hall toward the exit.

"It never hurts to take out a little insurance."

I punched Steve on the shoulder. "Your sister is not in the least like that."

"Watch it! You'll get yourself arrested for assaulting an office of the peace."

I snorted.

"Oh, that was ladylike. I'll bet Jim loves it when you make that noise."

"Jim is no longer seeing me, if you must know. But there are some who find my snorting quite appealing. I'll thank you to keep your opinions to yourself."

"As if. What are you up to now?" He opened the door for me. "Back to the paper to write up your story?"

"Something like that. Thanks."

"Thanks for what?"

"Sitting through that interview with me, and opening the door."

"Ain't no thing." He saluted me as I walked through the door.

*****

I slid into my Toyota and patted the dash. I was feeling very affectionate toward my car today. I was feeling dang lucky to be alive. Between homicidal coworkers and wayward deer, I'd had quite a month. I sped down Route 107, but instead of taking Route 14 into town, I turned toward home.

I was sitting on my couch with my interview notes. Sunlight was streaming in the windows and warming me. I'd taken the dogs out for a run. Well, they ran, I trudged. We were wet and tired but happy to be in each other's company. I'd pulled on an old pair of grey sweats and a baggy maroon sweater that looked like it was left over from the eighties. I had on my fuzzy, pink socks, and my hair was pulled up in a half-assed ponytail. I was working on my story.

Annie raised her head off the couch and focused on the kitchen. There was a knock, and the door opened. The dogs leapt to their feet and surged into the kitchen, baying. I could hear them leaping and jumping. Someone grunted.

"Are you going to help me out in here?" It was Jim.

I whistled, and the pack ran back into the living room and looked at me with anticipation.

"Lie down. You're being obnoxious. I don't know why they're jumping all over you. Normally, they let you waltz right in without so much as a growl."

Jim walked in. The mood in the room shifted. The dogs all lifted their heads and gazed at him. This confused me. Jim was looking extra hunky. Nice-fitting jeans, form-fitting tee-shirt, and a hip length jacket. Surely the dogs couldn't tell he was showing off his bod?

"Come on in. Sorry I didn't get up. I'm worn out."

"I wanted to talk to you in the hospital, but you were never alone."

"Meg's very protective. Have a seat."

Jim sat, and I could have sworn I saw something move. Surely he wasn't that happy to see me. "Are you staring at my crotch? That's kind of forward, even for you."

I tore my gaze away and looked into his face. He was laughing at me. "You have something very strange going on in your pocket. You got a hamster in there?"

"A hamster? No. A Mexican rat, yes." He reached into his pocket and brought out a fuzzy, pale yellow ball of fur hardly any bigger than his fist.

"What is that? It's not really a rat is it?" I drew my feet up under myself.

"No. It's not a rat. He's a Chihuahua."

"Oh, my God. He's so cute. Can I see him?" I uncurled my feet and reached out.

Jim placed him in my hands. He was warm and wiggly. He licked my hand, and I brought up level with my face.

"You are something else," I told the puppy. I rubbed his little ears, and he stretched his neck and gave me a puppy kiss on the nose. "I think I'd better keep you. That nasty old man over there will do nothing but teach you bad habits." I snuggled him into the crook of my neck.

"I'm glad you like him." I went to give the puppy back to Jim, but he shook his head. "No, he's for you."

"For me? You bought this little guy for me?"

"I figured he could go to work with you and keep you company. In an emergency, he could bite someone on the finger, and you could get away. You might not always have a pony on hand to squish evil henchmen with."

"You heard about that, too." I cuddled the little dog in my lap.

"You can't keep secrets in a small town."

The puppy yawned, sticking out his tongue. It curled at the tip. His little brown eyes looked ten sizes too big for his face. He looked up at me and wagged his tail. Oh, my God. "What am I going to do with you? What did Jim call you, a Mexican rat? You're cuter than a Mexican rat. Are you wagging that tail at me?"

It wagged faster. His whole body squirmed with pleasure. "What's rat in Spanish? Would that be a good name for you?" I thought of all the ludicrous names I could use. Tiny, Duke, Tank, Pee Wee. I could call him Pee Wee Herman. Pip Squeak. Hamster. An oversized hamster. If I put him on the floor, Ranger would swallow him whole. Even Annabelle could swat him around.

I held him against my chest. He curled in my hands, tucking his feet under his oversized head. I lifted him to my face and sniffed puppy smell. Clean dog, unfouled by muddy ponds or cow manure. A dog that hadn't yet rolled in anything disgusting. No dead chicken. No rotting compost. Fresh, unadulterated puppy.

The Mexican rat lifted his head and washed my face with his tongue. His tail was vibrating like a hummingbird. This dog would never survive in a house full of oversized chowderheads that could swallow him whole. I handed him back.

Jim looked confused. "Don't you like him?"

"He's very sweet, but I can't keep him."

"Why not? You love dogs."

"I can't accept this kind of gift from you."

"There aren't any strings attached, if that's what you're worried about." He looked affronted.

"I think it would be sending the wrong message." How hard was he going to make this for me? Sometimes men could be so clueless.

"What message would that be?"

I took a deep breath. Then I looked him in the eye and said what I had thought he was smart enough to figure out on his own. "That I have forgiven you. That maybe we could be friends. That there's the possibility that we could get back together."

"Taking a dog would say all that? A mighty heavy weight for a dog."

"Jim." I closed my eyes and puffed out some air. I really didn't want to fight right now. I'd had enough drama for a lifetime.

"Bree, I'm not giving up. I made a mistake. That's all. A mistake. I don't believe that I can't make it up to you. There has to be something, some gesture, something I can do that will make you understands."

"This isn't about understanding. It's about feeling. Do you have any idea how I felt when I saw you with Lucy Howe?"

"Not any worse than I felt when I saw you at the video store with Beau Maverick." His voice was getting louder.

"I didn't know you were at the video store."

"That's because you were too busy groping each other."

"I'm getting a headache. Can we please stop this now?" Ranger woofed at the door, and the little dog in

Jim's lap lifted his head. The kitchen door banged open. "Just what I need, somebody else walking in without knocking." I was starting to get up when Beau appeared. He nodded to Jim and came to stand near where I was sitting.

"Aren't you supposed to be in California?" I asked him.

"I am. I'm ahead of schedule, and the other team needs to catch up. So I came home for a few days." He sat on the arm of a chair across from me.

"Tom told you, didn't he?"

"That you were attacked by a maniac with a pair of scissors? Yep. He told me."

"It's been kind of crazy around here."

The puppy squeaked and jumped out of Jim's arms and off the chair. He ran to Beau and jumped up and did a four-legged jumping dance until Beau leaned over and scooped him up.

"Who's this? Don't tell me you have another dog. Aren't you afraid Ranger will eat him?"

"I'm not keeping him. Jim just brought him for a visit."

Beau looked at Jim. "I didn't know you were a puppy kind of guy. What's he going to do while you're at work all day?"

"I got him for Bree." Jim set his jaw. "But she doesn't want him, so I'll return him."

"Bree doesn't like this little fellow?" Beau turned to me. "You don't want this baby? I'm surprised."

"It's complicated." I widened my eyes and tilted my chin ever so slightly at Jim. I was trying to tell Beau to shut up. This was embarrassing me. "Besides, he wouldn't be safe here with the big dogs."

"You could just take him with you. He's little." Beau wasn't taking instruction.

"That's not the point. Just shut up, Beau."

"Well what is the point?" The furball had rolled over, and Beau was rubbing his tummy.

"I've had enough." Jim got up. "Give me the dog. I'm going." He took the puppy and turned to me. "I'm not giving up on you, Bree, but I'm not going to try and talk to you while he's here." He jerked his head in Beau's direction. "I'll see you later."

"He brought you a puppy as a peace offering." Beau was grinning.

"I don't want to talk about it." I had the sinking feeling I was going to be dealing with this rivalry for a while.

"Wish I'd thought to bring you a puppy. I only brought See's Candy."

"I don't need another dog. What's See's Candy?"

"These really great West Coast chocolates. But I left them at my house, so you'll have to come visit me to get them."

"You brought me chocolates, and then you left them at your house? That's tacky."

"I was so distracted by your injuries that they completely slipped my mind. I hope Tom told me the whole story, because if I find out anything else scary happened to you while I was gone, I'm going to have a heart attack. I've half a mind to load you up and take you with me so I can keep an eye on you." He ran his hands through his hair until it was standing up.

I smiled at him. "You like me."

He came and sat beside me on the couch. "Almost as much as I like that little dog. You should have kept him."

"If you like that little dog so much, you should keep him."

"I will, if it make you happy. But he'll have to stay with you whenever I'm away."

"Ranger would eat him." I couldn't believe we were playing this game. "I'm tired, Beau. Could we talk about something else?"

"I think we should talk about you coming to California with me until my job's finished." He slipped his arm around my shoulders and drew me to him. "Because I'm finding it impossible to work and worry about you at the same time."

"Everything's back to normal. There's nothing to worry about anymore."

"The queen of chaos is telling me there's nothing to worry about."

"Life got out of hand for a while, but it's all okay now."

"The minute I go back, Jim will be sniffing around here with another present. A horse, next time. Could you say no to some poor, abandoned horse? No. I can't risk it."

"I'd have to find someone to come and stay with the dogs." California. Warm California with beaches and dry ground. No mud patches or manure for me to roll around in.

"We could take the dogs with us."

"You'd let me bring my dogs to California?"

"If that's what I need to do, you bet."

"I'll think about it." I snuggled into his shoulder. "I'm too tired to make a decision right now."

"Well, then, I'd better take you upstairs to bed."

Meet Kate George

Born in Northern California, Kate George now lives in rural Vermont. She shares an old farmhouse with a husband, four kids, three dogs and three cats. She started writing because of a dare, and now she makes the rascal who dared her read through her rough drafts.

Ms. George earned a Bachelor of Arts degree from the University of California, Davis, and writes about things with which she has some experience. These include working as a typesetter, paste-up tech, and motorcycle safety instructor, as well as in the housekeeping department of a swank hotel - among many, many other unusual occupations.

Use this handy order form to enjoy other chillingly good mysteries from Mainly Murder Press.

Title	Qty.	Cover Price	Subtotal
Waiting for Armando-Ivie		$14.95	
Murder on Old Main St.-Ivie		$14.95	
A Skeleton in the Closet-Ivie		$14.95	
Moonlighting in Vermont-George		$14.95	
		Subtotal:	
		CT residents add 6% tax	
		S&H @ $2.75 for first book, $1.00 each additional	
		Total enclosed:	

Mail with your check and shipping instructions to:

Mainly Murder Press

PO Box 290586 • Wethersfield, CT 06109-0586

or use PayPal to order online at
www.MainlyMurderPress.com

LaVergne, TN USA
04 March 2010
174982LV00001B/59/P